The
Witness Tree

The
Witness Tree

a novel
by
Terry L. Persun

Cover art and design
by
Kimberly Torda

Implosion Press
4975 Comanche Trail
Stow, OH 44224

Acknowledgments:
It is with the utmost gratitude that I thank the following people for their continual support, honest comments, and, in many cases, hard work: Marie for her help in editing this novel; Terry and Mark for their support throughout my life; Jerry Spinelli, Steve Berlin and Kenn Morris for their friendship; and Bruce Boes, Joan Renner, and Willard Rowe for reading and evaluating this novel in manuscript form. And finally, a very special thanks goes to Terry Capuano whose gracious support made this edition possible, and to Cheryl Townsend who held this manuscript until she was able to produce it.

For

Catherine,

holder of the key.

Chapter 1

I remember clear back to the first day they began to move in the trucks and other heavy equipment. In the clear, pink morning, at dawn. It was early spring. All the animals became alarmed. Squirrels jumped from tree to tree, chattering and scurrying across branches; grouse fluttered from brush to brush, unable to locate a place where they felt safe; snakes moved too, some very slowly in the cold morning. Everything shook, from animal to plant. I felt it. It moved throughout common thought. The grass and fields, the saplings, trailing pine, moss, mushrooms, the largest trees trembled inside, unsure of what was about to happen. The disturbance lasted for weeks, until they were finished with the cutting.

A place had been cleared, a hole dug. Many trees were allowed to stand, even though eight squirrel dens were destroyed and the territories of two bird families disrupted. The ripple of territorial changes lasted for months afterwards.

Along with the equipment came the men, laborers of one sort or another. I've learned their types by what they do: workers with cement, wire and wood, shingle and siding. The house went up quickly, and by the end of June a human family lived within the clutch of common thought. That's when I got to know Lewis and Jeffrey. They were twins, but even as the bond between them was strong, they thought in altogether different patterns. Lewis was the much more sensitive one and therefore vulnerable, not just to his brother, but to the world.

They were nine when they moved in, had just finished fourth grade in the city and were to start fifth in the fall in the country school. Day after day for the first few weeks, the boys explored further and further from the house, following the old tractor road, as they called it. In fact, it was an overgrown road on which the farmer who once owned the land had driven his tractor to the field which harvested oats about a hundred yards north of where I stand. It had been years since he worked the field, and years after his death that the land was sold, a piece at a time, first to the Marshals, Lewis and Jeffrey's parents. The tractor road was hardly visible by then. It had once passed right by me, but by the time Lewis and Jeffrey moved in, it appeared to end right at my trunk, as though the tractor had driven right up to me and stopped. Early in planting season, he'd head towards the field, bouncing by me in the tractor, wearing a tee-shirt and flannel shirt, red hunter's cap. His thin hands on the steering wheel, lowering the plow, tilting his cap back. He hummed and sang and whistled while he worked through the cold mornings. He smiled at the silence when he stopped the tractor for a quick lunch. His wrinkled face was like bark itself, his thoughts as easy as wind. He was a good man.

But the Marshal twins, that's who this story is about. And it's good to start it that first day they came, loudly, up the old tractor road. Their voices echoed through the thin morning air.

"Slow down."

"No. I want to see what's up here."

"A field, Dad said, an old field."

"Good."

Lewis rushed to catch up to Jeffrey who kicked up leaves and slapped tree trunks as he half ran up the old road, grass growing tall down its center, weeds on either side, some as tall as the twins. Eventually, as the path thinned and the weeds, underbrush, and new saplings overtook the old indentations in the soil, Jeffrey slowed. They had reached the bend in the road. Once they turned it and walked on twenty or so feet they'd be heading straight for me.

"That's it," Lewis said. "We've been here before. The end of the road."

"It can't be. There's no field," Jeffrey said.

"So, it's grown in."

"No, look!" Jeffrey pointed. "That's oats or something growing over there, the road must have gone around those three trees there."

"Hey, I think you're right. There's a patch of mud where the tractor wheels must'a sunk in."

They both walked cautiously through tall briar bushes, holding back the arcing briar stems with thumb and forefinger as they walked around the trees they had spotted at the bend. When they finally glanced far enough down the path, they saw me.

"Boy, look at that," Jeffrey said.

"Neat."

"Let's climb it." Jeffrey took off as fast as he could through the underbrush, the thinned briar bushes tugging at his shirt.

"Wait up. Wait 'till I get there too."

But Jeffrey didn't wait. He no sooner broke through the weeds then he was reaching for a low branch to hoist himself up and onto. His soft face and hands were close against me. His tiny muscles tightened and tugged, his hands clutching any bump or branch they could. Lucky for Jeffrey, though, Lewis eventually pushed him enough to let him overcome the strain and he was finally sitting on my lowest branch.

"Help me up." Lewis jumped, reaching for Jeffrey's foot, but Jeffrey moved it out of the way. "Don't!" Lewis lowered his head and puffed out his lower lip. He touched my trunk with his little hand. He wanted, badly, to be beside his brother. I could feel the hurt he felt by what Jeffrey had done. There was so much action going on inside their little bodies, so much between them not being expressed that it excited all of common thought. It buzzed with tension and emotion. The power which was exerted when Jeffrey moved his foot away so Lewis couldn't reach it, the pain Lewis felt, each act between them a movement in common thought, a disturbance. Even Lewis' pout carried the strength of a hard rain or a strong wind inside him. And it could all be felt by common thought, so close to me, that it was loud, louder than the tractor engine, louder than all the heavy equipment that came in to build the twin's house.

Lewis looked around and felt trapped. It was like him to feel so. All he saw were briar bushes along the old road, glimpses of puddles, brown dead leaves half rotted from a winter just past. His hand trembled and tears began to fill his eyes. "You have to help me," he said to Jeffrey, his face still not looking up.

"Okay," Jeffrey said. To him the view spread far into the woods, down at the weeds and briars, the underbrush. Further to the north, the trees thinned out, and beyond them was the clearing which had once been the farmer's field, now mostly filled with weeds. For a moment there was no conflict, no competition between them; Jeffrey's expanded range of sight made him superior to Lewis, so it was easy for him to help his brother. He reached down to Lewis and pulled him up.

Lewis didn't want to stand at first, but Jeffrey urged him on, slightly taunting. Lewis gave in and backed close to my trunk, twisted his body all the way around, then inched his way up my side, touching the crevices of my bark a little at a time as he ascended. His fingers explored the tiny finger holds just as his mind did. Without really looking, he could see each place his fingers searched with uncanny accuracy and depth. For a brief moment, I felt his mind, felt it touch common thought. It sent shivers through the forest, reaching the overgrown field and beyond.

Once upright, Lewis turned his head and looked out across the wonderful distances just as Jeffrey had done. A sigh slipped from his mouth and his grip loosened. "Wow, this is great."

"Isn't it?" Jeffrey had made his way further out on my branch. He started on all fours, but reached up towards another branch that hung down near him. There was a moment between holding my lower branch he stood on and grabbing my branch above him where he stood balanced between the two, not holding on to either. That moment was exhilarating, it was a moment of flight, the letting go that birds do upon lift-off. He actually lingered long enough to become unbalanced, then pushed up with his legs and grasped my low-hanging branch to catch himself from falling. His heart raced for a moment, but he held tight as my branch settled. He couldn't see any further because he was essentially the same height, but when he looked back at Lewis and saw his brother cowering near my trunk, his shoulders squared and he stood straight. "You sissy, Lewis."

"What? I'm standing."

"Look at you, though, squeezing that tree like it's your mom. You look like a baby scared to take his first step. Are you scared?"

"No. I just have to get used to it."

"Does this help?" Jeffrey bounced up and down, but there was little movement of the branch close to my trunk.

"It doesn't matter. I can't feel it." Lewis turned and put his back to my trunk. He still held on. His hands behind him, clutching, his fingers deep in the crevices of bark. And his feet were planted close together. He could feel only the slightest movement, although Jeffrey bounced up and down a distance of about half the length of their bodies.

"Come on, Lewis, walk out here. I dare you."

"Stop bouncing then, and I will."

Jeffrey abruptly stopped. Both branches trembled for a moment, then stood still. He said slowly, daring his brother, "All right. I stopped."

"Don't move."

"You afraid?"

"No. I just don't want you moving. I'll fall."

"So," Jeffrey said. "It's not that far. You won't get hurt."

"You don't know."

"I do so."

"Still." Lewis loosened his grip.

"Come on, Lewis."

"I am." Lewis let go and stepped. Even Jeffrey hadn't tried such a balancing act.

Lewis took another step, all the while watching where his feet were placed. For a moment it seemed he was on level ground. It seemed he was safe. He looked up and smiled at Jeffrey, proud of his progress, but his smile quickly turned as he lost his balance. He looked back down at his feet, but there was nowhere he could put them to correct his balance. The branch was not thin, but it was not broad enough to help Lewis. Jeffrey yelled once and reached out. Lewis quickly burst into tears. His knees buckled. He forgot himself, forgot to try to land on his feet, and just toppled over. When he neared the ground his arm went out to break the fall. One arm, against all that body weight, just snapped like a dead twig in the road.

Jeffrey heard the sound loud and clear. He dropped to my branch and lowered himself to the ground.

Lewis lay on his back, his arm twisted unnaturally behind him. His palm open and pointing upwards as though waiting for something to drop into it. He had stopped crying, but his face was twisted in pain to match the twist in his arm.

Jeffrey didn't know what to do, so he helped Lewis to stand, told him to try not to move his arm, and then led him away, back to their home.

Although it was weeks before they came out again, I could reach them through common thought. So, I listened to them play inside their house. I followed their emotions while Lewis' arm healed.

The sound of voices broke through the early evening air like rocks clacking together underwater. No time of year is more perfect than evening at the early part of summer. The squirrels were out, playing among fallen trees and leaves. They chattered, ran and stopped, fluffed their tails and twitched them, then ran off. Jeffrey and Lewis were returning, anxious to go beyond their last adventure. Lewis' arm was still bound and slung. There would be no climbing this time.

"I'm waiting for you, this time. See," Jeffrey said.

"I know."

"I'll even hold back the briars."

"You don't have to," Lewis said.

"I don't want you gettin' hurt again."

"It wasn't my fault. You probably moved."

"Did not."

"You didn't realize it when you did," Lewis said as though it were a known fact.

"I didn't move." Jeffrey stopped walking and put his hand out to dramatize. "I was per-fect-ly still."

"Then the wind," Lewis said, giving in.

Jeffrey began to walk again, holding briar bushes aside for Lewis. "You just slipped, lost your balance. That's all. So quit gabbin' about it. It's over, isn't it? And I don't care."

"But you seemed mad. Like you blamed me, and it wasn't my fault."

"Right."

"It wasn't!"

"Drop it, Lewis." Jeffrey pointed. "There's the culprit."

"Yeah," Lewis said laughing, "it's the tree's fault."

"The tree monster shook its branches..."

"...and the brave adventurer slipped from its limb," Lewis added.

"You're not a brave adventurer," Jeffrey said.

"But I want to be."

They stood together, looked up at me, and simultaneously reached out and touched my trunk.

"What kind of tree is it, Lewis?"

"A white oak. The leaves are split, with rounded ends. Look." Lewis pointed.

"That means white oak?"

"It's a white oak. I know it."

"Look, you can see the sky through its leaves."

Lewis looked up where Jeffrey had his eyes fixed. "It could be a lake with leaves in it, or a sky."

"You're so weird sometimes." Jeffrey turned and sat at the base of my trunk. "It's just a sky and a tree. I don't know where you come up with some of this stuff."

"It's just in my brain. I think that sometimes a tree wants to be a lake, just like people want to be what they're not. Like Dad wants a new job or Mom wants to be like Mrs. Nichols."

"And a lake wants to be a mountain."

"Yeah."

"Sit down, Lew."

Lewis sat down next to Jeffrey, both of their heads pivoted back so they could see through my leaves to the sky.

"Did you ever wonder what you're going to do when you get older?" Jeffrey asked.

"I'm going to paint."

"Are you?"

"Yes. That's what I want."

"I thought you wanted to be an adventurer."

"That too," Lewis said.

"That's two jobs, you can't do that."

"Why not?"

"Because. Pick one."

"I'm going to go on long adventures and paint what I see."

Jeffrey laughed and pushed Lewis.

"Watch the arm," Lewis said, a wide smirk on his face.

"You bum," Jeffrey pushed him again, then again. "Where do you get off being a pansy just 'cause your arm was broken?"

Lewis got up and ran towards the field. Jeffrey chased him. Past the white birches and maple saplings they ran to the stone fence which bordered the field. After all those years, it still stood straight. The flat stones on top were as level as the day they were placed there. Only a few stones were out of place along the whole south side. Twenty to thirty feet to the left of where Lewis and Jeffrey stood was a wide opening, where the road had actually led into the field, but they weren't interested in the opening. Side by side, they stood looking over the stone fence, out across the wide, five acre field. Both their mouths were open. "God," Jeffrey managed to say.

"It's beautiful." Lewis stared. The sun had begun to fall behind the hills to the west. Light made of gold and orange fell across the old field. Besides the weeds that grew there now, the oxalis, dandelion, crow's foot and even milk weed, there were patches of oat grain which soaked up the light and sparkled and glowed. A calm breeze pushed and pulled at the climbing stems of life and made them sway like a calming symphony. Lewis was awestruck. They had arrived at just the right moment to see the field at its most spectacular, ablaze in light, swaying to invisible music.

Jeffrey wanted to run through it and slap at the weed blossoms. He wanted to touch the oat grain stalks, but Lewis merely wanted to look at it.

Jeffrey climbed onto the rock fence, "Come on, let's go in," he said, as though it were a river and not a field.

"It's too beautiful." Lewis watched the play of lights and shadows which changed moment by moment as the wind blew and the sun lowered.

"It'll make a great ball field," Jeffrey said while jumping off the fence and into the high weeds.

"Why cut it to make a ball field?"

Jeffrey noticed how mesmerized Lewis was so he added, "Not all of it, Lewis, only enough to play in." Then Jeffrey ran into the light and out of the shadow of the forest.

Lewis noticed how the light touched Jeffrey, how it mixed his colors with the colors of the field, how it took him in, lighted him up. Lewis climbed over the fence, careful of his arm, and dashed out past where Jeffrey stood.

"Hey, where you going?"

"I wanna be in the middle of the field," Lewis said as he ran. Jeffrey followed, and in the middle of the field they both stood, arms stretched out to their sides, as much as possible for Lewis, the two of them twirling around in the orange light of dusk.

It became easier for me to know what Lewis felt, to see through his eyes. That day, something connected Lewis to common thought. Something deep inside him shifted slightly, made contact and held. It all happening as the twins twirled. Lewis got lost in the moment, totally submerged in the wonder of the light and wind.

Jeffrey stopped abruptly and smacked the head of a tall weed. An array of dried particles burst from it, surprising the air with more sparkling lights. He smacked another one and another puff of dried particles entered the orange light. "Watch," Jeffrey said as he smacked another and another. Lewis stood watching the tiny fireworks as light ricocheted off the scattered particles. Jeffrey walked slowly back towards the stone fence and the darkening woods. Lewis followed, every once in a while holding his hand out to catch the light Jeffrey had slapped out of the weed heads.

Lewis wanted the light to stay, but the sun dropped and the woods became dark. Fireflies came out near the edge of the woods, blinking their warning of nightfall. Lewis stopped to watch them for a moment or two. He tried to follow the path of one firefly, but lost it in the maze of blinking lights. He turned for a last look at the field before following Jeffrey over the stone fence. The field had lost its color. A dull gray and brown hung amidst the weeds and wild-growing grain. Suddenly, nothing seemed important to Lewis. The sun would always go down, leaving everything dull and back to normal.

"Hurry up, space boy," Jeffrey yelled from inside the woods. "You look like you're about to float away."

Lewis turned and stared into the woods, but he couldn't see Jeffrey. Once he climbed over the fence though, Jeffrey stood right there.

"Quick, it's getting dark."

"Look at all the fireflies now," Lewis said, pointing into the field.

"Yeah."

"They come out of nowhere. Thousands of them."

"Let's go, Lewis, or Mom and Dad won't let us come out here again."

Lewis turned and followed Jeffrey. As they passed, Lewis touched my trunk and I could feel that he understood more than Jeffrey. He was somehow still connected to the field, the fireflies, to me. He could sense common thought, was a part of it, yet he didn't quite understand what it was. I could see into him, through his eyes, and followed him through the woods seeing what he saw.

Jeffrey didn't wait up. He became impatient. "Stop walking so slow. I can't just stand here."

But Lewis took his time. He looked at everything, each tree and each bush. He watched as the darkness swallowed the openings between briar stems, how the haze above the forest darkened. When he broke from the woods, Jeffrey was almost to the house. Lights fell through the front windows onto the porch and grass. Although he heard nothing, Lewis imagined the low conversation of his parents, like he heard at night after he and Jeffrey went to bed. The house was like a fairy tale house at the edge of the woods, happy lights, friendly talk. He wanted it to stay that way, just as he had wanted the field to display its orange and gold sparkles forever. But he had to end his dream and follow Jeffrey inside. He had to get into the picture instead of looking at it from a distance.

When he walked to the porch and opened the front door, I let go of his thoughts. I felt a quick tug I'd never felt before and knew that Lewis felt it too. The door closed and I turned my attention to the coming of night.

Common thought allowed me to sense, through other plants and ani-

16

mals, for a long distance. Animals, just as humans, most times, were more difficult to reach. Their common thought being slightly askew, yet animals were typically easier than humans to understand and feel. I had never been so close to human thought as with the twins, especially Lewis. There was something special about what was inside him that connected us together through common thought.

As the night wore on, the moon passed through the sky like a slow beacon, and I pondered what I had learned from humans, from Lewis, who was even more attuned to nature than the farmer had been. I wondered how such things happened. How those closest to the earth could not connect, while someone not born with the earth could connect so easily? Lewis had become an anomaly.

Through the night I probed for his thoughts, into his house and into his dreams. I wanted the connection to grow stronger without disturbing him. Over and over again I reached, regardless of how difficult. The connection was important. I didn't want to lose it for fear it would not return.

Chapter 2

It wasn't long before Lewis and Jeffrey made friends, even though school was out, and before you knew it there were twenty or more kids traipsing up the old tractor road towards the field. Mr. Marshal had rented a side cutter and, sweating uncomfortably in the hot sun, cut a large area for the boys to play baseball. Jeffrey had remembered his promise to Lewis and insisted that his father leave part of the field alone. That was no problem. To keep the entire field cut would have been a long, time-consuming job of which Mr. Marshal was not partial.

Where all the children came from was a wonder. There had never seemed to be that many children around before, yet, there they were with their bats and balls stuffed inside a long canvas bag. Each brought his own glove and sometimes girls showed up too, but they seldom played, except for Lorrie Watkins who was sort of shaped like one of the boys and often played a better game.

Lewis never played and Jeffrey always played. In fact, Jeffrey took the lead role as captain of one team, while Lewis wandered along the stone fence, the entire periphery of the field, discovering all sorts of bugs and insects, all sorts of plants. He even began to bring a small, spiral-bound sketch pad along, which he perched on his bent knees as he sat, leaning against the fence, drawing whatever he saw: bugs, leaves, trees. There were many drawings of the stone fence, one of the rest of the children playing baseball, although his human figures didn't come out well.

The games started early in the morning. Kids would show up a little at a time, on bicycles, on foot, sometimes eight or ten were dropped off, not in front of the Marshal's house, but right near the woods, at the beginning of the old tractor road, by a tired woman still wearing a house dress or robe.

As soon as enough kids showed up, the game would begin by choosing sides, the throwing in the air of a bat for the opposing team's captain to catch, then the hand-over-hand contest ending in pinching the tip of the bat handle to see if it would slip loose and fall, or hang safely between forefinger and thumb.

On most days a light-gray ground fog, caused by the sun blistering off the previous night's dew, lay over the flat stone bases which had been stolen from the fence. Canvas sneakers stuck to the ends of thin poles of legs quickly became dew soaked and squeaked against small feet as the children ran.

There was excitement those days. The high-pitched cries of small boys and girls, the loud crack of the bat hitting the ball, then the excited yelling for children to run, for others to catch, where to throw the ball. The early morning air held the voices for a second in the fog, then let them rush on and mix with dew-damp squeaking feet and the silent summer sun. All day they'd play, yelling in delight, stopping only to eat a quick peanut butter sandwich or to gulp down water from a mason jar or green plastic canteen. The field had changed from the lonely sanctuary left after the farmer's death, to the perfect baby-sitter, the greatest children's social auditorium.

In the evening, as the sun fell slowly and the air cooled, Lewis always tried to find in himself, and in the field, the brilliance and comfort of the first evening he and Jeffrey had seen the field. He tried to sketch the light as it fell over the field, his back to the ball field and everyone playing, but the field was never the same as that first time, nor would it ever be. He wanted to blame his father or Jeffrey for changing it, but at the same time knew it wasn't their fault. Even if the exact climactic conditions existed, the exact emotions, recent experiences would change the event. Lewis reached for the past, a past not far away, yet one which he couldn't grasp. He sketched, and eventually painted, the field over and over, whenever he longed for the sad depth, the complete awe of existence, he felt that first day.

It was on one of those days when he was totally lost in his search for the past, and in the sadness of his failure to reach that place inside himself, that he remained oblivious to the approach of other children. The game had ended, and Jeffrey, holding his finger over his lips, led the others to where Lewis, lost in himself and in the clutches of common thought, sat drawing quickly over his sketch pad with a number two pencil. He never noticed the sudden silence in the game or the rustling footsteps creeping up behind him until he heard Lorrie Watkins exclaim, "That's beautiful!" It was his first real praise from someone outside the family.

Lewis was so far removed from the reality the other children had been in, that he let the completely honest words she said slide down the long hollow corridors of his consciousness and into his being. It was something, a perfect sound maybe, that he would never forget. When he looked up, there were children all around him. "You're really good, Lew," Michael said. He was a fast runner and good catcher. "It's great," Lewis heard another child say. They all agreed.

"Told you he was good," Jeffrey said, proud to be Lewis' twin.

Lewis, slowly pulling from common thought, disconnecting like the slowing of water through a spigot while turning the handle, began to smile up at them, then stood and accepted their acknowledgment of his talent with a flushed face and down-turned eyes. Yet, he allowed them to look at what he considered a failed understanding of the uncut portion of the field. On the walk back down the old tractor road that evening, Lewis set the pace as the other children asked about his drawing. For once, the baseball game had been forgotten.

The next morning, however, when Lewis got up from bed, he couldn't find the drawing. It had been torn from the sketch pad. Tiny pieces of paper were still left behind, stuck inside the spiral. When he had lifted the pad, a strip of torn paper stuck out the end. He recognized the remains of the torn page, but didn't remember pulling that page out. And he always cleaned the spiral using his pencil point to pick the excess paper from it.

He looked around the room he shared with his brother when he realized Jeffrey wasn't there. The clock. It was late. No one had awakened him. Jeffrey must have slipped out quietly. Lewis thought that Jeffrey may have removed the sketch to show to their mom and dad. Or the other kids may have asked to see it again. But why would he leave without waking Lewis?

Lewis sat on his bed and stretched. It didn't make sense. Lewis felt alone. He had always been left alone by the other children, but this was different. At those times the children were at least around, yelling and screaming in the background. He could always go over and talk with them. But now, he was completely alone. Sure, his mom would be downstairs. That wasn't the same.

Lewis walked to the bathroom to brush his teeth.

"Is that you, Lewis?" his mother yelled up.

"Yes, Mom."

"You feeling all right?"

"Yeah. I was just tired."

"The other children went out to play hours ago."

"I know." He shut the door and turned on the faucet. In the mirror, he saw Jeffrey's gray eyes and sandy hair. He saw Jeffrey's round-shaped head and full lips. He wished, for the first time in his life, that he could get Jeffrey out of himself. He wanted to know what he'd look like without Jeffrey. He had been reminded of Jeffrey his entire life. Even at school, almost daily, someone would slap him on the back, mistaking him for his brother. He touched his own face, looked into his own eyes, tried to see deeper. Who was he if not just a quiet, reserved Jeffrey? Lewis brushed his teeth and washed his face.

Back in his room, he dressed quickly, then grabbed the sketch pad and sat on his bed to pull the strips of paper from the spiral. He imagined going to the field and seeing that they'd tacked the drawing onto a tree, sort of a mascot to their game, a sign which belonged only to them. They would have a place for him to sit and draw, he thought, as he placed another piece of the torn paper on the bedspread near his thigh. When he was through cleaning the spiral, he crumpled the paper strips between his hands. On the way out of his bedroom, Lewis dropped the paper into the trash.

Two steps into the hall and he realized what had happened. He went

21

back and pulled a large crumpled paper from the trash. As he slowly unraveled it, knowing what he had found, his last drawing of the day before came into view. It had not only been torn from the sketch pad and crumpled, it had been x-ed out. Jeffrey! Lewis pictured himself in his head. He and Jeffrey looked the same in every physical detail, so why didn't he destroy Jeffrey's possessions?

Lewis crumpled the paper back up and threw it hard into the bottom of the trash. He wanted to hit Jeffrey, but knew that for some reason Jeffrey always won fights. How was it, he thought, that they could be identical twins and Jeffrey always win when they fought? Why couldn't he just lose once? Lewis puffed his lip out, but no one was around to see it. He pawed at the corner of his eye when a tear came, but that was the end of it, a single tear. He was more angry than upset, but as he thought about what had happened, how Jeffrey must have felt as he x-ed out the drawing, he became sad.

Downstairs, his mother had a bowl of cereal set out for him. She stood next to the kitchen sink looking out the window. "Eat your cereal before you go out."

Lewis sat down at the table, picked up a spoon and began to eat. His mother turned around. "What is it now, Lewis?"

"Jeffrey ruined my picture."

"Oh, you two." She touched the back of his neck. "I thought twins were supposed to be close."

"It wasn't his picture."

"I know, honey. Try not to think about it. He was probably just angry about something."

"He's always angry."

"Now, you know that's not true."

"I know, but it makes me mad." Lewis ate his cereal quickly, expending his anger on eating.

"Getting mad never helps. Why don't you just stay away from him today? Find something else to do."

Lewis finished, then picked up his bowl to take it to the sink. "Maybe I will."

"Here, let me have that." His mother took the bowl and spoon and placed it in the sink.

"I'm not going to go out where they play ball, and when everyone asks why, I'm going to tell them that Jeffrey ruined my picture. They'll hate him."

Lewis' mother laughed. "I don't think they'll just instantly hate your brother because you two had a squabble, but they may find you both amusing."

Lewis paid no attention. He was already near the stairs. He ran up them two at a time, ran down the hall to his room and snatched up his sketch pad and pencil. Back downstairs he yelled, "Bye, Mom," as he slammed the front screen and ran towards the old tractor road.

He quickly made it to the stone fence, but stopped a few yards into the woods and watched the others play for a few minutes. Then he decided to go around the field. He stayed just inside the woods, following the stone fence around the field. Each step he took, the ground cracked and snapped with the sounds of crunching leaves or snapping twigs. All around him trees bent down and saplings stretched. Brush, which rose from the crevices in the hard gray stone, fluttered into the summer breeze. The air filled with bugs, but they congregated outside the cooled woods, rising in the sun like a hazy army looking for an enemy.

Lewis watched the bugs fly and wondered why they just hung in the air and did not go anywhere. He reached a hand out to try to touch them and they moved only a few inches away, then hung there. He didn't want to be a bug, all confused, going in circles, yet he realized the similarities between the gnats and the rest of the children playing ball. Both groups ran in circles, chattered or buzzed and seemed confused, and lingered in the same general area under the hot summer sun the entire day.

On the far side of the field, Lewis walked deeper into the woods. Still hurt by Jeffrey's obvious show of jealousy, Lewis wished to be far away from the excited screams of the others. When their sounds finally died out in the distance and became faint memories rather than intrusions, Lewis heard other sounds, at first mistaking them for talking. As he listened closely and walked further, the noise increased. It was water. A short distance away he saw the water, a thin, gurgling run down through the woods. All around the run stood tall pines; a pine-needle floor covered the ground, soft under his feet. Very little sunlight made it through the many thick branches only to splatter patches of light which moved left and right with the wind. A few rocks protruded from the ground, almost like furniture strategically placed in the cleared forest room. The water ran quickly as though it were going down a steep hill, yet the ground was level. Lewis rushed over to it and noticed how the ripples deflected off the rocks that protruded from the ground. He watched drops of water fly into the air. In an area near the edge of the run, a shallow, quiet patch of water held thousands of minnows. He bent and touched the water. Minnows scattered and were gone to regroup in another area only inches away, tucked closely together, almost touching like the gnats had done. He backed up and grabbed a loose twig from the ground and reached with it into the center where the water ran gurgling and gulping on its way. The stick was quickly torn from his hand and jumped further downstream before it got lodged between some stones where it made another place for the water to catapult loose drops acrobatically into the air.

Lewis placed his sketch pad on the shore, near a large rock, then sat and watched the water. He breathed slowly. It relaxed him to sit there amid patches of sunlight, watching the water move smoothly over the rocks, occasionally spitting a drop into the air, only to land further down stream and continue on with thousands of other drops.

Lewis sensed a kinship with this run which was, like him, calm on the outside, to the eye, and in a rage underneath. He was in a rage much of the time, but not outwardly like Jeffrey. They were twins, they had similar emotions. It was just that Lewis was locked inside while Jeffrey, somehow, had been locked outside. As he sat quietly watching the stream, he slipped once again into common thought. My night-after-night intrusions had loosened him, opened him up to accept what was already within him to accept. He almost fell into a trance, sitting on the soft pine blanket in the cool woods, watching water bounce and play and then run smoothly over rounded rocks and gravel bed.

Lewis bent to common thought and common thought held him close. Then animals, sensing no danger, began to come out. Squirrels chattered and played over a nursing tree lying near the edge of the run. Five saplings were growing from it. The squirrels pawed and preened, then ran one behind the other, stopping only to chatter, their fat tails puffed up and shaking. Birds flew into the clearing and perched on low branches, landing on the pine needle bed and hopping around, searching for food.

Lewis listened to the sounds of the running water, the wind, and the squirrels. He saw a black snake crawl from further upstream over the stones bordering the run and into a small rock pile. The wind started at the tops of the pines and worked its way down through to the bottom branches and then over the ground near where Lewis sat, throwing needles into tiny piles, baring the forest floor in brown spots. Lewis picked up a handful of needles and let them go, let them float away in the wind. A few needles stuck in his hand and he pulled them out and let them float also.

He rubbed his hands together to relieve the slight itching caused by the pine pricks and noticed that when he moved, the animals didn't instantly run away. He wondered about the animals, as I forced my thoughts, through common thought, into him. He relaxed and accepted it along with the animal's fearlessness, even though there was a hint of needing to fully understand what was happening. When a raccoon stumbled down from a nearby tree, I almost lost Lewis, but somehow it was within him to accept that the raccoon would be so close and unafraid. Maybe it was the fact that all the other animals accepted him into their realm which allowed Lewis to so easily let the raccoon be a part of the menagerie. Or possibly it was the enchantment of the place itself that pulled Lewis into common thought and held him there.

He reached out a hand. I could feel all the animals questioning his intrusion and, along with the rest of the grove, attempted to ease their fear. Animal common thought is slightly askew from the rest of nature, but is much easier to reach and influence than humans. The playing squirrels stopped and stared at the trees. They sensed concern. The raccoon dropped from a low branch and waddled towards the stream. Lewis pushed his hand out further and made a quiet kissing noise with his lips. He seemed to know what to do. The raccoon let him know what sounds were soothing. Lewis kissed again, with more air in the noise, almost silent. Slowly, the raccoon waddled towards him, closer and closer. I

25

tried to use common thought to keep Lewis safe, knowing it was almost impossible to have any control. I didn't want the raccoon to suddenly bite him. When the animal got close enough to touch, one squirrel chattered a warning. I pushed a feeling of calm into common thought hoping to reach the squirrel, and it quieted. The raccoon waited. Lewis turned his hand slowly, palm down. He tried to pet the raccoon which quickly jerked back, "Not the ears!" And Lewis heard it, I know he did. His eyes widened, logic dumped into his head as he thought he imagined the words. Again, slowly, he ran his hand along the raccoon's side. It felt smooth and soft. I was feeling what Lewis felt. The fur pulled back as Lewis' hand went over it, as though the raccoon were being tickled. Lewis touched him lightly once or twice more, then suddenly felt fear. I felt his fear, too. I don't know how it got in, or why, but the fear grabbed him around the throat so suddenly that the raccoon jumped back, then Lewis jumped back. Before long, the birds fluttered off and the squirrels scurried up a tree into the high branches to reach the sun. The raccoon, surprisingly, sat back for a moment and looked at Lewis, its pale belly and black feet facing him. Both Lewis and the raccoon cocked their heads. I had lost contact with both of them during the rustling noises of the other animals leaving the area. Yet, Lewis and the raccoon were still together. They had connected, excluding all else. What was going on between them? What was passed from one mind to the other? I pushed forward using common thought, tried to unlatch the door they'd shut, but nothing happened. It was too late. I was locked out.

Lewis reached out towards the raccoon. I waited. Please don't let it bite him, I prayed. That would destroy all the progress I'd made. Lewis could be lost to common thought forever.

The raccoon chattered quietly and leaned forward onto all fours. It shook its fur and took steps towards Lewis whose hand and arm was stretched to its limits. The raccoon came close and sniffed at the boy's hand.

Don't bite! Don't bite!

In a moment, a small pink tongue licked at a finger. Lewis stared, but didn't move. The tongue licked again, then the raccoon's head pulled back, it turned, and loped to the tree it had dropped from. Once into the branches, Lewis' arm dropped and his mind opened so wide Lewis felt as though he was in free fall. I felt it, too. He closed his eyes for a moment and placed both hands on the ground, one on either side, to hold himself steady. The ground brought security, the solidity of earth, the permanence. Lewis' mind let common thought engulf him and all the trees in the grove toppled in, the bushes, too, and mushrooms and grass. Lewis looked up, this time with the knowledge of the grove. He sensed the wind roll from branch to branch. In Lewis' mind he could almost feel the wind currents, the rubbing of branch-to-branch, needle-to-needle, the comfort of roots and trunks. He felt me, my many years, thick limbs, rough bark. Nothing was strange to him that grew. What the grove felt, Lewis felt. All the strangeness of nature, plant life, that was not known to him became available in an instant.

I don't know what tool the raccoon used to open Lewis' mind so completely, what trick of concept, but I imagined it to be a link in a long chain from human to animal to plant. I could never have reached him so well without the raccoon, could never have been so fully a part of him. I tried to sense what he sensed and became dizzy. He was dizzy. It was like a revelation, hearing God, seeing an angel, a wood nymph. The forest had become an enchanted place for Lewis. His eyes literally saw differently, like a psychic sees auras and knows when something is right or wrong with a person through that knowledge. Not that Lewis could see auras, but he could sense his connection to common thought. He could see each tree as an individual. He would, from that point forward, know the raccoon he first made contact with, and connect to me like no human ever has.

Chapter 3

The summer sun grew hot while the rains brought refreshment to common thought territory. To say that the woods remain the same from day to day because it looks the same, filled with the same plants, is a foolish thing. Not only does the forest floor of leaves and needles shift its patterns through wind and animal interruptions, there's the continual newness of branches and buds, leaves, new sprouts and blossoms. There is the tragedy of branches broken by the weight of rain and grip of wind, the death of trees and bushes, trampled or eaten mushrooms, old deer dying off and fawns being born. Birds are quick to come and go, even humans have beginnings and endings. An old man in a far farm house died on July 27th.

The forest and field shaped itself around a dozen or more children that summer. Paths were cleared, grass and weeds worn away from base lines, trees cut into, saying Joe and Sheryl, Eddie and Sue, with crooked hearts and straight arrows through the hearts. When a ball game ended, or lulled in the high-noon heat, the cool woods became shelter and a place to tell stories about the dead rabbit found near third base, the big snapping turtle the children rolled out of the playing field using sticks. Robert Hershon's black eye. The one he got while trying to stop a line drive to center.

Lewis, from the day Jeffrey had thrown away his drawing, had kept separate from the other children most of the time. His interest in them grew and subsided like breathing in and out. He went through cycles of emotion, often linked to the amount of life and death in the forest, though he never realized the source. He never told anyone about that needle-laden clearing near the brook where he had first made contact, through the raccoon, to the rest of common thought; the place he began thinking of as the enchanted forest. Lewis visited there often during that first summer and never told any of the other children. That summer, while Lewis became more of an introvert and Jeffrey separated himself from nature, shutting it out, I pushed further into Lewis' being and began to feel what he felt, hear what he heard, smell and see whatever he smelled and saw, often to the exclusion of my own senses. This total involvement warped my thoughts to see things through the eyes of a nine year old. But I did not have access to everything, pieces were left out, or altered because of Lewis' interpretation. At times when Lewis was away, such as church or shopping with his mother, I would probe upon his return and get only what he remembered. What's worse is that my understanding may also alter the facts. And, in cases where pieces are missing, I have no choice but to skip them altogether or create the situation based on the emotions passed through common thought.

It is during the school year that Lewis and I were first separated for long hours. His memories of the day were cluttered with Geography or Math lessons. He disliked History, all the dates and names of famous people to remember, people whom he hardly saw reasons for remembering. While one led a battle, another invented a machine no longer in use. Even Alexander Graham Bell. "So he invented a telephone. Do we need to know this?" Lewis asked Jeffrey one night.

"You do if you want to get out of school some day."

"Are we going to have to memorize all the inventors of the world?"

"Not quite." Jeffrey lay across his bed, Lewis across his.

"Do you like this stuff?" Lewis asked.

"It's okay. I like the Civil War stuff. Generals and battles. Pow, Pow!"

"What about the rest of it?" Lewis rolled onto his back, his History book held above him.

"I just memorize it. No big deal."

"So, do you know who invented everything?"

"Whatever's in that book."

"Who invented the car?"

"Ford."

"The washer and dryer?"

Jeffrey just threw a weird glance at Lewis and made a face.

"The television? The computer? The telephone pole? Without the telephone pole how would they string lines? That's an important invention. So is the highway. Who invented that? Swimming pools? Great for summer."

"You're goofy, Lewis."

"No I'm not."

"You are too, everybody says so."

"No they don't."

"They can't figure you out. You're too weird."

"Nuh, ha." Lewis threw down his book.

"What are you two doing up there?" their mother yelled.

"I dropped my book," Lewis yelled back.

"You'd better finish your homework or there won't be any television tonight."

"Okay."

Jeffrey stuck out his tongue.

Lewis picked up the History book and put it on the desk. "I'm done reading."

"You'll fail the quiz on Friday."

"So, who cares?"

"What are you going to do, draw yourself into the future?"

"Maybe."

"You can't major in art in college if you never get into high school."

"I'll finish."

"Not if you don't study."

"I'll study enough."

"Suit yourself, space boy." Jeffrey went back to reading. Lewis picked up his pencil and sketch pad. He had already begun to draw as well as some of the high school students, but he seldom felt satisfied with what he turned out. Periodically, and from memory, he'd go back to the field, remembering that first perfectly timed day when the sun was at the right angle and he and Jeffrey had first come onto the field. He'd draw, sometimes illustrating a weed head during its explosion just after being smacked by Jeffrey's hand, trying to catch the sparks which emitted from the weed. The golden glow of the field could never be done well in pencil, but Lewis tried, building in him a frustration, a knowledge of the inadequacy of humans to recreate nature. Lewis also produced drawing after drawing of the enchanted forest, the brook, the snake, even the raccoon. Although Jeffrey let him alone with his art most of the time, he still scoffed at Lewis and put him down for his constant attention to it.

"Back to the drawing board," Jeffrey would say with a snide tone in his voice.

"I'm trying to show the personality of the trees, not just a generic tree, like generic corn or beans Mom buys at the store."

"Oh, so trees have personalities?"

"If you get to know them."

"You're goofy as shit."

"Don't say that."

"Why, you gonna tell Mom?"

"No, just don't."

"Shit, shit, shit, shit, shit," Jeffrey said into Lewis' face.

Lewis gripped his pencil and broke the point on the sketch pad.

"Gettin' pissed?"

Lewis' lips drew tight. "No."

"Yes you are," Jeffrey said. "You're always pissed. You just never do anything about it."

"So."

"That's 'cause I'll cream you."

Lewis put down the pad and leaned over it to erase the mark he'd made by breaking the pencil point.

Jeffrey pushed Lewis' elbow and Lewis' arm jumped. "Stop it!"

"No," Jeffrey said. "Make me." He did it again.

"Jeffrey!"

Jeffrey poked at Lewis' ribs, then cuffed the back of his head with the flat of his hand.

"Asshole," Lewis said.

"Woooo, you are getting pissed."

"Just stop it."

"Or what?"

Lewis dropped his pad and pencil, got up from the desk and swung at Jeffrey, but Jeffrey stepped back and pushed Lewis aside. He tripped on the throw rug and went down against the bed frame. His head cracked loudly. Lewis blacked out.

I tried desperately to see through Jeffrey's eyes, but got little more than foggy images from him, so I attempted to get closer using a maple which stood outside their bedroom window. Either way, through Jeffrey or common thought, it was difficult, no link seemed close enough to Lewis for me to fully understand what had happened. I had become used to seeing through Lewis himself, these substitutes were relatively ineffectual. Lewis' blackout was deep and dreamless. Through Jeffrey's jumpy, foggy mind and Mrs. Marshal's, once she arrived on the scene, I found out that Lewis had cracked his skull badly.

Before long the loud ringing of an ambulance siren filled the air spaces between all the trees. It was a frightening, constant sound that packed into the woods like the insulation that had been blown into the Marshal's house walls, pushing obnoxiously deeper as it grew closer to the awaiting household, who were ringing their hands while standing on the front porch.

When the sound stopped, I pushed towards Jeffrey. He had calmed and I could see blood in his memory. Although I couldn't really feel his emotions, the fact that his mind balanced between clear and foggy indicated nervousness. His memory was recent and the blood ran along the floor below Lewis' bed. When they finally brought Lewis from the house I let go of Jeffrey and focused on Lewis through common thought. His sandy hair was matted, with dark blood, to his fragile head. Blood also stained the stretcher. The two men hurried him into the ambulance and in moments were off. Jeffrey and Mrs. Marshal followed in their own car. Mr. Marshal hadn't returned home from work yet. The smell of their supper drifted onto the air, dissipating into the smell of a warm autumn night. There was no way to reach Lewis now.

Jeffrey moped around while Lewis was on his mind, then totally rejoiced in his own plans and thoughts between those times of guilt, which became fewer and fewer as the days went by. He adapted quickly to

Lewis' absence, moving his things off the desktop and onto the floor beside the bed. Jeffrey also folded down Lewis' school photos. The sketch pad, the latest one, had already been removed. Lewis had asked for it almost as soon as he awoke from his initial blackout. "He didn't seem to care where he was," his mother had said.

Those days were difficult for me. The woods and field weren't the same with Lewis gone. The leaves made different sounds, animals played less, even the brook flowed quieter, as though waiting for his return. Then, one day, I felt a sadness rise from the enchanted forest and searched it out. The pines stretched, reaching for the morning sun, accepting the weak rays from the cloudy sky. I focused on the squirrel population hoping to sense the problem, but even they seemed a little confused. Some ferns and moss emitted a short, quiet sorrow, and, searching closely, I found it. The raccoon. It lay near the trunk of that first tree it had climbed from on the day of Lewis' connection. But it lay still. Dew had accumulated on its fur. A shiver rustled over its back, and a weak cry came from its dry mouth. For some reason, I knew it had waited for me. When I probed, it shook once, then calmed, as though even common thought was painful. The raccoon was old, something I hadn't noticed, hadn't cared about, that day in summer. While trying not to die, its mind pulled and stretched to the physical world, holding on with claws of faith. Once with him, I let go and opened. The connection was strong and I could feel pain like never before. I thought my roots were being stripped from the ground, pulled from my trunk in violent jolts.

The raccoon placed Lewis' image into me and tried to make me understand how special their connection had been, but I knew, I felt it, too. It let me know how dangerous and difficult it would be to try to hold too tightly to Lewis, how life for humans is filled with many more emotions, pains difficult to accept or understand, and to try to ease up contact, let go of Lewis. The raccoon was warning me about the frustration of not being able to help, how dangerous the need to help could be to my own well being. Before he died, before that last struggle with the physical world, the final shrug of the shoulder, sniff at the air, I told him I understood. Then he was gone, a short life being the payment for mobility. I had, though, already decided that I would accept all the pain, all the frustration necessary, just to experience Lewis.

Upon Lewis' return home, Mr. and Mrs. Marshal had a small party. Children came from school. Many of them were the same children who had grouped together all summer in the heat and itch of the ball field, even though Lewis seldom played with them. A few others were new to me, new friends from school. Although Lewis had to take things slowly, the noise rose and the cake and ice cream, just like a birthday, plopped onto plates and was engulfed by the always-hungry mouths of children.

"What happened that you had to go to the hospital?" Brittany Sholes asked.

Lewis looked over at Jeffrey who stood in the corner of the room talking with his friend Larry. It was like looking at himself, only a healthier, stronger self. The person he couldn't disconnect from. The person who had pushed him down was always pushing him down. He felt an urge to throw something at Jeffrey, a bottle or plate, knock him over the head, but instead he answered Brittany. "I fell and hit my head real hard."

"Oh, did they have to stitch it up? My brother had his hand stitched up when he accidentally cut it on an arrow point."

"Did he?" Lewis said politely.

"Yeah, how about you? Did they stitch it?" Brittany leaned towards Lewis and reached to touch his head.

He turned so she could see the bristly spot where his hair had been shaved and was just coming back in. He let her touch it and could feel her soft fingertips probe around his wound.

Brittany smiled and exclaimed, "Your hair feels funny."

"Funny?"

"Good funny."

Lewis had never had the attention of a girl before, except for Lorrie Watkins at the ball field, but only when he hung around, which hadn't been often towards the end of summer. But this was different, even for a nine year old. Brittany's closeness carried with it a sense of intrigue, interest, which didn't come through while hitting a ball and running bases. Lewis suddenly found words more difficult to mold in his mouth and fumble-tongued a question about how school had progressed without him, which came out, "How'd ya do, okay, in the last months?"

"Huh?" she said.

"School, I mean," he mumbled.

"School?"

But before he could regain control of his own tongue, Mrs. Marshal clapped her hands for attention and announced the arrivals of the first parents. All excitement and talk hesitated, then changed course as children found their coats and got ready to leave. Most said something about being glad that Lewis would soon be back at school, a few just said "Bye" and "Thanks," before rushing out the door. Jeffrey glared at his twin, who was getting all the attention, and slowly built yet another wall of brick between them, one on each side of the personality fence, opposites as much as twins are expected to be identical. Neither seemed to want to recognize the other in himself.

Lewis milked his sickness to its fullest. It was the best way to keep Jeffrey in check. By feigning a feeble slowness, or intense pain, Lewis easily spent long hours in peace. He did begin school again, though, and had to put in extra study time just to catch up. That fall, he'd slip out for walks to the field, and often spend time sitting at my base, leaning against my trunk, just thinking, or sketching. His thoughts typically wavered around Brittany, and I could tell that his bringing up her image let it slide deeper into the ruts of his brain, making it important where it otherwise may not have been.

It was here, under my bared branches, that together, we experienced the first snow of that winter. Lewis had brought a blanket with him and sat on part of it, the rest he pulled partly up under his arms and around his front. The warmth of the blanket, added to the thickness of his shirt, sweatshirt and coat, felt secure. Most of the early winter wind was blocked by my trunk. Only occasional swishes of wind made it all the way around enough to flip pages in his sketch pad.

Lewis was the type of person who decided his life goal early, and had the drive to continue regardless of obstacles. His art went with him everywhere, much more than could be seen by a mere sketch pad and pencil. When Lewis looked at anything, there began a dissection of the object into distinct shapes and colors. Where others would see green grass with white highlights and interpret them, logically, with green high-lights, Lewis would see and interpret, properly, the white. This occurred over and over in his mind, so much so that, at points, there seemed to be nothing to what he saw but a contorted mess of shape and color. But just as in great paintings where distance brings the true picture together, so it was with Lewis. But this phenomenon went further than truth, or is it further than reality, and deeply into truth? For Lewis, and I can only imagine from seeing other works through Lewis' eyes, there was color and shape even in emotion. Later, Lewis would drag emotion in by alter-ing reality. That is what he did: alter reality to uncover truth. And I felt it in him, felt much more. I sensed what nothing physical could show. The tension, love and hate, understanding and confusion, sight and blind-ness, even in the thin, developing mind of the now ten-year-old boy.

One evening in early winter, Lewis drew emotion onto his sketch pad. It seemed guided to him by thoughts of Brittany Sholes. He had been digging that trench into his memory, focusing on her featureless young face and the feel of her fingers on his wound, when the bright haze overhead, caused by snow-filled clouds, burst into flakes. Lewis had his head skyward at the time. His hands were lying across the sketch pad resting on his lap. In the soft glow of that early winter evening, in the added security and snugness of a warm blanket over his clothes, and mingled with the flowery thoughts of Brittany Sholes, Lewis watched as those first flakes of winter fell. He watched them come down like slow parachutes, from the second they came into view, to the time they closed in around him, dotting his blanket and pad with quickly melting, moist hexagonal shapes. Because it was a dry snow and the flakes were not bunched into globs, each pattern exploded into clear sight just before melting. As they reached the leaves around him, the crystalline shape lasted longer before falling from grace, into a mere wet dot.

After a few minutes of pure amazement, Lewis hunched over his sketch pad and began to put his feelings onto the paper. And to him, unfortunately not seeing that the talent was his alone, Brittany had a great part in it. But it would be years of frustration before he could let her know that she had helped.

Chapter 4

The years, like days, moved by quickly. I watched as Lewis and Jeffrey became only slightly more civil as they entered high school. One became so much the opposite of the other that if it were not for their physical appearance, a stranger would not accept that they even belonged to the same family. Yet, even living at arms length as they did, the two were bonded with a closeness which grew once they passed the sibling rivalry stage which had plagued their childhood. As teenagers they were in competition, but with the added tension of a deep-felt love for one another, which occasionally caused violent disagreements and un-called-for ruthlessness.

Lewis had remained true to his interest in Brittany Sholes. Jeffrey, on the other hand, played the field. The twins had grown into handsome young men of average height, sandy blonde hair and gray eyes, Lewis' appearing much deeper. Lewis would stare, unnervingly, at people as they talked, often causing them discomfort, while Jeffrey used his eyes to coax and tease, winking, looking away. His eyes sparkled as they darted around. He moved quicker, thought faster, and was more deliberate and practical. Lewis pondered, stared, operated as though he were always confused, not sure what he should do, or what he wanted, besides painting and to eventually marry Brittany.

"Brittany?" Jeffrey laughed after saying her name. "You can't be serious."

Lewis had broken down, could not keep Brittany a secret any longer, but with Jeffrey's initial response wished he'd kept quiet, or told someone else. "Why can't I be serious?"

"She's not your type."

They walked along the well-worn tractor road. It was September, their final year of high school, Senior parties and graduation ahead of them. Jeffrey tried to help in his own brotherly way, but Lewis wasn't listening.

"You don't think anyone's my type, so why should I listen to you?"

"She's too flighty and free. You need someone quiet, serious. Brittany's more my type than yours. Ha! I'd say we should think of swapping. Marsha is the quiet type. I think she's annoyed with me anyway."

"Great, I get your leftovers."

"No, Lewis, don't be this way. I just mean that we're two different people."

"Wouldn't know it by looking at us." Lewis turned his face to Jeffrey and smiled to show he was joking, then turned back to walking with his head down thoughtfully, his ever present sketch pad under his arm.

"Maybe not, but it's true and you know it. You need a quiet girl and I need a gad fly. Let's face it, we're going after what's bad for us."

"Maybe for you."

"And for you. Marsha will slow me down, bring me down. I'm not used to thinking about things like she does. She worries too much about the ozone layer, whales, rain forests."

"They're important," Lewis said.

"See. You two are alike."

"Maybe, but Brittany might help me open up. I know I seem spacy all the time. I know I focus too much on art, but I have to, it's what I am. Maybe she'll drag me out of myself sometimes."

"Is that what you want?"

"I don't know. You're always telling me to open up."

"I don't mean it." Jeffrey stopped and put his hand on Lewis' shoulder. "You're not me. Sometimes I'm actually jealous that you know where you're going, what you want."

"You know what you want."

"Yeah, I want to make money. Lewis, it's not the same. You've known about your art since you were a little kid. When I tell you to open up, I'm saying it out of jealousy. If you opened up too much, you'd probably be unhappy."

"But, I'm in love with Brittany."

"God, Lewis, you don't even know her. She'll destroy you."

"We talk all the time."

"It's not the same. A relationship with her is an emotional battlefield for someone like you. Trust me."

As they headed towards the field, Lewis listened but never changed his mind. He wanted Brittany Sholes, needed her to continue painting. If the school year ended and he didn't have her, Lewis knew he'd never paint or draw again. So, right there, while going along that familiar path, Lewis began to plan. He had the school year, September to June, early June, to gain Brittany's affections or end his career at eighteen.

"Look," Lewis pointed to the sky along the Western treetops. The trees were on fire with the evening sky blazing against golden autumn leaves. The twins had made the trip often between the ages of nine and seventeen and every time they saw it, the sunset amazed them. Jeffrey followed his brother to the field, sensing that something there belonged only to Lewis. I could feel, at times, Jeffrey's awe of Lewis' confused, yet directed, drive toward a single goal. That awe, stretched thin as a rubber band ready to snap, was never inside him without a glint of jealousy and rivalry, yet it was there often. I felt it that day, even though common thought didn't penetrate Jeffrey so well as to know its origins.

The two of them rushed like chickens into a feed yard, towards the field. Lewis wanted to catch the golden glow of sun kissing weeds. He felt urged to sit in that sunlight, conjure, like an old magician, Brittany's smooth face, as the wind leaned gently against the weeds and tall grass, nudging them. What Lewis wanted most was to dive into common thought. He didn't know it exactly, but he knew the feeling, could shout when it and he were one, when everything changed, as though he were in a trance. He'd draw emotion out of the weeds, the trees, the sun. He'd falsely use Brittany's image to guide him, momentarily forgetting the enchanted forest and his meeting with the raccoon.

The moment Lewis jumped over the stone fence and burst into the pool of gold the field made, Jeffrey stopped following. He knew that Lewis was gone. Their brotherly conversation had ended abruptly, turning into a dazed mumble as Lewis broke loose and accepted common thought.

Jeffrey had seen it happen before. "I'm heading back," he yelled after Lewis. "Happy sketching."

Lewis waved. He was already turning and sitting. His pad opened, his pencil working to rough out what he'd drawn or painted thousands of times already, many of them gone into the waste basket.

Lewis had, by his senior year, already won many art awards at school, yet he had never recaptured the field, and he never would. It destroyed him a little each time he failed to recreate the feelings behind that first visit to the field. He imagined his own destruction as a cancer, a voluntary one. He knew that each time he tragically attempted to get those emotions on paper, they pushed further away from him. Yet, he had to go back to that time, he had to try. Within the boundaries of pain and failure, of the cancer of himself, there was also security and comfort, but it was the failure, that feeling of eating himself alive, that was the part of himself he recognized easiest, and felt closest to.

Lewis struggled with the drawing against time. The sun would disappear quickly, vanish behind the hills, and leave him alone in the dulled afterglow. He would let go of common thought, and sit, exhausted, until he felt he had to leave.

I can see him still, sitting as a young man, his hair brushing along his face, his eyes searching as much inwardly as out, sketch pad lowered, face turned up, almost in prayer. Never could I reach out and touch his shoulder, comfort him. I often yearned for the short sentence of mobility, even if I could calm his turmoil only once, and then die.

Like a volcano, his senses bubbled and churned and built up pressure. He shook like a tremor, two great stone plates under the ground, two brothers, grating against one another, yet bound in grit and dirt. Lewis wanted out, to reach outside himself and get away. He wanted to understand everything, transfer it to color and shape, but most of all to understand himself.

On the way home that evening, Lewis stopped by me and pulled a pocket knife. Why he'd never done it before, I don't know, I often begged through common thought for him to carve his name into my bark. That

40

night, it was a conviction, a promise to himself and Jeffrey, and I suppose Brittany, as he carved his initials and hers, a broad heart, straight arrow. I would carry that heart like it was my own, trying, year after year, not to let it fade.

Common thought allowed me to follow Lewis out of the darkened woods. Able to see him from any angle, I did as much: from left, right, above, and below, from behind and in front. There was no angle I hadn't seen Lewis from clearly, like seeing myself, and seeing myself through his eyes. It was as though we were one. But I couldn't escape my immobility, couldn't reach out to offer a comforting hand, a word of understanding. Immobility has its benefits if only through the use of common thought, but often I would give up common thought and long life for the short-lived mobility of humans and their ability to reach out to one another.

Lewis walked slowly, taking in his surroundings, letting color and shape wash through his mind. There were images in his head, scenes he would paint, not always as perfectly and brilliantly as in his thoughts, but beyond other artists, into a realm only he could reach. I know of no other who has ever shown that he or she had come so close to common thought. Somehow, Lewis was able to express it in his work. I saw nuances of the field and grove of trees in the enchanted forest, of the brook, in paintings where none of those elements were present in image.

On his return home that night, at seventeen, soon to be eighteen, a young man past puberty, future paintings snapped into his mind as clearly as watching a slide show. His head filled with ideas, overflowed with paintings which would take years to complete. In the cooling darkness of the woods, everything from Maxfield Parish-type semi-surrealist to Mondrian and Miro, from O'Keefe to Wyeth, passed in and out of Lewis' mind, paintings he'd seen, mixed with ideas of his own, variations of their works, brought into fuller understanding with slight changes carried out using the brush in his mind. Lewis exploded with pent-up energy screaming to escape. He couldn't spend enough time with a brush, a sketch pad, charcoal, to release all that grew at exponential rates inside him. And although I received this second hand, through Lewis, after the fact, I know that it was that increased explosion waiting to happen that forced Lewis to pursue Brittany.

Many thought she was beyond his reach. Even Jeffrey had expressed it that night on the old tractor road, but Lewis was driven. He planned and watched. He deduced that Brittany was pursued primarily by the egotistical athletes, the pushy quarterback of the football team, Ben Johnson, the state wrestling champ, Greg Botini. Other kids let her alone as though there was a cage around her, an envelope of energy. Yet, Brittany did tease the jocks, she even dated some of the other kids, Larry, Jeffrey's long-time baseball-playing friend for instance. It was the "Lonely Beauty" syndrome Lewis had seen in movies. Brittany scared the boys, all of them except those few who were so sure of themselves that they actually cared more for her as a monument to their virility than they did for her as a person. Lewis knew, one day when he over heard Brittany telling a friend, "I don't think he really cares about me, the me inside," that he had to strike, had to overcome the banks of his own shores.

"So," her friend, Sue, had said, "he's cute. Any girl would date him."

"I'm not about to be any girl," Brittany retorted. "There are other guys."

"Haven't you already dated most of them?"

"Fun-ny, Susie slut. That's because most of them are jerks and I drop them as soon as I find out."

Lewis eavesdropped while standing near a friend's locker. Although I couldn't connect with common thought that far away, I can see him standing there with his books, his ever-present sketch pad in the pile, his head down. Welling up inside him was the pressure of fear, excitement, lust, all the things associated with young men on the verge of pursuing love for the first time.

When Brittany left her friend for class, Lewis did the same. "Oh, I gotta go," he said, rushing off to fall in behind her.

"Where to? Class is this way," his friend yelled.

Lewis heard, but didn't answer, didn't stop.

Brittany's blonde hair swayed with her body as she walked. Lewis had seen her move, talk, smile, many times in his mind. Now, following her, those memories helped to bring her to life inside him. The longer he followed, the more he filled with her, the greater his conviction that he needed her for his art to survive. "Brittany!" The ice was broken.

She stopped and turned. They had talked before, but her face betrayed her, that she saw something new, unusual in Lewis. "What's wrong?"

Lewis swallowed and his knees felt weak, there was a twisting in his groin.

"Lewis?"

"Brittany."

She smiled at him. "Are you all right?" She stepped closer and put her hand out to touch his forearm. He felt the same sensation he always did with her touch ever since the time she touched his head after he returned from the hospital.

"Will you go out with me? Saturday?"

"Are you serious?"

Lewis felt like he was about to fall over. "Yes. Why? I've always wanted to. Since we were kids. Since I got back from the hospital," he exploded.

"When was that?" she didn't remember.

His heart sunk. "It doesn't matter. I need to go out with you."

"Need?" She pulled back her hand and looked at him quizzically. "Is this some kind of dare. Is someone making you do this?"

The thought that someone would have to make anyone ask Brittany Sholes on a date was ridiculous. Lewis laughed, "God, no, Brit." The laugh calmed him, steam oozed out his ears, nose, and mouth, the pressure subsiding, the stillness after the minor eruption settling in. I imagine his eyes getting softer, more inviting. "Brittany," he repeated, "I've always wanted to date you. I just didn't seem able to ask."

Bam! The truth came out so evenly that, in Lewis' memory, Brittany appeared to be overwhelmed. Lewis hadn't been the first to tell her such a thing, even he knew that, but he was probably the first person she considered a friend to do so. It must have been a new feeling for her, because she said yes.

"Yes?"

"I like you, Lewis, you're nice."

That night Lewis rushed home, threw his books onto his bed and ran up the old tractor road. When he approached, his arms spread wide. He hugged my trunk, his face close to the heart he had carved before the school year had started. "Oh, Brit, I love you so much. I knew it would work."

Of course, nothing worked, not yet, only that he managed to get a date with her. Nonetheless, Lewis had broken through. It wasn't just excitement and love for Brittany which broke through, but his personality. He had asserted himself. It may have been the first time other than once, when Jeffrey pushed him to the point of a fight, the two of them wrestling on the floor of the forest, leaves sticking to their sweatshirts, dirt kicked into piles until they both tired. Somehow, that may have been a start of his opening up, though, because they both tired. Jeffrey was no longer the stronger, only the more aggressive. They got up and actually shook hands afterwards, in congratulations of Lewis' expressing aggression, or for mutual respect, it didn't, at the time, matter why.

Lewis' personality was let loose for a while, you might say. After so many years of being locked up and pushed around, the escape inevitably came with no written instructions and few social guides.

After kissing the heart, each initial actually, one, two, three, four, Lewis let go and ran to the field. He leaped entirely over the stone fence, not touching the top flat stones at all, and slammed excitedly into the field. It still being winter, the ground crunched under his feet. The bent weeds and grass from fall winds and rains, stood stiff against his legs, unrelenting in the cold air. Nonetheless, he twirled in ecstasy, saying "Brittany, Brittany, Brittany," over and over until he became dizzy. Lewis slowed and walked further, towards the opposite end of the wide field, through the taller, uncut weeds, towards the dark clutches of his enchanted forest. As he walked, the grasses and weeds, trees and ferns, became part of his thinking. He slipped into common thought, to him a meditative realm of calm. He wished he'd not left his sketch book home, but when he looked skyward, he realized it was getting too dark for that and the enchanted forest would be even darker, with the pines looming, protectively, overhead.

Lewis ran part way to the enchanted forest anyway. The pine clearing opened before him, with little underbrush and the thin brook worked into the forest floor. Darkness swooped down and became ominous when he entered the pine grove. His eyes adjusted slowly as he walked deep into the clearing. He found the rock he first sat near and kneeled next to it. In front of him was the tree the old raccoon had plumped out of. For a moment, as Lewis turned his head to listen to the running water's trickle under thin bands of ice along the bank, he thought he glimpsed the raccoon. His reaction, instead of pulling back, was to fall deeper into common thought, only slightly askew, into the animal version, nonetheless still connected to me. His reaction was more than mere falling, it had elements of instinct, elements of a deeper knowledge as to what he was doing. I felt within him a confidence and understanding which hadn't been there before. The memory of the raccoon had drawn it out. A set of perfect circumstances had arisen, the right person in the right place at the right time: Lewis, the enchanted forest, in a deepening darkness where illusions coming from within easily slipped out into reality, exposing themselves to the physical world.

Lewis had not actually known that the raccoon had died quietly near a bush. For some reason, he never wandered in the direction of the carcass, even one time when he smelled the fading body and wondered of its origin. But, for the second time, it had been the raccoon who had opened Lewis further. It seemed that each time the pure opening of Lewis', shall we say heart, or soul, happened, a bigger part of him became available to more of common thought, and equally, more of common thought opened up to him. And it was his progress to this point that allowed him to project, no, recognize, the raccoon. For after all, in common thought, as along the thread of time itself, the raccoon had never really left that spot. In many senses, it was at the bottom of that tree, the kerplunk sound of its body landing on the soft needles, its appearance, its movements, its openness, all of it together being the key to Lewis' full understanding, his conversion to door opening as a way to live as opposed to door closing. Even Lewis' newfound personality of a higher degree of aggressiveness (and this, truly, is where I am leading) was as much a part of his understanding and acceptance of common thought, as it was the well-known egotistical human opening of the personality. Lewis, opened within and without, embraced common thought in a visual sense, around its

45

raccoon-shaped body and ran blindly with it, into the realm of human personality. The combination almost exploded inside him, the explosion not showing through, because as he kneeled near that rock, as he saw the raccoon out of the corner of his eye and in his soul, as he listened to the brook gurgle under leaves of ice, like a Thai chi dancer, he was calm on the outside.

The pine grove, miraculously knowing how different Lewis was, just as I and the raccoon, squirrels, birds, and probably brook water knew, helped Lewis to hold to the image, to grasp it. For Lewis, the enchanted forest stood tall to its name. He focused, was it inward or outward, past or present, on the raccoon and it came further into view, even though the remaining light would have caused the opposite had the raccoon still been alive.

The raccoon waddled to within a foot of him and, for a second time, licked Lewis' fingers in the present time (or was it a repeat of the past?) then used its key, a key which had not been used for nearly eight years. Another explosion occurred inside Lewis. Suddenly the enchanted forest was a realm of colors linked to emotions, colors bursting into intimate recognition to particular elements in nature, not just tree or stone or bird, but particular, individual tree, stone, or bird. He tossed his head back, sat down on the icy cold ground which forced a chill into the images he saw. Then, just as the feel of ice can be cold or hot, Lewis saw heat. Saw the color of it, and made it, and the cold, part of himself.

The raccoon was gone, the sky black. Common thought swirled around Lewis and through Lewis as easily as wind or thought. Tears crept down his face. When his eyes focused, he stared at his own hands, barely able to see them in the pitch black color of the night, under the canopy of evergreens.

Chapter 5

"Lew, don't take this date thing to heart. She's just being nice to you. Probably feels sorry for you or something."

"Say what you want."

"I'm only trying to help out my brother. You've gotten cocky lately, because of this date thing."

Lewis laughed out loud while combing his hair.

"Well, I don't find it so funny."

Lewis turned and leaned his face close to his brother's. "You're jealous," he said.

"Asshole," Jeffrey said. "I don't know what's gotten into you lately, but I don't like it."

"Nothing's gotten into me." Lewis walked past Jeffrey, the sharp odor of cologne lingering in the bathroom doorway.

Jeffrey turned. I saw the vague shape of Lewis walking down the hall through his eyes, but felt nothing. I believe I get this far because they are twins. As Lewis passes windows or house plants I see him, and always, I have Lewis' senses and emotions to guide me. If odor lingers in his nostrils, it must in Jeffrey's as well.

"You know what you are?" Jeffrey yelled down the hall at his brother's back. "You're arrogant, loud, egotistical and snotty."

When Lewis turned, Jeffrey's angry face appeared in view. "More like you than you'd care to know."

Jeffrey, in a flash of realization, let out the truth, "More animal than me."

Lewis slapped the wall with the flat of his hand as he ducked into his room.

Jeffrey walked behind him in a huff, "Brittany's too much for you. You'll never keep her."

Lewis tightened up. He knew, at this point, that he must keep her. She was too important to his art. As chauvinistic as it sounds, Lewis needed Brittany, not because he loved her, but because he needed her. She was fuel for the fire inside him. And without that fuel, he would fade to embers.

If I could have sat with him and explained how she only came into mind right before or right after he communed with common thought, would he even have listened? After all, what he felt for Brittany was not healthy for him or her. Nothing could be done. As much as I cared, I could only be a spectator, intimate though I was.

Lewis said nothing back to Jeffrey, so Jeffrey repeated, "You'll never be able to satisfy her enough to keep her. You don't have it in you."

"Look in a mirror, Jeff. I am you. I've got just as much in me."

"What's outside doesn't necessarily reflect what's inside. That's been proven before. And, I'll tell you right now, she's out of your league. Being cocky for a few days doesn't prove anything."

"I don't have a choice."

"What?"

"It has to work between us."

Jeffrey's facial expression suddenly changed to confusion. "I don't get you."

Lewis told him, "Without her, I die."

"You're weird, Lew. You're nuts." Jeffrey backed away, his hands raised to keep Lewis back. "What if I told you I liked her too?" Jeffrey played his trump card. "Who do you think would win her?"

"You'd be killing me."

"You're wrong. I'd be saving you. Probably from yourself. You just don't know it."

"You don't."

"I still don't get you. Why Brittany?"

"I love her."

"I saw what you carved in the tree, but that doesn't mean love. Neither does wanting." Jeffrey walked around Lewis like a cat circling prey. "And what makes you think she'll want you?"

Lewis' newly acquired, more aggressive personality pulled back, but the animal inside him remained strong. "Everything," he said calmly.

"You'll never keep her."

Lewis pushed past Jeffrey. "Gotta go." He ran down the steps and grabbed a coat from the hall closet. He picked up the car keys Mr. Marshal left on a stand in the foyer.

His mother appeared in the doorway to the living room.

"Hi, Mom."

"You have fun tonight, Lew."

"Thanks, Mom." He felt favored.

"Be home by twelve," his father yelled from inside the living room.

"I will." He looked at his mother's face. For the first time, he saw her, not as his mother, but as a woman. He noticed creases around her eyes and lips that he hadn't before. Her eyes were gray like he and Jeffrey's. Her hair was darker than theirs, speckled with gray. She smiled warmly. He should try portraits, he thought, try to capture his mother's face before it aged any more. He shook the keys in a loose fist. "Gotta go," he said.

"Have fun."

"I will. Thanks again." He walked onto the front porch and pulled the door shut behind him. He let the screen door slam. It was cold, and he pulled his collar snug around his neck and cheeks. The quiet night air was clear and hollow. The porch-boards snapped and creaked under his weight. The moon was not visible, but its light brightened a spot over some trees lighting a patch of leaves and exposed branches. Lewis looked back over his shoulder, wished now that he didn't have to go. But a lump welled up and lodged itself in his chest. Brittany's face appeared. He should paint her, he thought, echoing the feelings he had had towards his mother. He could already see the various colors of Brittany's skin, her cheek, its shape and highlights. In a dim light, she would glow with beauty. He tensed his muscles and forced himself to run down the few steps and get into the car. This was it, there was no turning back.

With the window cracked open at the top, the smell of the country circled inside the car. The headlights lighted the road and sometimes patches of woods, when he turned into a curve, where small animals jumped away or sat and stared, their eyes glowing magically, reflecting the headlights. The road twisted intermittently amid woods and fields, over a set of unused train tracks, then further on and out of my reach.

Regardless of what I wished for or what I've said, I was not a part of him, not a physical part which could travel with him like a mouse in his pocket. I could only reach as far as common thought allowed, and although there is common thought everywhere, it fades with distance just as a voice fades, or the sound of a train departing the station. What little perceptions common thought can pass from one boundary to another is often not reliable. I prefer as direct a contact as possible. A relayed message might as well be no message at all. I would wait until he returned and probe his memory.

Apparently, Brittany was ready when he arrived, a relief to Lewis who didn't want to sit uncomfortably in front of questioning parents. Although, when he saw her rushing from the house almost as soon as he pulled up out front, it also crossed his mind that perhaps she didn't want her parents to meet him.

"Hi," she said, the passenger car door half open, her face peering in at him. "You look nice."

"You look even better, but I'm sure everyone tells you."

Brittany sat down and closed the door. Her long hair was partially pushed into her coat in the back. Her legs looked thin through the black slacks she wore. "You haven't told me." She settled herself, "But now you have. Thank you." She seemed excited, glad to be with him.

"We're off then." He pulled from the curb into the street. "Thank you for going out tonight. You didn't have to agree to it. That was nice of you."

"Don't be dumb, Lewis. I wanted to. You've always been nice to me. We should have gone out long before this."

Lewis felt slightly uncomfortable hearing her praise. He twisted in his seat to try to get comfortable, but the discomfort came from inside not out.

Brittany zipped her jacket open and exposed a mint green blouse with fake, plastic antique buttons. She reached over and turned off the heater fan. "It's hot. Do you mind?"

"No." Lewis shrugged. "Not at all."

"Good." She sat back, settled in more comfortably, and crossed her thin legs. She leaned into the center of the bucket seats, resting her elbow on the armrest between them. "So, what are we up to?"

"The usual, I guess. Dinner. A movie. You're probably used to the routine."

"Like I'm used to people complimenting me?"

Lewis noticed an edge in her voice. "I suppose," he said, not knowing what else to say.

"Let's take this date like there's only two of us. Me and you. No others, just two friends."

Friends, Lewis thought. "All right. I'm sorry if I offended you."

"Stop." She put out her hand. "You're too nervous about this. It's not like we've ignored each other through the years. Like we're complete strangers. Ease up."

"This, well, it's different though. Not the same."

"I know what different means. What you mean, though, is that it's a date, not a friendly visit. What I mean is it's only a date. We're not going to get serious in one night. We're friends, Lew," she pleaded then slapped his arm, leaned in and smiled, then touched his cheek with her finger and whispered, "Don't be so worried. I'll tell you when you've done something wrong. And I'm sure you won't."

What? Wrong? What'd she mean?

"So, how's school?" she said.

"Ah, fine."

"Still winning art awards, I hear. Mr. Whitestone wants you to try for a scholarship, but he's afraid your record in other classes will hold you back."

"How do you know?"

"Heard him talking in the hall. I forget who with."

"I've tried to study and keep my grades up. They're not that bad."

"No, but you've got to admit your grades aren't anywhere near Jeff's."

Lewis felt hurt that Brittany would even know Jeffrey's academic record. But why not? Everyone knew Jeffrey. He was popular and smart. "He has different work habits."

"You mean he studies," she smiled playfully. "That's okay."

Lewis pulled into the parking lot at Winnaby's. "Jeffrey has everything." He parked in an open space near the back of the lot.

"What, because he studies harder? Well, he doesn't have a date with me."

"I'm surprised. He's more popular. And Larry..."

"Larry's nice. I don't like the way Jeffrey treats you. Never did. I think he's mean."

"Really?" Lewis left the dash light on and turned the engine off. Brittany's hair sparkled. Her face glowed. A warmth came from her eyes and smile. Lewis stared at her, ran the shape of her cheekbone and jaw, her forehead, eye sockets, nose, through his mind. He drew her, sketched in the light from the dash, the outside lamplight at the edge of the lot.

Brittany swallowed and averted her eyes. Lewis was staring. She put her hand on his arm, where she'd playfully slapped him earlier. "That's why I wouldn't go out with Jeffrey and agreed to go with you. You're kind."

"He asked you?"

"Yes, two weeks ago, the first time."

"The first time?" Lewis was beaming. He'd actually managed to outdo his brother. This grounded his conviction that Brittany and he were meant for each other. He felt blessed and thanked whichever supernatural being may be responsible. No wonder Jeffrey had made such a fuss, following him from room to room, trying to dissuade him from dating Brittany. It was jealousy. And defeat.

"Yes, he asked again last week. I hope this doesn't make it worse for you."

"Not at all. I feel privileged."

"Privileged?" She leaned her head back and laughed loudly. "I'm not a privilege, I'm a problem."

That disturbed Lewis. A problem is just what Jeffrey had called her. Why? Was she only playing with him, and this was his cue? Was she already planning to break his heart, even before the relationship progressed? His image of her, the one sketched in his mind, took on new angles of light, converting her to a darker, more menacing, vampire-like person. Lewis shook his head and got out of the car.

Brittany leaned over and turned off the dash light, while he circled the car to open her door. She let him take her hand and they walked into the restaurant together. While waiting to order, they hardly spoke, even after ordering they remained silent. When their salads came, rather than avoid one another's eyes by looking at menus or rearranging the table utensils, Brittany asked, "Why so quiet, Lew? I was waiting for you to say something. Mother tells me not to talk so much, not to try to control the conversation. When you quieted, I thought something was wrong, that I talked too much, so I waited, but I can't wait any longer."

"You said you were a problem."

"I didn't mean anything by it. Actually, I'm more a problem to me. I never seem happy with anyone."

"Does it bother you?"

"Sometimes. Everyone's so, well, worried about scoring me, like I'm a game card, a sport. I hate it. That's why the other day I asked if they dared you. I thought, now there's something Jeff might do just to get at us both. You because he's always mean to you, and me because I wouldn't go out with him. But that wasn't it. You asked on your own, and I've gotta tell you, I'm glad."

"I've wanted to ask for years. You never really seemed interested."

"I was," Brittany winked while lifting her fork to her mouth. Lewis took the cue and they both ate in relative silence until their salads were almost gone. Eventually, the conversation progressed. Lewis became more comfortable and Brittany even more talkative. There's no need to go through it all. What's important is that, to Lewis, Brittany became more human and less fantasy. He saw insecurities which he had never attributed to her. Most notably was a lack of confidence in her own personality, that it could be liked by boys, rather than just something they had to accept to get at her body.

Yet, it wasn't really her body, Lewis thought. It was more her face and hair. Brittany was just a skinny girl. Her legs were tooth picks under her pants, her breasts small, but noticeable, there wasn't much of a butt to speak of. But her face was beautiful, her eyes had that perfect gleam, the first eyes you noticed when you came into a room, beacons. And it was the way she carried herself. Regardless of how she felt, she displayed all the outward appearances of being confident, the walk, the sway of hips, movement of the hands and head. She was what every boy or man wanted.

Lewis continued to listen to her, even though he often didn't hear what she was saying. She jabbered. Most of the talking that night came from Brittany. Lewis kept his eyes on her almost continuously, drilling her features into his mind, noticing her movements, the sound of her voice. He listened intermittently and still knew where in the conversation she was. He still followed her thoughts easily.

Brittany loved to talk. Her hand was always reaching for his, just to touch it. Her head cocked teasingly, letting her eyes sparkle. She bent to look straight into his face for emphasis whenever she said something that she thought was funny. Brittany's arms were always moving with signs of interest, excitement and mystery. As she moved and talked, Lewis soaked it all in. He already, after one date, felt himself to be part of her life, and felt that she would be part of his.

Upon his return to the house that evening, there was a strong sense of accomplishment, yet with a trace of sorrow. Something about her made him sad, but he refused to accept it. Instead, he focused on the color and shape of her, and the sound of her voice. It was not her that he loved as much as what he pictured her to be. Image and sound. Color and shape. Yet, Lewis shrugged it all off and called what he was feeling love.

I'm being too critical here, I'm sorry. I must say that he did love her, in his way, and even after that first date, she must have, somehow, loved him also, whether for his listening ability, his appearance, or because of what I've always believed to be essential in their relationship, the presence of the raccoon inside him, the mystery of common thought, animalistic understanding, plant understanding, and don't let me forget, his complex understanding of beauty, shape, and color, which was his own gift.

I must also apologize for my theories being dispensed throughout this, but, admittedly, much of this story is my perception and not necessarily what actually happened. As much is true as I can make it. Forgive me the rest. I'll try to relay the story more directly and be less intrusive. Nonetheless, I believe that Brittany was attracted to Lewis because of that intangible part of him she wasn't quite conscious of. And, sadly enough, it was Lewis' closeness to common thought that helped to develop a distance between him and Brittany.

TERRY L. PERSUN

Chapter 6

Near the end of the school year, Lewis became more talkative, more proud. He and Brittany had become an item, regardless of that underlying sadness about her that Lewis carried with him everywhere. Mrs. Marshal adored Brittany, not only for her talkative and likable nature, but for what Brittany's personality appeared to draw out of Lewis. Then there was Jeffrey, who eventually accepted defeat by being jokingly light-hearted about the apparent mismatch.

One day, Lewis came running down the stairs. "Mom?" he said.

"Yes, honey. I'm in the kitchen."

"Is it all right if I take one of the cars and run over to Brit's?"

"I think so. I don't plan on going out today. I think Jeff left with Larry already."

"He did?" Lewis grabbed an apple from a bowl on the table and bit into it. "Thanks," he mumbled. "We're gonna talk about college."

"I thought you decided on the Philadelphia College of Art?"

"I did. But Brit's not sure what she's doing yet."

His mother leaned backwards against the counter next to the sink. She had been cleaning vegetables for a salad, and green, orange, and red debris lay around her. Her hands were wet. Lewis liked the soft, domestic picture created by the aliveness of the color against the soft hues of his mother's dress and apron. "Do you need help cleaning up?"

She smiled broadly, "No, go on. I've got more to do first."

"Okay."

She turned back to the sink filled with color and plunged her hands back into work, as a splatter of moving colors roared through Lewis'

56

head.

During the drive to Brittany's, Lewis stopped by the creek bridge not far from his house. The creek's feeder streams came in from all angles and from all directions, one such feeder being the brook from the enchanted forest. Lewis pulled over and parked next to the road after crossing the short bridge. He got out. I could see into his eyes as well as through them. They were strange, almost transparent. He saw the weeds near the road as pins with large heads, like the ones used to pin new shirt sleeves to the shirt itself. The hills bending towards the creek became cement embankments. The creek itself was a wash of smeared color; rocks became arrows pointing upwards from the smear. There was no sound entering his ears but a constant ringing. The abstract lingered in Lewis' mind and he became afraid, or anxious, something welled up in him that I did not understand. What he saw was distortion of color and shape. Then, the weeds moved like waving fingers sticking up from the ground. The creek muddied, then lifted up on short legs and splashed in the pure white residue of itself. The muddy smear continued to flow quickly even though the feet moved slowly.

Lewis buckled at the knees and lowered his head into his hands. Through my lead, common thought tried to stabilize his feelings. There was little that could be done, so I tried immersing myself in his image, his mind, and found only confusion, distance. I pulled back quickly and noticed him jump involuntarily. Somehow he felt my quick departure. How? He stood back up and opened his eyes. The scene had slid back into normalcy. Light from overhead sparkled silver on the water and tall weeds near the road bent to touch his hand. His mind cleared. He was a realist artist, the abstract was foreign ground, horrible and frightening.

Lewis rushed back to the car and pulled his sketch pad from the back seat where he had thrown it earlier. He roughed out what he had seen, but something was missing. In the rough sketch there was a calmness, the calm of common thought, a richness to the odd images which did not belong to them, the edge was gone, the tension relieved. He tore that page from the pad and threw it out the window towards the running creek water. He dropped the pad onto the seat beside him and got back onto the road. Brittany would be waiting.

As soon as he pulled up, Brittany appeared at the door and ran out to the car. She always seemed to be waiting for him to arrive, and he was always surprised by her apparent, overwhelming interest in him. She opened the door and popped her head in. The same face, the same smile surrounded by blonde hair that he had seen over and over, came into focus once again. "Hi, cutie." She picked up his sketch pad and sat down. They kissed quickly. "You do another one of me?" Brittany asked opening the pad.

"No, sorry."

"But you were doing something." She paged through the front of the sketch pad, the beginning pages, and when she got to one she folded it back and held it up. "I like this one." It was a rough sketch of her that he'd done at school during lunch.

"Don't smear it."

"You worrier. I'll be careful." She flipped through more pages and stopped at a sketch of the field.

They were driving to the park near Brittany's home. "What are you looking at, there?"

"The field. Your sketch of it."

"Oh."

"Why do you do so many? And most of them without the baseball diamond?"

"I'm trying to get it right."

"They look fine to me."

"Yes, but they don't feel fine. Something's missing."

"And the ones of me?"

"What about them?

Do they feel right?"

Lewis reached over and put his hand on her knee. She quickly grabbed his hand and leaned into his arm. "They feel just great," he said.

It was a fresh smelling spring day and a lot of people were at the park just to be outside for one of the first really warm days since winter. Lewis took Brittany's hand as they walked. She had left the sketch pad on the car seat. Both her hands were touching him, the one not clutched by his hand was wrapped around his biceps. She leaned into him and he felt a continual drag from her weight half-resting on his arm. It always seemed peculiar to him that she actually, as the word implied, hung on him. At first he enjoyed her attention, but lately her blather and hanging made him wonder about her true affections, which seemed almost desperate, an odd thing to even suggest for such a pretty girl, but truly how he felt. He dismissed his thoughts with a shrug. "So," he said, leading the conversation into talking about college.

"Here we go again," she said.

"You don't like to talk about it, do you?"

"I'm just not sure what I want to do. I don't even know if college is right for me. You know? I've always wanted to be a wife and mother, stay home."

"You're seventeen."

"Eighteen. My mom was married when she was eighteen."

"But your dad was twenty three and had a full-time job. I'm going to be a Freshman in college."

"I'm not saying that we should get married."

"It sounded it."

"Well, what is going to happen in September when you go away? We just break up?"

"I hope not." Brittany was really pulling on his arm, so Lewis shook loose and placed it around her waist. His shoulder had begun to hurt. He felt frustrated, unsure of what he wanted from himself or Brittany.

"We could live together."

"Where? In the dorms?"

"No, in one of those little artist's lofts like on TV. You could do a whole series of me."

"How could we afford it?"

"Who cares? We'd do something."

Lewis couldn't figure what. He surely couldn't ask his parents to help him with an apartment so he and Brittany could live together. "Why don't you go to college at the University of Pennsylvania? We could see each other all the time then."

"I don't know. What would I take?"

"Take Economics or History, something you're interested in."

"But I thought I was done with school this year. I need a break. I need time to figure things out."

"There isn't much time."

Brittany kissed him on the lips. "For us there is."

They kissed again. The people passing by seemed to ignore them.

Lewis could see out the corner of his eyes the bright colors of spring. If the colors were not natural: greens, yellows, whites, they were synthetic: blue, orange, and red clothing. When he and Brittany hugged, Lewis looked down the long sidewalk which led over a small knoll and down to a lake. The sidewalk was mottled light and dark gray. The dark gray shadows, cast down by the overhanging trees, moved with the wind. Dandelions speckled the large grassy areas around the sidewalk and between the trees in clusters like small galaxies lifting from a universe of grass. The people, on the sidewalk in front of him as well as the sidewalk's tributaries entering from left and right, walked leisurely. Many were middle-aged with children following behind, some were of college or high school age. All of them, though, seemed to know their own lives, joys and sorrows, and accepted them. None seemed as confused as Lewis felt he was.

On one hand, Lewis loved Brittany. He had loved her from age ten. She was the impetus behind his creativity no matter how distant they had been in the past weeks. Her being with him now materialized his need for her. His spiritual need. Yet, the way she hung on him, her lack of enthusiasm about her future, and the constant blather about her girlfriends, clothes, shopping, her need to express herself in such an animated way that it almost became animation and not reality, all this bothered him. Yet, he kept it hidden inside, pushed it deeper every time it came up for air. Regardless of these bothersome personality quirks, I can assure you, Lewis was in-love with Brittany. He maneuvered his way around her hanging, her blather, and her animation, almost as though it wasn't there at all. The most he felt was that slight sadness he had always felt when with her, which he attributed more to himself than to her.

Holding hands, walking towards the lake, Lewis loved Brittany. She protested going to college, still thought they could make-it living together. She was unrealistically smitten by young love's ability to over-

60

come the harshness of the world, uncompromisingly optimistic. Furthermore, and most importantly, she had decided not to go to college at all. Her innocent outlook made her even more beautiful to Lewis. It brought out an inner light in her eyes and her hair, like the many suns of the dandelions as they were moved by the wind, which hypnotized Lewis into believing she may be right. Sitting at the side of the lake, they forgot, or pushed aside, all conversation centered on what they'd do after high school. There was a summer ahead of them, plenty of time for such decisions.

Although I received all this information second hand, it came through as though I were actually there with them, as though I was the tree they leaned against when they kissed just before going out to sit near the lake shore. So you can understand how intruded upon I felt when the following episode happened.

I recognized, inside Lewis, the presence of common thought, but rather than from my territorial range, it came from the park. It was like the rushing of air into a vacuum, and although I knew I could always hold a place inside him, this rush of common thought pushed into him with a vengeance, wishing to hold onto him and keep him. The park was aggressive in its probing, and I felt violated because of Lewis' own memories of me and the field and the enchanted forest. I knew that Lewis accepted common thought. That's what made him different, but this was the first time I was faced with another common thought becoming intimate with him. It was like lightning burning loose one of my branches, like squirrels hollowing out my trunk until the sap wouldn't run, like a woodpecker pounding, pounding, pounding into my side. There was no reason for me to feel the way that I did, but the feeling was there, standing alone inside me. It was not Lewis' fault for loosening himself, for opening the door, it was mine for feeling betrayed. After all, it was me who edged that door open, who picked the lock in the first place. Regardless of what I felt, Lewis gained immensely from his experience that day.

Sitting by the lake, holding Brittany, and letting go internally, Lewis opened his eyes and heart, to both human love, and common thought love in a way which advanced his work tremendously. Lewis, in his normal manner, mentally painted the lake, the trees surrounding it, the grassy edges at the borders, the sun shining across its flat surface, the reflections in the top, the small ripples caused by fish breaking the water's surface tension to eat bugs. Then there were the smells and sounds, from which he made his own shapes and colors. He included taste, added common thought, and love, and even more aggressive common thought, or, if I may, a different common thought personality. All this happened inside his mind, like the flash of a camera, a thousand dandelion heads blooming into super novas at once, the painting, almost like a revelation, burst into view.

"Where's my sketch pad?" he said, breaking the silence.

"In the car. I left it on the seat."

"I need it."

"Now?"

"Yes." He got up. "I'll be right back." Before Brittany could say anything, Lewis ran to retrieve his sketch pad. When he returned moments later, he was out of breath.

"God you're impulsive. I've never seen you like this."

"Something's happening to me," he said. It was the short, confused episode from the side of the road near the creek bridge. It was the experience of personality through something he wasn't sure he even possessed. It was love, beautiful love, but love the way it always arrives, with the razor's edge of confusion, sadness, and pain just under the surface.

While Lewis sketched the lake which had suddenly come upon him, as he tried to get the nuances of all those things he felt into it so that he could paint it later, Brittany sat quietly, her head on his shoulder, her knees bent and her legs tucked under her. Lewis worked quickly. By placing a line here or a curve or check there, he would remember what it meant and be able to translate it later. He had created, long ago, his own shorthand, used to transfer exact images from sketch pad to canvas. Color and emotion went down on paper, including the taste and sound and feel of common thought, all of it incorporated in a certain structure, a certain style. When he was through, he lay down the pad and pencil and sighed deeply.

Brittany, who had been quiet the whole time he worked, sighed also. "That was wonderful."

"How do you mean?"

"To watch you create that quickly, right in front of me. I feel such a part of it. Like I did it myself."

Lewis felt embarrassed and slightly violated. She had entered his world. She could watch, but not comment, not be part of it except as he wished it. That was a strange feeling for him to have after years of attributing much of what he'd produced to her, as though she had already been a part of it. But she hadn't been a part, not really. She had only been a necessary utensil, just as the pencil or pad. She wasn't allowed to take credit.

"It's not done," he told her.

"It looked it."

"You wouldn't know. There are pieces that aren't right." He was quick with her, blunt. "Besides it has to be painted. This one has to be." He pulled back from her.

"Don't be so mean." She pushed his shoulder with her hand. "Don't you want me to be part of it."

Yes and no, he wanted to say. She was a part, emotionally. He just didn't want to spoil a work which came from the depths of him with the arrogance of reality, with the intrusion of speech. The sketch, and eventual painting came from silence, it should remain there. "I'll do you," he said. He wanted the sketch to escape from her, slip away and be left alone, for him to deal with it later. He flipped to the next page in the pad, distancing her from the lake piece.

She conceded, "Where do you want me?" She loved being sketched, and Lewis, in his blind love for her, loved to sketch her, if only to make her happy.

"That tree over there," he told her, "sit next to it."

She got up and bent down to kiss his forehead. She ran to the tree and he followed.

"Now sit down and look over there, to that side of the lake. Watch that crow perched atop that tree near the edge of the water."

She turned her head and stared. She quieted. Just what Lewis had

63

wanted.

"Now, stay still," he said. Don't even talk, he thought.

And again he opened up to common thought and let it flow through him. Or he may have been pushed into it. I felt a pressure. But whichever happened, he drew Brittany, adding his shorthand notes into the piece. This would become the first painting of her he would do. It would have elements of love and aggression, hate and reserve. But for now, it would quiet her and it would calm him.

Neither wanted that day to end. As evening crawled across the western sky, they found themselves alone in the park, in one another's arms, watching the sun's final departure slip away in the splendor of the day, stretching its orange and pink arms across the horizon.

They kissed gently, then more forcefully. Their breathing became heavy. Lewis felt Brittany's hands slide over his back and shoulders, one hand tracing a line to the back of his neck, around to his cheek. His hands, too, roamed the softness of her body, trying to pull her closer to him, inside him. They breathed into one another's mouths and nose; their teeth met, their lips slipped like soap in a bathtub, almost no friction, only nerve endings. Lewis held her face while they looked into each other's eyes. As their lips pressed together again, his arms were caught between their bodies, his hands still on her face. She held him tightly, kissing him, then loosened enough that he could pull his hands down. When his hands reached her breasts, she pushed into him again and moaned. She shifted and twisted her body slightly so that his hands moved over her. Lewis squeezed, then pushed when Brittany made a tiny sound with her throat. They pulled back for air, but Lewis' hands stayed against her. She reached up and unbuttoned two buttons on her blouse. One of his hands easily slipped behind the cloth and cupped her bra as though his hand were another layer of material. His other hand moved around to her back. She twisted in his arms. They kissed lightly and his hand pushed against her, his thumb brushing the bare skin of her breast being pushed out the top of the bra. In an instinctual moment, his hand was completely over her bare breast, the nipple pushing hard into his inexperienced palm. They breathed and kissed as he rubbed and pushed. Their mouths were long tunnels, their tongues trains rushing to reach the other side. Each flick of the tongue pushed deeper into Lewis a sense of need. Every time he moved, or Brittany moved, the movement seemed to affect his groin. Even as his hand rotated on her breast, his groin felt the pressure.

As the sun sent up its last spark in the sky, some people further up on the hill talked. Their voices were low, and couldn't be understood, but the sound penetrated the privacy that Lewis and Brittany had placed around themselves.

Lewis jumped, his hand pulling from her breast as though it were a hot stovetop. They both turned to face the sun. Brittany, nonchalantly pulled her blouse together at the top and rebuttoned it. Together, they looked out over the sky where the sun had just disappeared. No more voices came from the hill. Lewis turned his head to look. "They must have been walking past on their way out."

Brittany looked into his face when he turned back around. What did she see? An artist? A man? Or just someone different? Was she really in love with him? It seemed so. She searched his eyes, nose, cheeks, mouth, with her eyes. Then she burst out laughing.

"What?" Lewis said, his mouth turning up into a wide smile to match hers.

"You look so serious."

"Well, they scared me."

"They sure did."

"You, too."

"I know. That's what's so funny."

He laughed. "That was funny. I wonder if they saw what we were doing?"

"How could they in this little light? Maybe they saw us kissing, but what more?"

"Probably."

They kissed slowly, Lewis leaned into Brittany, again feeling his groin as much as his lips. He opened his eyes and saw that Brittany's were closed. As he pulled her close, her hand fell to his thigh and an explosion occurred inside him. They pulled apart. "We should go," she said.

"We'll park the car somewhere."

"Okay."

Lewis had a difficult time walking back to the car. His nerve endings were all at the surface of his skin. Every step seemed almost painful. Brittany held his hand with both hers and leaned on it until it ached, but Lewis couldn't get himself to pull it away. He wanted to be very delicate with her. The situation demanded that things go smoothly between them, no wrong moves, even though he didn't quite know why he felt that way. Instinct took over. Even humans had it.

When they had the car parked off the road and into some underbrush, Lewis cracked the window open. The night air had cooled considerably. The smell of the forest lifted up and squeezed into the car. Brittany sat opposite him, against the passenger door. One leg lay provocatively across the seat. Lewis bent over the console between the seats and reached for her. She leaned and kissed him. His hands went straight for the buttons on her blouse. She helped. In a moment two white mounds with pink, hard nipples stared back at Lewis. He reached up and caught them in his hands. Brittany closed her eyes, sighed deeply. She propped one foot on the seat and let Lewis' upper torso slip between her thin legs. He could feel her thigh against his side as his lips kissed her hard nipples, as his hands traced her shoulder blades and neck.

"We should get in back," she whispered.

Lewis was hoarse and almost speechless. His actions spoke for him as he pulled away and let her crawl over the console to the back seat. He could smell the scent of her clothes as she passed. A cool wind shook the car. The sound of leaves rubbing together in the trees and of Brittany's movement across the seat mixed together in Lewis' head. Bright patches of blue car seat and white skin, jeans slipping down the long thin legs of Brittany.

Lewis fumbled and shook. He helped her off with her underwear all the while wondering how he would, in his condition, undress himself. He noticed a sparkle of light reflect off the moisture at her crotch, the soft, blonde hair, slightly matted, the musty odor. His wallet fell onto the floor, then he reached for it and for a moment Brittany helped him retrieve it and pull out the foil wrapped condom. Lewis noticed her cool smile, the pinks of her nipples, how they stood out, pointing at him, the wetness between her legs, the new shape her body took when her legs were bent slightly and open.

Chapter 7

Brittany did not follow Lewis to Philadelphia where he went to school, but, on two occasions, she did drive down to visit him. But most often, he drove the six hours to visit her. I remember him coming home during the cool, early-autumn days. He'd first come into the woods, up the old tractor road, and sit next to my trunk, or climb onto the branch he fell from, and just sit or sketch. Even before Brittany got to see him, often before his parents or Jeffrey, if Jeffrey were home from business school at the same time, Lewis ran straight into the woods. That's where he would recharge, by opening his mind, the door to his true self, where he would slip into common thought and let the wildness inside him flow like a raging river. In those days, Brittany was almost never out of his thoughts. He focused on her face often enough to keep her with him always, but neither she, nor anyone else, could rejuvenate him like common thought. Each time he walked through the woods to the field or the enchanted forest, the whole area took on new life for him. Subconsciously, he knew that it was the source of his deep understanding of nature, if not life itself. Lewis lived for this contact, and although there was common thought everywhere he traveled, there was none like his home, like me, the field, the enchanted forest. He would never forget the raccoon or the glow of gold spread over the field the first time he and Jeffrey went to find it. Before he went to see Brittany, he always came to us. This one time, something bothered him, which made it more imperative that he come into the woods and open up.

I felt his presence almost immediately. I didn't have to search for him, he was just there. Tired after driving all those hours, Lewis had already allowed common thought to swell around and through him. A meditative lull hung over him, yet inside, if you searched deeper, he was running, trying to keep up with the sensations bombarding him.

In common thought, all of nature swarmed around with its own understanding, its own personality. As I think of it now, for Lewis, it must have been like having other people in his head trying to take over his thoughts, but there was more to it than that. Lewis also connected to animal common thought, and possibly human common thought as well, even though it was often pulled back and hidden from me. Inside him there was the strength of numbers, and minimal probing uncovered that the sensations and, if you will, pressures, of common thought were almost constant now, coming at him from all directions. All he had to do is open up and focus. But here, I could help buffer his reception. I had some control because of our bond. Common thought outside my range could be extremely harsh to him, like receiving many things at once and not having the ability to sort them out. Lewis, while driving home, had grown fatigued by the ever constant pounding of common thought. It was so strong in his mind that I thought of pulling back to let him rest, but decided my presence could do no worse, could actually help to protect and calm him.

It wasn't until he got home that I realized he had brought paintings back with him. As he unloaded them into the house, I could see in his mind what they were. Out of eleven large canvases, which barely fit in his back seat, three were almost identical paintings of the field. I recognized this as a cry for help, a cry for everything to go back to the way it used to be. Each of the field paintings had only minuscule differences, hardly noticeable. Still, the feel of each was different, although, none had reached what Lewis searched for. The other eight paintings were split, four nature scenes and four portraits, one of Brittany done from memory and incorporating an unnatural, or unrealized, longing. All of Lewis' paintings had something extra, other than the visual, some you could almost smell or taste, every one had emotion and personality, as I said, even the three of the field had their own individuality.

He took them inside, carefully setting them under and behind his bed to protect them, then brought in a suitcase from the trunk, and a bag of dirty laundry. He moved almost automatically, as though in a trance. What he saw of the house, felt, as he unloaded the car, kept changing. It reminded me of the episode near the creek bridge off the highway. Occasionally, abstract images appeared, with them fear and anxiety came. Lewis brushed the thoughts away, sometimes by physically running his hand through the air in a motion reminiscent of shooing a band of gnats from his face.

Rather than take the bag of clothes upstairs, Lewis threw them in the laundry room off the kitchen. He rushed through the house and actually broke into a run when he reached the bottom step of the porch on his way out. By the time he ran past me, slapping his left hand over the carved initials, there were tears running down his cheeks. He leaped over the stone fence, fumbled and almost fell, but his hands stopped him and just as quickly pushed him off again, into a full run. Inside the enchanted forest, he stopped running and leaned against a tall, black-barked pine. The sound of the brook roared in his ears, the vibration of the pine, its life, hummed like an electronic motor under his touch.

He breathed heavily, adding an uncomfortable roughness to his throat. He coughed and spit mucous into the underbrush behind the tree. Images, blurs of images, raced through his mind. The tree held him up, his fingers parked between ridges in the bark. He cried loudly, a defeated wail. His hand went up to rub the back of his neck. Kneeling, he placed his face against the tree. In a few minutes, his crying slowed. He was tired. When he calmed, almost falling asleep from exhaustion, I saw into his mind and realized what had happened. He had betrayed Brittany with a girl from his school, an art student. She was plain looking and odd tempered. She dressed loosely, talked about politics as much as art, and how art should be anti-political in that it should show alternatives. Lewis had no idea what she was ever getting at, and didn't really like the girl. Then one night, in a light rain, she visited. I saw in his memory her matted hair and damp cheeks. He was nice to her and wrapped her in a blanket to fend off the damp and cold. He offered her a dry sweatshirt which she accepted. When he turned around with the sweatshirt, her top was off. She never wore a bra. He handed her the shirt and she took his face and kissed him. The odor of fresh rain, the feel of her cold face and breasts was still in his mind as clearly as it had just happened. He could have refused her, I saw it, and he thought briefly to do so, remembering Brittany, but I felt animal common thought well up in him. A different order of instinct took over. Human moral judgment was pushed aside as he took her in his arms.

Now, kneeling by the tree, it was moral judgment that he was fighting with. He had operated from a different order, one which he'd been accepting into himself for many years now, but one which had not taken over, had not, until then, reared up with any great strength inside him. He fought it and accepted it simultaneously, performing a tug-of-war with himself. He first felt as though he had betrayed Brittany, then he decided that he had only done what he had wanted. Both answers were right for him, both were equally represented inside him. He could accept both with total indifference, that was plant common thought coming through: the inability to act brought a certain amount of indifference into the picture. Mixed in proper proportions, plant common thought was good and could help Lewis, but he accepted everything so fully and whole heartedly that one could not overcome the pain of any other. Each emotion stood firm with equal force, merely switching places in line, confusing his perception, discoloring his ability to ultimately decide which way to go. He cried as much from the battle going on inside him as from his assumed adultery. Images of Brittany and the other girl, Susan, pounded at the inside of his skull, indifference rising often enough to let him rest only for a moment, then the pain would burst from his eyes again, like a volcano.

I wanted to uproot and go to him, would have even if it meant death, but I could not. I felt I had been damned to the soil by some impassionate god. My leaves began to wither as I willfully held back nourishment. Lewis was in great pain and therefore, so was I. As I pushed deeper into his mind, the only way I could touch him, I felt my root tips get numb, felt my branches sag. Never had anything so physical happened to me. At the same time I tried to will my consciousness into him, forgetting myself totally. The deeper I probed, the more my extremities became numb.

Once I pushed that far inside Lewis, things changed for me. It was almost as though I was Lewis and not merely a player inside his head. I remember reaching up to wipe Lewis' (my) eyes, the softness of our cheek. The ends of my fingers were dry from the paint, and scratched the corner of my left eye. The ground was cold, not because I was inside Lewis' mind and it had told me so, but because I was Lewis and I felt it, felt it on my knees. As Lewis, for those few seconds, I became terribly confused, body parts moved, I sniffled, scratched, my face wrinkled. Thoughts and emotions and physical movements became one. A twitch of the lips, the way the hand lifted, all connected intimately to emotion, visual images flashing in lightning speed through his mind. I felt nauseous. I wanted to lie down but couldn't. I couldn't! Then, I left him. Snapped back. I lost consciousness for a few seconds and when I gained it back, felt the numbness at my extremities. A few leaves fell from my grip. The darkness of my bark became blacker. Nothing inside me felt the same. And worse, I could not move. I could not go to him, couldn't even get inside his head again. I was exhausted, so I watched him from a distance. I didn't want to get too close for fear I'd probe inside him again. Humans were complex, too complex, but Lewis was not merely human, there were also the effects of common thought running through him like a vein. He fought the added complexity with the already complex problems of being human, but often the many things in his head were at odds. I waited and watched, trying also to bring myself back to reality, let the nourishment flow into me.

Lewis kneeled near the pine tree for a long while. His exhaustion finally let him stop crying for good. He sat flat on the ground, his legs stretched out and slightly apart, not moving. He leaned back against the tree and stared upwards. My first reaction was to get inside him and see what he saw, but I held back all the while wondering if any of the other trees, grasses, ferns were able to enter him without me, but as quickly as I wondered, common thought answered.

I don't want to get into the dynamics of common thought, but you need to understand that I was the contact to Lewis. There are complex reasons for everything, and just as humans question one another on the subject of God, I cannot be sure about all aspects of common thought. If I were to guess, I'd say the first contact is the one in control of contact, or the stronger one recognized, and I had probed continually those first days, placing myself further inside him. In reality, the way it feels, is just that we two clicked. I don't know what philosophical implications that brings with it: perhaps that we were together in another time, that each human has soul mates which also cross over the boundaries into plants and animals. If I were to philosophize, in fact, I'd stretch that to include the deaf and dumb rock, the brook, fallen leaves... Do leaves belong to the realm of common thought while on the branch, then transfer to another realm, the realm of the rock, when fallen? Does any of this even matter? No, I suppose not. What matters here is Lewis, and that I am in contact with him, at least until I pull away.

I watched him. He would have stayed all night if Jeffrey hadn't come through the woods looking for him.

"There you are," Jeffrey said, breaking the silence.

"I am?"

"Therefore you think." Jeffrey laughed at his own joke. "What is it, Lew?"

"I'm tired." Lewis still looked upwards, towards the partly cloudy sky.

"When did you get in?" Jeffrey only walked close enough to be able to talk comfortably and not feel as though he had to shout, as though Lewis were a wild animal which might quickly run away if approached.

"I don't know when."

"You been in here a while?"

"Yeah." He lowered his head and looked at his brother. "Sometimes looking at you is scary."

"How so?"

"For a moment I think I'm not me, that you are. That I've disappeared."

"Not a chance, Lew. Not a chance." Jeffrey shook his head back and forth. "You are definitely a unique person."

"That could be because I'm not really here. Just a mass of extra thoughts. You came out first. Maybe I was just an afterthought. Still am. Wandering in every direction."

"Who's wandering?" Jeffrey stepped closer. "You know, Lew, ever since we were kids you've known exactly what you wanted to be. Your whole life has been chosen. Mine's been confused, not yours. If anybody's wandering aimlessly, it's yours truly."

"But there's too much sometimes. Everything I do is so important."

"You're a fanatic. It's not all that important, you make it that way. You do that to yourself."

"No. It is important."

"Is it?" Jeffrey rubbed his hand over his chin, which could have been Lewis' chin. He looked down at his brother, shook his head. "What are you doing here? I came to get you."

Tears filled Lewis' eyes and he sighed long and deep. "I've cheated on Brittany."

Jeffrey rolled his eyes, raised his hand, and let it fall against his leg in release of energy. The loud slap got Lewis' attention. "You fucked somebody and you feel bad?"

"You don't understand, without Brittany..."

"You can't paint. Bull fucking shit. I told you you were a fanatic. For Christ's sake, maybe because of experience you paint better. You know about artists and all their lovers."

"Not all artists."

"Who cares? This is you! Don't ruin your life over something like that. It's over now, right? Put it behind you. If you're still devoted to Brit, then nothing's changed."

"You're so logical."

"I'm studying business. I'm supposed to make sense."

They both laughed. Jeffrey walked over and held out his hand. "You're my brother and I love you, but you're also one weird son-of-a-bitch."

"Fuck you," Lewis said while taking his brother's hand.

"Talk about Brittany, she's at the house. Worried. That's why I came looking for you."

"What'll I tell her."

Jeffrey gave Lewis a look of disbelief. "Nothing. You went into the woods like you always do the first thing you get home, and you fell asleep. That'll explain those bloodshot eyes, too. Maybe the drive was too much for you this time."

Lewis walked a little lighter. Things got better. Sometimes a loving brother is best. A tree is nothing, at best a mass of unconnected thoughts, not even recognized.

Lewis and Jeffrey talked and remembered together, wondering if they could still get the kids together for a ball game. They decided they probably could, but didn't want to. It was better just to remember them on the walk home.

"You look better already," Jeffrey said at one point.

"Thanks for the help. I thought I lost it out there for awhile."

"Sometimes you need logic," Jeffrey said. "Oh, and I looked through your paintings. They're great. I wonder if you really need that school sometimes."

"Me too. That's why I'm quitting."

Brittany was glad to hear the news and quickly forgot her previous worries. She actually jumped up and down clapping when Lewis announced his decision. "That's fantastic. Oh, my God. I can't believe it." She hugged him around the neck. Jeffrey smiled and was outwardly happy for them. Mr. Marshal shook his head and walked into the other room.

Mrs. Marshal leaned against the counter for a moment, then pulled a chair from the kitchen table and sat down. "What do you plan to do now, then?" she asked.

"Paint." Lewis said over Brit's shoulder.

His mother looked away, gained her composure, and turned back to look him in the eye. "You're going to paint from your bedroom? I thought you were going to be an illustrator, get a job. How are you going to take Brit on dates, get a paper route?" She slapped her hand down on the table. Mr. Marshal heard the loud crack and came into the kitchen. Brittany let go of Lewis and stepped to his side, her arm resting along his waist.

"I'll be okay, Mom."

"Will you? How? You're giving up college. How do you expect to get a job? Be a respected member of the community?"

"Respected! Is that what you want? I'm going to paint. That's what I do. That's me."

"Hear, hear," Jeffrey said, raising his hand as though there were a glass of wine in it and he was toasting Lewis.

"Don't egg him on," Mrs. Marshal said.

"I'm not. I just think he's old enough to make his own decisions."

"Don't tell me you're next with this nonsense," said Mrs. Marshal.

"Never. But I'm not Lew."

"Thanks," Lew said, "but the truth is I've sold a few paintings. A gallery near Philadelphia wants to show my work. And I'll find work illustrating. I don't need much."

"Neither do I," Brittany said, then she turned away in embarrassment.

"It's true, Mom. I'm sorry you're upset, but I'm not doing well in school anyway. All I care about is my work." He looked to Jeffrey who was nodding approval. "This way I'll be able to focus on just that, nothing more."

Brittany slid closer to Lewis, tightened her arm around him.

"Well?" Lewis said.

Mr. Marshal walked around behind his wife and placed his hands on her shoulders. "We've always been supportive of you two as individuals." He smiled weakly, then went on, "We're not always happy about your decisions, this one for instance, but we're behind you. Just remember that you can change your mind. If you decide to go back, we'll help."

Mrs. Marshal looked up at their father and placed her hand over his and patted it once or twice, then nodded. "If this is what you want, Lewis."

Chapter 8

Like the seasons, the cycles of life, and the cycles of emotion, there are mental cycles which arrive and depart quickly and others which arrive and depart more slowly. Like the unwanted quest, they do not go by strict patterns and may arrive at any time, and in the midst of other cycles, as well. These swellings and ebbings overlap, making the simple mind complex and the complex mind even more so. Inside Lewis, where things turned and swirled together, storms thrust him into rages, and calms abandoned him to lethargy. There was a time, not long after he moved back home, when happy and sad were the same mood emotionally. He worked on sketching out ideas for paintings or worked on actual paintings almost continuously, running himself ragged into the late evening. A second gallery began to request his work and he began to sell to magazines. For the science magazines he was required to be more abstract, and that's where confusion came in. He altered paintings by mixing human, animal and plant qualities. Eventually, he recreated the creek with legs from his earlier experience. Then he carried on by painting dandelions as their own universes, the pods rushing out like nature's own big bang. But inside him, emotions had to be manipulated, colors altered slightly, shapes distorted. In order to continue his work, he had to maneuver around his own mind like the Titanic in an iceberg-infested ocean.

He suppressed his short meeting-of-the-bodies with Susan and focused on Brittany for his inspiration, although she was only a jumping off point for him. Regardless of what she was to Lewis, whether the entire inspiration in all his pieces, or only a starting point, her image etched itself into his brain and did not let go. He became obsessed with her, a love-hate overwhelmed him, it built concrete castles in his chest, exploded his heart. Their lovemaking increased in frequency and he learned to include it in his paintings, the passion of thrusts and the tenderness of a hand slipping off panties, how a silk blouse hung over the back of a chair.

Lewis was written up in the local paper as the artist genius of Blattsfield, Pennsylvania. His paintings sold increasingly well.

One day while sketching the field, while standing in the early light of sun-up, he turned to a new page and laid out a two-bedroom cottage with loft where he and Brittany were to live. All he had to do was buy the piece of woods just west of the field and have the cottage built to overlook what, through time, had become his other obsession, the field. He vowed that he would search the expanding light across the horizon every evening for just the right feeling, the one he had the first time he and Jeffrey ran innocently into the field with wide eyes and open hearts. That feeling of delight and happiness he often confused with the odd melancholy inside him.

Brittany had pressured him about marriage, usually after lovemaking, sometimes during. "Do you love me?" she'd ask.

"Of course."

"Sometimes I think you're not going to marry me, that you're just going to use me then throw me away."

"Never."

"Do you think we'll be together forever?"

"I can see nothing else in my future but you," Lewis said one afternoon while sitting up in the cool air of a rented motel room. The bedspread lay on the floor, knocked off during play.

Brittany stood near the mirror. I saw this all from his memory of it. She had very skinny legs and thin arms. Her about-average-size breasts were firm, but sloped slightly downward. To Lewis, the pinks and pale whites of her, the blonde of her hair and bush, colored the morning in its own light. Her standing there before him brought on a great weight, the heaviness and sadness of never really loving, but of the obsession of need. He told the truth when he said he could see nothing in his future but her, except that she could have been an ornament on a shelf.

"Then some day we'll get married?"

"Definitely."

"You sound so sad when you say that."

"Not at all, just serious."

Brittany smiled. She walked over to him and took his face into her love-scented hands and kissed him.

He had played that scene in his mind many times, always with the same curious interest, as though he were merely trying to understand it and not hold it as a cherished thought. When he thought of marriage, a thickness of the chest, not unlike that received when he was about to paint, overtook him. And what did it mean? Wasn't marriage a dangerous thing for most? I would suspect it was even so for Brittany, but she seemed to want it badly.

"We could be together forever, me in the kitchen cooking or in the living room playing with the children, and you in the loft painting, becoming more famous by the hour."

"In the loft?"

"Of course, all painters have lofts where they paint."

"Oh, yes, of course."

"Don't you want a loft?"

"Yes, I do." He looked into her face from his position on the bed. Her hair was like the flames of the sun. Sometimes when he looked at her, she took on the appearance of that little girl who touched his sutured head wound, the little girl who seemed so caring and so sensitive. She held him and he wanted to melt into her hands and face, but it was sadness he would feel, not warmth and happiness, because that sensitivity between them seemed to be gone. Maybe it was never there. Lewis never thought that, I did, I extracted it from how it felt to me. As I said, happy and sad were the same thing to Lewis during that time.

He told her about his layout and sketch for the cottage. It looked like the one he imagined she thought of when she mentioned the kitchen and the loft.

"Do you have it here? Can I see it?"

"In the pad." He pointed to the chair where their clothes were draped. Under his jeans, the spiral of the pad protruded out over the edge of the chair.

Brittany went to it immediately. She remained completely nude, un-afraid, un-shy about her body. She brought the pad over and sat next to him, handing it over. Her legs spread and one leg was placed along the bed in front of Lewis.

He looked down into her soft blonde crotch, pink protruding from the puffed folds, a glistening of moisture.

"Find it," she said.

Lewis flipped through the pad and opened to the sketch.

"It's beautiful!" She exclaimed. "Just as I pictured it." She moved closer to him, an acrid smell rose between them.

At once, Lewis wanted to tear the sketch apart and drop it into the waste basket. He didn't understand the feeling and suppressed it almost physically.

"When did you do it?"

"The other day."

"Were you planning to surprise me?"

"With what?" He knew what she was getting at and wanted to avoid it, but couldn't.

"The cottage."

"No, I just... It wasn't meant..."

"You didn't mean to let it out."

"Not that."

"Ohhhh," Brittany hugged him and shook her head. "You're so sad-looking sometimes, like a puppy dog. If you wanted to surprise me with the house, you should have. But I know you, you couldn't wait."

"It's not like that. Don't misunderstand."

Then she got serious. "Misunderstand what?" She pushed away. "You didn't mean for me to live in it with you, did you?" Her accusation came at him like the shot from a rifle.

"Not at first," he admitted. "Until I could afford it," he said trying to ease the pain he saw in her face.

"I thought you wanted me. I thought you loved me." She bent her head at an angle.

"I do. But I need to work for a while longer."

"Maybe we should just break up for now if you're not ready."

"But I am."

"Are you?"

He began to shake inside. His obsession with needing her in his life clicked in like a light switch being turned on. He couldn't let her go, but didn't want to be pushed into marriage either. "I'm just nervous," he said. "I wanted everything to be perfect."

"It will be."

"Not if it's too soon. Not right away."

"I've always wanted to be married to someone famous," she said.

"But I'm not famous. I've only just begun to sell regularly, and I'm not sure I can keep it up."

"You can."

"How?"

"If you have a wife and baby who depend on you, you'll have to. It's the best thing."

"Can I take that pressure?"

"It'll make you even better." She leaned into him once again.

Lewis felt defeated. He wasn't positive what he wanted. He put his arms around her and felt the soft skin across her back. He wished he could just suck her into his body and have her there, not have to deal with her on the outside world, not have to feel manipulated.

Brittany pushed him over onto the bed and kissed him. "Forever," she whispered.

The word echoed inside the caverns in Lewis' mind. For the first time, forever fit only his work and not Brittany. For the first time, it was difficult for him to see her forever. Maybe for the rest of his life, until death, but forever dragged more than mere mortal time with it, and he was uncomfortable with the thought. Brittany must have seen forever differently, more temporary.

As they kissed, his mind slipped off into another realm, the one of sex, where little else mattered but the senses, and that final wild release where all color, all sound, all sensation, met and merged.

Afterwards, Lewis rolled over onto his back. Brittany took his hand and said quietly, "Forever." She had not forgotten, and needled him with the word.

Lewis tightened up. His mind clamped around the word and held it like a vice, not letting it go any further inside him. Marriage was one thing, forever another, and Lewis struggled with the distinction while Brittany slowly fell off for an afternoon nap.

While she lay sleeping, Lewis slipped off the bed and took a shower. He let the water fall over his face and head for a long time, closing out all other sound, the road outside, the buzzing light over the small vanity, the flapping corner of the shower curtain. He stood in the tub and dried off, looking at his body in the mirror. He seldom stared at himself that way, the real him lay inside the body, in a tangle of color and shape. Outside, he was Jeffrey, strong-limbed, sandy-haired, gray-eyed, like the gray of the sky just before rain. Not black thunder clouds before a storm, but the gray of an all-day drizzle.

As he dried off, Lewis watched how his arms worked, how his hands grasped, his penis swung, and his thigh muscles tightened. He had done the same careful watching with Brittany, his father and mother, even the kids at school, the boys entering the shower after gym. Once he watched so intently, trying to collect those movements, that he was discovered and called faggot by a few of the boys. That soon subsided though, as they realized Lewis didn't care about their taunting. He was already introverted and the teasing didn't irritate or amuse him, so the boys gave it up. At the bathroom mirror, Lewis remembered that time and the difference in movements between one boy and another. In the mirror, though, all he could detect were similarities between he and Jeffrey. He slipped the towel over a wrack near the door and went into the room to dress.

Brittany slept on top of the blankets, her tiny butt sticking up, one leg bent at the knee. Her body twisted slightly on the bed and her face turned towards the window, her mouth open, her full lips pink against the white pillow case.

The way the dark blue bedspread was tucked under her, it looked as though Brittany was outlined in blue and that she was lifted, held above the bed by the bedspread. The negative space created an interesting effect. Lewis dressed quickly and began to sketch out the offering, the bedspread holding Brittany out to him, for him to take. Like waiting for the next song on the radio to see what it said you should do with your life, like believing that you heard your name called when it was completely quiet, like any expected God-send or total mystery, Lewis was ready to believe, did believe, that Brittany was being offered to him, handed to him from the dark-blue platter of the bedspread. He drew her fuller than what she was, added weight to her butt and legs, a larger mound to the shape of breast pushing out from the weight of her torso. After he was through, he closed the pad and set it back on the chair. He went over and slid his hand over the small of her back and onto her butt where he cupped each cheek one at a time. Then he leaned over her small face and kissed her, his hand now on her shoulder and shaking her. "Brit, wake up. Brit."

"Lew?"

"Yeah. Are you awake?"

"Silly question. I'm talking, aren't I?" She rolled over so she was pushed against him. He watched as her breasts swayed first one way, then the other, and how her arm moved and her legs parted, the blue bedspread still holding her white-skinned body out to him. "I guess you're awake then," he said.

"So?"

"So, what?" he tightened.

"So, I guess we better go."

"Right."

She ran her fingers along his cheek and jawbone. "I had a lovely afternoon."

"Me too."

"We should do this more often."

"It's expensive."

"Not if it were in our own home."

"Then marry me." He couldn't believe that he'd actually said it.

Brittany's mouth gaped open and stayed that way for a long while. "No."

Lewis' face wrinkled quizzically.

"I mean, no, like you can't be asking me, not no like N-O."

"But I am." Another surprise.

She sat up. "Oh my God. Lewis, you're actually proposing."

He lowered his head. He wanted her and didn't want her. This may have been the only way, what he must do.

"I accept. I want to. I'd love to." Brittany bounced on the bed, her arms waving as though she were in a parade, stark naked, waving to a million on-lookers. "There's nothing in the world I'd rather do more." Then she asked, "When?"

Lewis hadn't thought about it. "Later, when things are ready, once I feel set."

"After the house is built?"

"I haven't even looked into it yet. I have a sketch, That's it. And not a very good one."

"Maybe our parents will help out."

"My mom and dad can't do much."

Brittany became solemn faced. "Are you trying to put this off?"

"Not long."

"Only until everything's perfect." She crossed her arms. "Well, it's not going to ever be perfect."

"Not perfect," he protested.

"Then when? Have you even thought about it?"

"Yes." But he hadn't. "A year."

"A year? That's long enough for you to change your mind. You'll get more sales, more women will come around. Bam, I'm out-a-there."

"No, Brittany." He moved to touch her.

She scooted over and got up from the bed and began to dress.

Lewis turned. "Don't be like this. I just have to get some things straight." He was a hurtling ball of asteroid inside, watching the earth rush into his face at increasing speed, feeling his body overheat with air friction. "Any time you want then," he said, his arms outstretched and pleading. "We'll talk about it and decide together."

"I don't think you mean it. You're not ready."

"That's not it."

"Then what is?" She halted, her jeans halfway up her legs, her breasts hanging like two bells swaying, ding-ding, ding-ding.

Lewis found it difficult to think. He couldn't lose her, and getting married didn't seem right. Not yet. Not now. He needed to build first, try to get the field perfected. His hesitation worsened the situation. He was looking at Brit's breasts, not really letting the conversation sink in.

"Well?" Brittany asked.

"What?"

"That's what I want to know. What is the problem? Why aren't you ready?" She pulled her pants up and buttoned them, then picked up her bra and slipped it over the bells. The blouse was next.

Lewis stared. He went to her and took her arm. "I'm sorry." It must have sounded like he was breaking up, sorry about letting her go, when he was only trying to erase the tension.

"Ohhh," Brittany squealed and pushed past him, her blouse half buttoned. She grabbed her purse and walked out.

Lewis stood there wondering what had happened. How could he let her go? Then it dawned on him. She had to be waiting outside. He drove. Lewis picked up his sketch pad and followed in her footsteps outside the door and down the stairs. He saw her get into the car, so he rushed down two stairs at a time.

She sat in the car with her head down and her hands folded in her lap. He had never seen Brittany in such a state and didn't know what to do, where to begin. He got in. "Brit."

"No. Don't."

He quieted. His hand touched her shoulder.

"Please, Lewis."

He removed it. "What can I say?"

She was quiet. Her head lifted and she looked out the side window.

"Brit, what can I do? I don't know what happened in there. What do you want?"

"Nothing," she said into the window.

"But..."

"Just take me home. Enough has happened. And the afternoon had started out so perfect."

"Can I see you tomorrow?"

"I'm working at the store."

"I'll come to the mall to see you."

"No. Not for a while. I want you to be sure." She turned her head to look into his eyes.

Lewis felt her eyes penetrate him. They appeared similar to an angry animal's. He wanted to sketch the look, but didn't. There was little else to do but start the car and drive her home. All the while he drove, she was silent. This was the first real fight they'd had. Brittany usually didn't think much about anything and, therefore, didn't take issue often. She wanted this marriage, he thought. And he did, too. So why was he balking? He feared that if she left, he couldn't paint. How could he? She had been such a part of it for so long. When he pulled up to the front of her house, he reached out once again. "We'll marry as soon as you want."

"No. You're not ready. I wouldn't want it that way."

"But Brit, I am ready. I don't know what was wrong back there. I don't know what I was thinking."

"Sleep on it, Lew." She looked at his hand, still clutching her forearm. "I've got to go."

He let go and she stepped out of the car. He watched as she walked to the house without even a glance back. His heart fell. When she was inside, he turned the car and drove home. At home, he threw his sketch pad across the room. He slammed the bedroom door.

In no time Jeffrey came through the door to see what was up. "What is it, Lew?"

"Nothing."

"You came in in such a rush, my papers flew all over. So, what is it?"

"Dammit."

"Brittany?"

"You guessed it."

"Only thing it could be. Women are the only things that can do that to a man. I've felt it numerous times with Marsha."

"And you're still dating?"

"Can't leave her now. Too much investment." Jeffrey had, of late, adjusted his outlook on life to fit into his studies in business. He often spoke of Marsha's assets as though each year they depreciated.

"I can't leave either."

"You've invested more in Brittany than I have in Marsha."

That was a fact. Marsha always seemed to just be there whether Jeffrey spent time with her or not. His attitude towards her was such that he seldom went out of his way.

"It's not just the investment," Lewis said.

"I know, I know. I've heard it for years. You can't work without her."

"Don't mock me."

"I'm not. I just don't believe it, never have. You're going to work no matter what. You have to. I can see it, Mom can, Dad can. That's why they laid off soon after you decided to quit school. They know you're doing what you must do. You have a purpose. Me, I'm going to make money. If I had a purpose like you, it'd just bog me down."

"I don't know."

"Well, Lew," Jeff slapped him on the shoulder, "you're going to have to find out sooner or later."

"Why? We're still together. It was only a fight."

"Can you work now, while she's pissed?"

"I don't know."

"Bet you can," Jeffrey smiled and punched at Lewis' arm. I'd bet you could do it without her too."

"Don't think it." Lewis turned towards the bed. He looked for the sketch pad, he'd thrown. It lay bent and spread open, so he picked it up and straightened the pages. He flipped through some sketches and remembered her eyes. An impulse to get it down pushed through him like a strong heartbeat. "Maybe you're right." He had relinquished to the logic of his brother.

"I am." Jeffrey waited for a moment. "I envy you sometimes. What you have. It's a gift. We all know it."

Lewis looked at him. Never had Jeffrey said such a thing.

"It must be hard, though," Jeffrey said.

"Not so much. Just sometimes. Sometimes I can't stand it. I can't stay in this world."

"Sounds scary."

"I don't know."

"Where do you go?"

Lewis looked at the ceiling, at the specs of sand that were purposely in the paint to add texture to the ceiling. "There's a completely natural world. It's everywhere. I can feel it. Like I'm always being watched."

"Really? Me, too."

"You mean it?"

"Yeah. I sometimes think God is watching. I'll be doing the oddest things and get this feeling like someone's watching me. Like I'm in a play. This whole world's in a play, like Shakespeare said."

"Mine's there all the time. Almost. It is nature, though, not God. I don't think there is a God."

"Because of Brit and you? That's stupid."

"No, no. I mean all the time I think that." Lewis sat on the bed.

Jeffrey joined him there. "You don't believe in God?"

"Not really. I believe in nature."

"Trees and junk? Wood spirits, like the Indians?"

"Maybe not spirits. I don't know. I just know that sometimes plants and animals seem to just talk to me. Not in words, but in pictures and feelings. It's hard to explain. It's not the same as how we communicate."

"I could believe it from looking at your paintings. There's such an organic... ah, closeness, oneness to nature."

"Ha, that's what that article said. You're quoting."

Jeffrey laughed. "It's true, though. They do. Really."

They both laughed then. Jeffrey threw his arm around Lewis' shoulder and patted it. "You shouldn't worry about Brit so much. She's kind of dizzy sometimes. She'll get over it."

"You think?"

"Yeah. But it still doesn't matter. You'll paint no matter what. The world could cave in and there you'd be," Jeffrey made imitation brush strokes in the air in front of them, "painting away with flames and screaming people all around you."

They both laughed again.

"God," Lewis said, "you seem so fucking optimistic. How do you do it?"

"Balance."

"What's that mean? You're balanced and I'm not?"

"No. We're twins right?"

"Okay so far."

"This might sound dumb, but ever since I was little I thought this."

"Go on."

"In most people, there's a balance of good and evil, right and wrong, optimist, pessimist, introvert, extrovert. Now in twins, the same balance is there, but it's spread between two bodies. Not always, but with us, one gets more of one thing than the other. So, individually there seems to be a slight imbalance, but together, balance."

"A little far fetched. What about people who have an imbalance and don't have a twin?"

"Mental birth defect. The only birth defects we recognize are physical, except for retardation. Slight personality anomalies we miss."

"You've been thinking about this a lot."

"I had to come to terms somehow."

"With what?"

"Our differences. I was always jealous of your... gift."

"I was always jealous of yours."

Jeff laughed. "What gift?"

"To make friends, play ball. You were always a team captain. Always an important player. Always better at school. You had more discipline. I was never important to anyone."

"Except Brittany?"

"Except Brit."

"That's not true. Eventually, your art will be important to lots of people, you're just going to be detached from them. But you've got to know that what you do will touch them much deeper than anything I could do."

"Are you still jealous?"

"No. There's balance. I don't think, at this point, I would want your gift. I've gotten used to myself. I'm comfortable."

"I'm not."

"I know. I wish you could be, but I don't think it'd be you. You'd lose something in the transition."

Lew stared and listened, letting Jeffrey's voice sink in. When a silence lingered, he said, "Sometimes I see everything in color, just color, no lines around them to define them, just color slapped onto a canvas at will, everything abstract, then when you pull back, something emerges and takes form."

"Sounds weird."

"It's been my world for so long that everything else is weird."

"At least you've gotten used to yourself."

"It's not just me, though, it's everything. Like I said, nature has its own voice, look, sound, smell, and touch. Along with that, nature has its own psychic energy, its own sort of ESP."

"I know, it talks to you."

"Sort of."

"What's it say?"

"I don't always know. But it's there. Almost always."

"Like I said before, it sounds scary."

"Plants and animals are very special. Like that old white oak, there's something about it. It's special. It has its own feel to it."

"The clearing where I found you that day?"

"A different feel. I remember a raccoon there who came up to me."

"A wild one?"

"I was a little kid. I swear it told me not to touch its ears, or head or something, but I heard it. I know I did. Not words exactly."

"You're spooking me, Lew."

"No. It's all right."

"You were a little kid. Maybe you imagined it."

"No, I know the difference."

"Do you, if you're not in this world a lot of the time?"

"I do. It's not like I'm dreaming or hallucinating, it's just shifted slightly. Not much."

"Let's talk about Brittany and Marsha, women, something I'm comfortable with, something I understand."

"Okay." Lewis knew that he had talked more than he normally did. He may possibly have said too much, but it felt good to get it out.

For me, it felt good also. Whatever Lew felt was good for me, a new experience. There was a relief that came with Lew's confessions, a relief for Lew and me. But the problem with Brittany wasn't over yet.

The next day, Brittany still wouldn't talk to Lewis. He followed her out of Katy's Clothes and into the mall, one step behind her. Little came out of his mouth. He had run out of things to say and couldn't grasp any words except I'm sorry, but those were sounding old even to him.

Brittany wore a mint skirt and mustard top. She walked fast. It was her break, and she had only fifteen minutes to go down to the food court, stand in line, and buy a soda, which took about ten minutes. She'd have to drink it on her way back to the store.

Lewis tried to get close, but the way she swung her arms and turned corners, left him little room. Finally, he got close enough to reach out, but when he did, his foot accidentally stepped on her heel and she stopped abruptly. Lewis flew past and halted on the other side of her. "I'm sorry, Brit." His arms reached out to her.

"Can't you just stay away from me? Stop following?"

"Yeah, buddy," someone in the crowded mall said, but Lewis didn't see who it was.

"But..."

"But I asked you to leave me alone for a while. Don't you think I'm hurt, too?" Her face twisted as though she were ready to cry.

"But, it's so simple to clear this up."

"No it isn't."

As they stood in the mall aisle, people stared as they walked past. Lewis wanted to hide and hoped no one he knew walked by. He heard some of them talking, changing from previous conversations into: "Oh look, they're fighting."; "I wonder what's up with those two?"; and, "You think everything's all right?" He wished he could tell them everything was fine, but would be much better if they'd just get on with their own lives and leave his and Brit's out of it. What they needed was privacy so they could talk and straighten things out. But privacy wasn't on the menu that day; in fact, what was served was frustration and anxiety on a platter of disappointment.

Finally, with Lewis struggling with words and trying to ward off the fear of exposure in the mall, Brittany just slapped him hard across the face. The stillness held until the initial sting of his cheek subsided. Brittany looked right at him. There were tears in her eyes. Her hand must have stung as much, or worse, than his face. Then, she reached out and touched his cheek tenderly and walked away.

Lewis watched her walk past. There was nothing more he could do. After standing there for a few minutes, he left the mall and drove home.

In his bedroom, he set up his easel and began to paint Brittany's eyes, the globes of moisture pulsing up through tear ducts, filling every cavern in every corner, just before breaking loose and falling down her cheek. He painted them at their brink of overflowing. Light glistened off the tears, slight strands of yellow hair at the sides of her face hung near her eyes, delivering the idea of sunlight to the painting. Reflections of color and shadow glanced off the tears in their own mirror-house repetition, or like a jazz song where there's always the sound of the original tune underlying the entire piece. Brittany's eyes became pure pain, exhaustion. The eyes were at their end of understanding and wanted to be left alone. One canvas, one pair of blue, tear-filled eyes, along with a few strands of blonde hair, said it all. Lewis worked on the painting well into the night.

Jeffrey let him alone, coming upstairs late and going straight to bed without comment or question. As their previous conversation had indicated, Jeffrey had learned to accept Lewis as part of his own balance, sibling rivalry seldom interrupted their relationship any longer.

Chapter 9

Some things happen more quickly than others, and for humans, whose time is often measured relative to action, the movement of time can compress months into weeks. So, in two short months of spring, Lewis' paintings became popular sellers in the Philadelphia and Blattsfield galleries, and were picked up the J. J. Max Gallery in New York. All told, more paintings were sold in those months than the entire year prior. All this at age twenty-two. During those months, and because of his sales, Lewis procured the land for the cottage, his father helped him hire a contractor, and the building had begun. At Lewis' insistence, the least number of trees were cut. Two. We all felt the pain. I believe firmly, no, I know as fact, that Lewis also felt the loss as well.

Daily, he called Brittany to ask for her hand in marriage. His obsession with her had not lessened, even though he found Jeffrey's prediction true. In fact, without Brittany, he painted from a low drone of pain which heightened his emotions and his sensitivity to his art. Further, her absence gave him more time in which to paint.

Each day, Lewis walked out to the building site, always passing me, usually touching me where he had dug the tattoo into my bark, sometimes elsewhere. The cottage was small, quaint, and went up quickly. Lewis sat in the woods for hours, out of the sun, watching. He sketched the progress, two sketches ended up as paintings, one a close-up of a young boy of about fifteen or sixteen perched between two roof rafters nailing up a cross brace being held by someone who looked to be his older brother. The father, at least for the painting, stood watching from below. The other painting was produced from a sketch made early in the morning. Even in the painting you could feel the cool, dew-damp air, the notion of the warmth that would come with the sun. All on the site was quiet, a pair of squirrels sat atop a small stack of two-by-sixes exploring the new arrival, a lone bird perched on the tip of the roof peak. In the painting, Lewis felt accepted by the woods, as part of common thought.

Towards the end of the second month, Jeffrey rustled his way through the woods, rather than take the skinny road which had been used by the contractor and his sons and helpers, and which would eventually be paved with stones. He came upon Lewis sitting on the stone fence, still undisturbed by the new cottage which sat back in the woods about fifty yards from the fence and field.

"News flash," Jeffrey announced upon arrival.

Lewis, unshaven and slightly rumpled, looked up at Jeff with baggy eyes. "Hi."

"You look rough. Ever hear of sleep?"

"Not lately. What is it?"

"The news of the day, received from reliable sources. Not the best news though, "Jeff sat next to Lewis, "depending on your viewpoint. Kind-of mixed news, actually."

"All right," Lewis sounded tired, "give it to me."

They stared at one another for only a second, until Lewis was reminded of himself looking badly, as Jeff had suggested. Jeff looked fine, fully rested, shaven, dressed in khaki, loose-fitting pants and yellow golf shirt.

"Brittany's pregnant," Jeff said quietly, almost as though he were sorry he had made the trip.

Lewis turned back quickly, his eyes wide, more alert to his world than he had been in days.

"It's true. About three months or so."

"She must have known..."

"The day of the big fight." Jeff finished the sentence.

"Why didn't she tell me?"

"Don't be dumb, she wanted you to be sure. When you balked about marriage, she probably felt betrayed or something. Who knows how women think?"

"But it wasn't that I didn't want to."

"I know. You told me, and I believe you. Brittany's another story."

"God."

"Don't ask him for help. You don't believe in him anyway."

Lewis' shoulders slumped noticeably.

"Sorry, wrong timing for jokes, I suppose."

"What'll I do?"

"Don't know. She still refusing your calls?"

"Yes." Lewis stood up and turned around, first taking a step in one direction, then the other. "We've got to get married."

"Hold on there. Don't go off and rent a tuxedo yet. Decide what you want. This is too important for you to just make a quick decision. Make up your mind first."

"I've gotta marry her."

"You don't have to do anything." Jeff stood and took his brother's shoulders in his hands. "Look, you're tired right now, worn down. Too much has gone on the last few months. Maybe you can't handle making the decision right now. You should rest. Sleep on it for a day or two."

"No. I've wanted to marry her, she just hasn't listened."

"Remember, she's known about this for a while. You just found out. She doesn't feel the same urgency, obviously. Besides, she's still not talking to you."

"She has to."

"Not so far. Listen to me. Rest and think. Think of why you balked in the first place. This is big stuff. The rest of your life."

"Exactly." Lewis took off down the road, Jeffrey close behind protesting all the way.

When they reached the house, Jeffrey stopped at the porch and sat down on the top step. There was nothing else he could do. He sat, looking exactly like Lewis on the outside, except that he was cleaned up, but on the inside he was all human, not a trace of common thought, animal or plant. Yet he had his own strength and optimism. And he was still connected to Lewis.

In less than an hour, Lewis came out the front door, clean-shaven and dressed in freshly washed jeans and tee-shirt.

95

"You look better," Jeff said, turning towards the sound of the opening door.

"I feel better, to tell the truth."

"What a difference appearance makes to your psyche. Boosts it."

"I guess."

"Before you go, give me five minutes?"

"Don't try to talk me out of it."

"I know better. It's been Brittany, whether I liked it or not, for far too many years for me to have an effect now. Just like your painting, you know what you want."

Lewis sat down next to his brother. "Okay, what?"

Jeffrey slapped his palm over Lewis' knee. "I've been thinking. The further along you get with your painting, the further apart we become. I know I'm headed in a different direction in life than you. Nonetheless, we're twins. Sometimes I miss being brothers as we grow older. You're just so driven. Nothing gets in your way."

Lewis looked away from Jeffrey, to the side of the house, then looked back.

Jeff must have noticed Lew's impatience. "Well look, with you building a cottage and now getting married, I want you to know I love you. You're my brother."

Lewis forced himself to put his arm around Jeffrey. Not that he didn't love Jeff, but to Lewis those deep feelings were so strong with common thought that he felt them differently, maybe even more strongly, except that they were all part of a whole, and were expressed only through his art. He seldom fell into one emotion without dragging others with it and then setting them all down on canvas. "Me too," he said rather matter-of-factly. "I mean it," he added to make up for the coldness he had sensed in his own voice.

"I know. Now, you can head off and rescue your maiden."

"Thanks." Lewis got up.

"What are you going to do?"

"I don't know. Force my way into her house?"

"Want a suggestion?"

Lewis wanted to run off, but he knew his brother would be logical in

96

coming up with a solution. "Yes, I do."

"Buy a diamond, a big one. Do it right. Few women can refuse that. It's like you really mean it. Go out of your way."

Lewis' eyes darted to the side. That would take time, and he was ready to go get her now."

"Do it, Lew. You won't have to force your way in. She'll open the door."

Jeff was right and Lewis knew it. "Thanks, Jeff. If it works, you get to be best man."

"Hey, I'm the best man anyway, and don't you forget it."

They both smiled, then Lewis left.

Much later I found out how things went, after Lewis returned that evening and I probed him. But for the rest of the morning, I soaked up the sounds of the workers. The hammering and sawing reminded me of the time just before Lewis and Jeffrey moved in. The hollow sounds of young and old voices driving deeply into the woods was soothing. I stretched towards the sun as it rose across the sky and could feel growth, something humans and animals miss because they are always wrestling with the freedom of movement. I listened to the sounds of common thought, felt the field, the birds, heard the leaves clicking together in the morning breezes.

Jeffrey remained seated on the porch steps for a long while after Lewis left. Occasionally, I focused on him, but could not get inside him. He looked sad and lost in thought. I realize, up to this point, I may have insinuated that Lewis' contact with common thought furthered and enriched his life far beyond that of other human's, but that is not to mean that other humans don't have deep feelings or thoughts of their own, only that Lewis used his differently.

Jeffrey sat on the steps, deep in thought. Whatever was inside him, it had a tight hold on him and was wrenching his soul. Possibly, as twins, he was so closely linked to Lewis that he tried, for himself, to resolve what he felt were Lewis' internal anxieties. I don't know, but I don't want to downplay what Jeffrey might have felt.

When Lewis returned home, he went straight upstairs. By that time, Jeffrey was out with Marsha, so the room was empty. Lewis wanted to talk to someone, so he left and went to the cottage, which by the time he arrived, was bathed in orange light and strong angular shadows. He walked between the frame studs of the front door, over to the center of the floor which would eventually be a wall to separate one of the bedrooms from the kitchen, and sat down. He lay back onto the floor and watched the colored clouds twist and bend with the wind.

Brittany had gone to work with hopes of getting off early so that she could visit him. He was happy with the turnout, yet tired from all the days of little sleep. He had many paintings to show for his time though, and open wall space in several galleries for them. As he lay back on the plywood floor, he could smell the odor of forest floor float over him whenever a breeze made its way down through the trees. The field rippled with delight and relief as the wind bent its stalks, stretched its membranes and cooled it down.

Lewis recalled the day's events, and what he didn't recall, I probed into his more recent memory for details.

After taking Jeffrey's advice and picking up a diamond, Lewis drove to a parking spot in front of a white house two blocks from Brittany's. Holding the small ring case in his tight, white-knuckled palm, he rushed over the uneven sidewalk to her front door. There would be no way for her to see him coming unless she were staring out the window. He knocked. Brit's mother came to the door and smiled at first sight of Lewis, then frowned. "I don't think she wants to see you."

"Give her this, then. Please." He held out the case, his arm inside the partially opened door.

Brit's mother looked down, then swept the case from his hand.

"I want to do the right thing. I love Brittany."

A smile returned to the mother's face. "I know you do, son. Wait here." She closed the door.

Lewis stood with his hands folded in front of him. He didn't know how he felt, but was on a mission. Only the mission mattered. Only what he came to do was important. As that thought pushed a wide road through his brain, obstacles popped up: What if Brit refused the diamond? What if she really didn't want to marry him now, after the past months? What if her mother didn't approve? What if she didn't return?

Lewis plowed through his thoughts until he felt stymied just standing there and decided to try the door. It was unlocked.

Lewis stepped inside to the familiar sight and smell of Brit's house. He had been there often, its feel second nature to him. In a half run, he climbed the carpeted stairs to the upstairs hall, turned down the hall and went directly to her bedroom and pushed open the door. "Brittany, I want to marry you. Now, stop all this nonsense and say yes." As soon as the words left his mouth he felt embarrassed. His face felt like it turned red. He found that in all the excitement tears had formed in his eyes, which increased his embarrassment tenfold.

Mrs. Sholes stared at him and Brittany held the ring between her thumb and forefinger. Both looked surprised at his entrance.

Luckily, time did not slow.

"Yes," Brittany said. "Oh, yes, yes, yes. I will marry you." She was smiling at him. Her face half made up, mascara sitting on the makeup table, open and ready to finish off her face. Then she and her mother broke into laughter as though the last two months had culminated into a huge joke. As though, Lewis rushing into the room, teary-eyed, blushing, and announcing his unfettered love, was the punch line.

The urgency he had felt quickly subsided. He felt conspicuous. What should he do with his hands? He took one step, then stopped.

Brittany bounced up and down in the characteristic way she did when she was excited and happy.

Her mother smiled so broadly Lewis couldn't see her ears. He gave a half shrug, not knowing what to do next.

Brittany closed the gap between them and hugged him, kissed him. "I've missed you so much," she said, and everything inside Lewis began to calm and feel better. In a half trance, he came home.

As Lewis watched the sky, the tree tops at the corners of his vision, an occasional bird fly by, and listened to the sounds of chirping and cawing, he allowed himself to fall deeply into common thought. He felt the trees sway in the wind, which pulled at their tops only to be dragged down through one lower branch after another, until only a breeze reached the forest floor. He listened for the squirrels and chipmunks and snakes, searched inside common thought for their whereabouts and found them.

There were several deer nearby. He lingered around them. Like calm meditation, Lewis let himself go where he may, linger wherever he felt like lingering. His exhaustion helped him to remain calm and accepting. There was too little energy left in him to become confused, too little energy to deal with fear or anxiety. He held onto his meditation and recognized it as the best he'd felt in months. Working to the point of exhaustion had become a blessing.

As he roamed the forest and ferreted out deer, chipmunks, bushes, as he explored the enchanted forest with its brown pine-needle floor and trickling stream, a wary, yet determined Brittany walked up what would eventually be the road to the cottage. She stepped over rocks and logs placed in holes dug in by the contractor's trucks. She tip-toed through slightly muddy areas, her arms out to her sides for balance. A wind rushed down the road and tossed her blonde hair away from her face. In the soft evening light, she appeared to be glowing. She was an unsure traveler who turned at every noise, and at every noise rushed a little more. When she arrived at the cottage site, she yelled, "It's beautiful."

Lewis barely heard her voice. He still roamed the woods, determining which colors he would need to mix together to create the idea of deer or snake. Slowly, recognizing her voice as she said the word beautiful over and over until he looked up, Lewis wandered back, not wishing to disturb anything along the way. He raised his head, and I saw Brittany, once again, through his eyes. Freshly back from common thought, Lewis saw only his love when he looked at Brittany. And she, he thought adoringly, was pregnant with his child. He sat up and his smile broadened. Brittany had her hands on the floor and was climbing up and over the edge one foot at a time. Her hair fell over her face and, when she stood on the floor, she brushed it back with her hand.

"You got off early." Lewis' voice had the calm one has when there is total peace within.

"I just had to be with you."

"Welcome to your new home." He lifted his head and spread his arms out in welcome.

"It's just as you drew it."

"Almost."

"It's perfect." She walked over to where he lay, her heals clacking on the plywood.

Lewis reached over and held her ankle. She wore black slacks and a thin green blouse, the colors of the forest at night. A splash of moonlight fell over her head.

"I'm sorry about the last two months. I don't know what I expected of you."

"It's over now."

"You seem so, so calm about it now, like you're out-of-it."

"I'm tired, Brit," he dismissed her query. "I needed you here. I love you."

She bent down to her knees and kissed him. "Oh, Lewis, I am sorry."

"Me too. I should have known I couldn't live without you."

"You were fine."

"Not inside. I feel fine now, now that you're back."

Brittany sat next to him. The sun dropped further behind the mountain behind the cottage. "This is beautiful."

"It's perfect, isn't it?"

"How did you swing it?"

"Dad helped. I bought quite a few acres, the field, some woods, all the way back to Mom and Dad's."

Brittany brushed her hand across his cheek. Lewis slipped an arm around her waist and lay back down, pulling her into a prone position.

"There are stars out," she said. "Stars over our house." Her voice was dreamy.

"There are stars in your eyes," Lewis said.

"You're not very original."

"Should I be?"

"Not right now."

They kissed and Lew's hand slipped up along her stomach to her chest.

Brittany sighed long and deep.

Their mouths met. Lew's hand searched through her blouse for a breast.

Brittany pulled him over onto her and held him tightly. "Are we alone?"

"Only the trees," he said.

They made love on the plywood floor of the partially built cottage. No animals stirred in fear, none worried of danger. In his final ecstasy, Lewis dropped back into common thought allowing us all to know his joy.

By the time they walked back and Brittany left for home, the sky had become very dark with clouds. A cold Canadian wind had picked up and brought the threat of rain with it.

Lewis patted the window ledge of Brit's car. She sat behind the wheel, the engine running.

"I had a wonderful evening," she said.

Lewis smiled. "Me, too. Maybe when the house is finished we'll try it again."

"Before then, I hope." She placed her hand over his. "I missed us."

Lewis bent down and kissed her, his head resting against the top of the door.

"I'll have to work tomorrow."

"That's all right, we're back together."

She held up her hand. The diamond sparkled from the light coming from the house behind Lewis. A kitchen light was on. "I love it," she said.

"I'm glad."

"I better go."

"Good night, Brit."

"Good night, loverboy."

When she pulled away, Lewis, instead of going into the house, walked up the old tractor road. The darkness was almost absolute under the canopy of dark green, but he knew his way well. There was a slight clearing where I stood, partially caused by my expansive spread of branches. The underbrush was thin there.

Lewis came over and climbed up onto the branch he had first fallen from. The height was no longer threatening. He sat in the crook and put his back against my trunk, drew his legs up to rest along the branch. His eyes closed and all energy seemed to slip from his body. The only activity going on was in his mind which traveled out across common thought, listening and learning more about the way nature works. Lewis just sat and accepted everything, often converting sounds, tastes, feelings, into color, twists in shape, spirals, lines. Common thought was a well to drink from, to stuff inside him the waters of understanding. Not only good happened in nature. In the short time he sat on my branch, animals killed and ate other animals, plants died. He took it all in and converted it to color and line. The wind picked up through the forest and the loud crack of thunder snapped Lewis from his meditation. Lightning flashed again and a few seconds later another loud crack spread shock waves through the area.

Lewis shivered and folded his arms across his chest and drew his knees up tighter to his body. He pushed his head into his knees and closed his eyes again. Intimately, he felt the wind caress him. He focused on the enchanted forest. Needles swept across the dirt to form little mounds. Branches shifted in the wind. Leaves twisted and tried to pull loose, some did, floating for long moments in the wind. Lewis waited for the next crack of thunder, but before it came, the rain began to fall. The wind separated the foliage and let the drops penetrate to the forest floor. Pellets the size of small stones fell all around, dampening the ground and Lewis. He sat in the crook of my branch, getting colder as he got wetter. Something about the feel of the rain against his body made him stay. He wanted to know it better, that sensation. What color was it, a transparent blue with green and red portions? How much did each drop weigh? How long did each stay wrapped in its own surface tension before splattering in all directions, or soaking into a new being? Lewis listened and felt and smelled. He tipped his head up to taste the drops and watch them fall. When lightning came again, the clearing opened up in a brightness beyond day, then closed off into deeper darkness. He stared. Again, lightning struck and he saw something, someone, standing, raising his arm. Lewis sat up straight and stared. I waited with him. Again, the lightning flashed before the thunder came. The man, dressed in loose-fitting Indian garb, had his arm out and a finger pointed at Lewis. The man was old. Lewis stood, hugging my trunk.

At first, I did not see the man, nor feel him. He didn't appear in common thought, only inside Lewis. Through Lewis' eyes.

When the next flash hit, he was gone. Lewis had changed everything that came to him, through his senses, to shape and color, had fallen into abstraction on several occasions, but never, up to that point, created something so real. Lewis blinked and waited. Rain had soaked his head and streamed down his face and into his eyes. When lightning flashed again, there was still no one there. It had been a spirit. That's what Lew imagined, or knew, a human spirit. I had never seen one, hadn't seen this one except through Lewis. Common thought had no memory of it. I don't know how human spirits worked, but Lewis had either seen one or had conjured one up, as he was more than capable of doing. Whichever had happened, Lewis, instead of showing fear of the unknown, felt awe, felt as though he had been chosen. In the darkness, he climbed down and slowly started back for home. I went with him, and tried to understand what had happened. His exhaustion had reached a critical state where he easily fell into common thought, accepted whatever death or life was there. He also began to hallucinate, and accepted that as real, too. As he walked towards his home, he was on the verge of collapse. The cold rain penetrated his clothes, soaking his skin to a tacky dampness. Rain trickled down over his eyes; he walked like a man possessed, a zombie. Before he made it back, he collapsed onto the old tractor road, into the soft mud.

Chapter 10

Early the next morning, Jeffrey jumped out of bed screaming. "Mom! Dad!"

Mrs. Marshal stepped from her bedroom door in a robe. "What is it? What's wrong?"

"Lewis didn't come home last night."

"Don't you think he's with Brittany?"

"No. I don't know why, but I feel something's wrong."

"Okay." She turned and went back into the bedroom. "Honey, get up, Jeff says Lewis is missing."

"Yeah, yeah. Why, what happened now?"

"Nothing. He just has a feeling."

"Fine. I'm gettin' up."

Jeff appeared at their door in jeans and sweatshirt, dressed for a search. "I'm going out to the cottage."

"The cottage? You think he's there?"

"I don't know. It's just my first thought. I'll come back by way of the old oak. He may have gone there, too. Can you call Brit's just in case I'm crazy?"

"You're not crazy, dear. I'll call, though."

"Great." Jeff ran down the stairs and out the door, leaping over the porch steps. He ran all the way back into the woods where the cottage stood in the foggy morning light. When he arrived, he slowed his pace and looked around all sides of the frame, behind equipment, near the stone fence where Lewis sat to watch as the cottage was being built. The contractor hadn't shown up yet, but just as Jeffrey was about to leave, he heard the loud hum of the truck, and the loud creaking of its shocks and splashes of water as it bumped through rain-filled holes in the makeshift road.

Breathing heavily from his run and frantic search, Jeffrey ran to the truck as it approached. "Have you seen my brother this morning? He's missing."

Jack, the contractor, leaned forward to look across his two sons at Jeffrey. His face was serious, as though, instantly, he could sympathize with Jeffrey's predicament. He had salt and pepper hair, cut short, and a rough-honed face. "We ain't seen 'im yet this mornin', but we'll watch for 'im. If you want, we'll help search the area."

Both sons bobbed their heads in agreement with the father.

Jeff tapped the truck roof and thought for a moment. "Not yet. I'll keep looking. In an hour or so if I can't find him."

"Fine with us. You'll let us know, then."

"I will."

"Good luck," Jack said.

"Yeah, good luck," the other two spoke up.

Jeff was off, leaping over the stone fence to make a quick run around the field. He stopped and looked in one direction, then the other. I knew he was torn between going to the enchanted forest or to me and down the tractor road. I tried to project an image into Jeffrey's mind, of the road with Lewis lying in it, but couldn't tell if it worked. Regardless, that's where he went. In a full run, Jeff leaped over the stone fence again and didn't slow down to a jog until he neared me. His eyes shot in each direction in perfect sync with his moving legs. When he started down the road toward his house, Jeffrey slowed because of the briars that attached themselves to his sweatshirt. About half way home, he saw Lewis on his back in the mud and ran over and kneeled next to him. "Lew!" He picked up Lew's head and shook his shoulders. He placed his hand over Lew's forehead, then took off his sweatshirt and wrapped it loosely around his brother's shoulders and chest and arms.

I tried, as I had all night, to get inside Lew's head, but only received small amounts of acceptance. Throughout the night, Lew had gone from a complete blackout to a semiconscious state which led to horrifying images of giant flowers talking in low, indecipherable voices, and flying wood hitting his head and arms, then to images of Brittany screaming at the tops of her lungs, and after a few moments of that, another blackout.

Jeffrey's chest and arms quickly got prickly from the chill air, even though he had been running and had sweat across his worried brow. He hesitated for a moment, shook Lew again, then patted him on the chest and ran back to get help.

In very little time Mr. Marshal drove up the path in his car. Miraculously, he didn't get stuck. He and Jeffrey lifted Lewis into the car, while Mrs. Marshal sat in the back seat with a blanket to put over him. The two men sat in the front and Lew lay across the back seat, his head on his mother's lap, her fingers in his hair. He began to come to again. He moaned and tried to talk.

"Shhh," his mother said.

"Hold on, Lew. Take it easy," Mr. Marshal said while backing out of the road.

Soon, they were off to the hospital. I followed as far as I could, then, like falling off to sleep, faded from Lew's mind, and they were gone.

Back to the solitude of my life. By solitude, I mean without Lewis. There was still Jack and his boys to watch. I could listen to them, or delve into common thought for sensations from other parts of the forest, but sensations in common thought weren't as exciting as the mental activity in Lewis. Nothing since I was a sapling was like the complexities I found in the combination of Lewis' mind and motion.

Lewis had hardly moved since his fall, once just to roll onto his back. When Jeffrey found him, his legs were still in the same awkward position as when he first rolled, one partially bent up, the other straight out. Slight movements of the head only irritated his nightmares, his odd hallucinations. I began to doubt the existence of the spirit he had seen earlier, since it had only appeared inside Lewis and nowhere else. Had it been an early signature of things to come, of his eventual collapse? Those warning signs often appeared in nature, why not in humans?

To curtail my concern for his health, I dropped into common thought to meditate and let myself wander wherever I seemed to be pulled, just as Lewis had done the night before. New animals were born, old ones died, trees died from insect infestation, moss grew, weeds grew and pushed their beautiful flowers, their healthy bulbs of sun-loving membrane, into the open air. I was a favorite tree for the birds in my common thought territory, and different types, red-wing blackbirds, wrens, even robins came to place their delicate clawed feet over my thin branches.

It may seem that I sometimes go on about my world, but I am fond of it and all its intricacies. And this, after all, is where Lewis takes what he needs to express much of his genius. To understand it is to better understand Lewis. He has learned to accept death, as well as rejoice in new life, born screaming as though their souls had been torn from them. Life here is balanced by death. Take the rain which Lewis walked through before his collapse. It felled several trees within common thought reach, some were not fully dead, only partially rotted. The lightning brought down the tops of two trees, the largest branch of another. Baby rabbits drowned in their flooded den. The mother saved only a few. All night there was death, even while Lewis was watching. I feared, at times, that he would become too accepting of death, and lose his instinctual will to live. My worry was unfounded, but I didn't know that until the Marshals returned home.

For the longest time they did not speak of him. They went along about their business of cooking, cleaning and, for Jeffrey, studying. For a while, it was as though Lewis had never been born, had never lived in that house. Then Brittany drove up. She jumped from the car practically before the engine was off and ran to the house, knocking loudly and pushing the doorbell.

Mrs. Marshal answered the door. "Oh, come in, honey. You must be worried."

"Jeff called from the hospital."

"I know. Lew asked him to."

"What is it?" Brit followed Mrs. Marshal into the living room.

"He didn't tell you?"

"No, he just said Lew was in the hospital, but that I couldn't see him until tomorrow. Then he said something about them taking him somewhere, mumbled and hung up."

"It's pneumonia."

"Pneumonia? How'd he get that? He didn't even have a cold."

"The doctor said he was run down. He never sleeps."

"How bad is it? Is he awake?"

"They're optimistic."

"They said he'd be fine," Mr. Marshal corrected, coming into the room and sitting in a stuffed chair. He looked like an older Lewis and Jeffrey, but they definitely had Mrs. Marshal's eyes.

Brittany turned her attention back to Mrs. Marshal. "How long do they think he'll be in there?"

"Not long. Now sit down. We heard about the engagement."

She smiled shyly. "Oh, that's right." She held out her hand to show off the diamond. "I just assumed..."

"Don't assume anything as long as Lewis is around." Mr. Marshal opened the newspaper. He didn't look at either of them.

Mrs. Marshal waved a hand at him to dismiss his comment.

"I'm sorry," Brit pulled her hand back.

Mrs. Marshal leaned forward following the hand. She took it into her own. "Don't worry about that." She leaned closer. "It's very nice, isn't it? Lewis has artistic tastes."

"He does."

"What the hell was he doing out last night anyway?" Mr. Marshal stood up and threw the paper into the chair before leaving the room.

Brittany looked a little worried.

"He's just upset. We all are."

"I know."

"He was calm until the doctor said that Lewis would be all right, then he got angry, as though Lew had done something to him instead of to himself."

"I'm sorry."

"Don't be. That's the way he is. He and Jeff are alike in that way. They're both very practical and businesslike. Things done irrationally, in their minds, are just plane crazy. Jeff seems to handle it a little better."

"Well, they're brothers."

Mrs. Marshal looked away. "I suppose they are."

"So, why can't I see him tonight if he's going to be okay?"

"They want him to rest. Told us all to go home."

Brittany lowered her head and shook it back and forth, "Why does this stuff always happen to him?"

"I wish I knew. I'd change his diet."

They laughed at the ridiculous sound of her statement.

Mrs. Marshal put her hand over Brit's knee. "I think you're good for him."

Their eyes met and held. It looked as though they were examining each other's thoughts, or true feelings, eye to eye. They pulled apart simultaneously, as though there was a hidden signal they both adhered to. A grin flashed across each face in silent satisfaction.

"We know about the baby and all. It's okay."

Brittany shifted in her seat. "I'm sorry."

"Well, I hope not, dear. You shouldn't be."

"But..."

"But it takes two. I know how life is. Don't take me for an oldster who doesn't understand. It's too bad it couldn't have been planned, but don't be sorry. There's nothing to be sorry for. You two are in love, that's what matters."

Then they discussed other things, Brit's mother and father, the cottage, Lew's successes in the art field. They didn't mention his collapse, and Brittany never mentioned what I know she must have thought about, and that's their naked lovemaking at the cottage site the night before, the night of the collapse. I sensed a little guilt in her, that maybe she helped to push him over that edge. Or it may have been me projecting; although, I should have known it wasn't her, or anything about her, but more the cold wind and rain. Why he came to me, to sit through the rain, instead of rest, I don't know.

Chapter 11

Lewis returned home totally disoriented. Yes, he was on medication, but mild medication. He feared common thought, a cycle he had gone through before. Yet, I could always get in and probe. He just didn't open to me fully. If there was anything I could have done to hold him within common thought, I would have done so. But what could I do but try to ease his mind into wanting to stay? Like the man who wants nature to stay with him when he enters the city, so I wanted Lewis to stay with me when he went to the city.

Those first weeks home, Lewis remained in the house. He often felt tired and tried to get rest, his biggest problem, because when he got into a painting fury, he tended not to stop. He would have to be forced by Jeffrey or his mother to put down his brushes and go to bed. He ate very well though, gorging himself at every meal, and gained about ten pounds over what Jeffrey weighed. He looked a little bloated from the additional weight, but then I liked him lean.

Brittany visited more and more often as they planned their small wedding (family only) and set a date only a month away, mid-July. Brittany wouldn't be showing yet, so they figured she could still wear a regular gown. Lewis bought a new suit for the occasion, no tux for him. Everything up to the day of the wedding, July 12th, went very smoothly. For those thirty days leading to the final date, the house was filled with happiness. Brittany and Lewis' parents met for a cordial dinner and became friends in the process. The uncomfortable position of Brittany's pregnancy was set aside. Mutual friendship and understanding between the parents, apparent good feelings for one another's children, and the fact that Lewis was selling well, appearing in magazine after magazine, all made for a worry-free wedding and, in all their eyes, a happily-ever-after marriage.

The only one to show signs of dark within this white, fluffy cloud of happiness and acceptance, was Lewis, and maybe that was because I could see inside him and not inside the others. One evening near the wedding date, he and Jeffrey began to talk, as they had more and more often as they got older.

"So, how's the nervous groom?" Jeffrey had started.

"Unsure." Lewis was laid out on his bed flipping through his latest sketch pad.

Jeff pulled out and sat on the chair to their desk, the one they'd done homework on for so many years, the one Jeff still sat in to do homework when Lewis was out. "You're supposed to be nervous, not unsure. Unsure sounds like pending cancellation, calling it off. I'd heard of that being done before, but never in my wildest dreams could I imagine my obsessive brother in such a position."

"You sound like a lawyer talking like that."

"My persuasive business meeting tone. Long useless monologues."

Lewis smiled and closed the sketch pad. "I told you about our fight."

"Yeah. That was a long time ago."

"Did I hesitate to suggest marriage then because I didn't want to marry her, or because I was just nervous?"

"I don't know exactly. How did you feel?"

"I need her and I don't. Does that make sense?"

"No."

"I need her around, her image, her, her... feel."

"Let's not get into sex, she's already pregnant."

Lewis sat up. "No, the feel of her being around when I need her, being close enough that I can work. Not on top of me."

"Wow. On top of you? Is that how you feel she'll be?"

"I don't want her staring while I paint, saying things. Sometimes I need to be alone."

"You paint while I'm in the room watching."

"That's you. You're me. Maybe I'm used to you."

"You can get used to her."

"Maybe."

"She'll be taking care of the baby anyway."

"Maybe." Lewis flopped back onto the bed. "I don't know. I keep thinking of that Indian spirit I saw."

"Good God, don't start that again. You're starting to spook me."

"No, Jeff, listen. He pointed at me, like he was saying, you're it, just you, alone. That's what I got from him."

"And the raccoon said, 'Not my ears'. I think you've been hallucinating most of your life, how else could you do some of that weird stuff you do?"

"The abstracts," Lewis said to the ceiling. "They're just a twist of reality. The real crazy stuff is still inside my head."

"Well let it out, I'll hit it with a hammer and we'll both be done with it."

Lewis sat up again and looked right at Jeffrey. "So what do I do with my insecurity concerning the marriage?"

"Swallow it. And keep it down."

"And keep swallowing?"

"If you have to. Don't you feel responsible? A little?"

"Of course I do. But do I want to make a mistake?"

Jeffrey brought his hands to his face. "No, not at all," he said quietly. They both sat staring at one another.

Lewis broke the silence. "I'll make a decision I can live with." He got up and headed for the door.

"Where you going this late?"

"For a walk."

"To look for your wood demon?" There was a definite sound of sarcasm in Jeffrey's voice where there had been a slightly joking sound earlier. Lewis noticed the contrast and felt hurt, mistrusted. He had confided in Jeff and Jeff didn't believe that he could make such a decision.

"Spirit," Lewis corrected, just to haggle him.

"Don't stay out late. I don't want to worry about you lying in filth again."

"Then don't worry," Lewis yelled up the stairs. When he passed the living room where his parents were watching the news, Mrs. Marshal looked up. "You're not going out this late, are you?"

"I won't be gone long."

"Oh, Lewis, why must you?"

"I have to think."

She sighed.

Lewis stepped into the warm summer air and high humidity, a moth flew by his ear on its way towards the light that reached through the glass of the front door. It fluttered almost like a bird.

For the first time in a long while, I could feel Lewis' willingness to open up fully, to lower himself into common thought. But what he expected from nature was too much, an answer to his problems, a catalyst to his feelings, something to "show him the way", and there was no such thing waiting for him. Without his imagined spirit to guide him, I feared he might revolt by blocking common thought out completely. He would become as all other humans were, lost in their private thoughts. Because of the link we had established, I expected to be able to read him most of the time, but I needed for him to accept common thought willingly or even that link might fade.

I followed him to the cottage. It was almost finished. Lamps and appliances, bedroom and living room furniture, had all been planned for and bought. In the loft were a second set of easels, stretched canvases of different sizes, a sofa, paints, shelves, everything he needed only in a larger room than the bedroom he shared with Jeffrey. He would no longer have to store paintings in the basement.

Lewis climbed the stairs to the loft and, in the darkness, stared out over the field. What did he search for, a revelation that would never come, one that nature could not supply?

I let go completely and waited for him to come to me. I watched him through the large pane-glass window in the top half of the cottage. Jeans and tee-shirt. Ruffled hair. He stood with his legs apart, a slight paunch to his belly from sitting around and eating. The urge to enter his mind, to see what he was thinking was great, but I held back. In a few minutes, Lewis was there with me, with us all. His mind searched the woods, searched the field; he lingered around squirrels, field mice, deer. Like a bird, he flew into the topmost branches of trees, like snakes he wriggled under rocks, like fish he swam along the stony bottom of the brook. Lewis had dived in deeper and with more trust than ever before. He wanted answers to his problems, but all we could answer was instinct: eat, drink, copulate, die. Was that enough? Lewis belonged to common thought. It was there inside him stronger than mere image or color, stronger than just a sensation. How long would it last? How long would we be so close? His human mind, just like animal thought, couldn't hold on forever, it would eventually have to turn to its own privacy.

The sky was dark around the cottage, the forest green-black. Lewis was on his knees with his hands against the pane, poised there. His eyes were open, but he saw only what we saw, what I saw. He wasn't used to being able to see many places at once. He even viewed himself from a distance, so used to seeing himself in Jeffrey that he wasn't shocked at the sight of himself kneeling inside the cottage. He eventually found me within common thought. I felt his presence. We were like two long separated friends finding one another in a dark alley, both scared until recognition kicked in.

"You," his mind said.

I was shocked by the sound of his thoughts, so strong, so sure.

"Have you done this?" he asked.

But he knew the answer, and I didn't know how to respond.

"How long?" He continued to ask questions, forcing his mind into mine as I had forced mine into him, except that he could never hear me. Could he? Still, I was silent.

"You must be the one." Then a flash of memory appeared and disappeared. It was the Indian spirit he had seen. "No," I said. "That was not me. That was you."

He could not understand me.

"No," I repeated. "No!" I pushed an image into him, the image of me from a distance. I suddenly felt exposed, and it felt exhilarating. There is nothing like nakedness, physical, mental, or emotional, to excite the soul.

Lewis accepted the image and understood it. He flashed pictures, memories, at me, and I acknowledged him. He remembered the feel of my bark, and I approved and verified his memory, hoping he understood.

Then he flashed the spirit before me. This time the spirit felt like me, had the look of me if I were human. It connected. The spirit was me, in his eyes. It was his way of explaining what he knew of me. Using images, he questioned me like a child just learning about the world, but I lacked the answers and a way to deliver them. I didn't know the why's of anything. It was all just natural, the way things worked. I'd get signatures of things to come, but even that was natural. I could only say what did happen, not why. Free will, as it related to humans, was foreign to me. My freedom stretched only so far, farther as my roots extended or as my top and sides grew, but minimally so. I could choose to shut off or open up, could enter animal thought only if allowed, and still have no control. No control. I tried to show him that, at least, he had control.

He asked of signatures pertaining to his future, but I could not see any. He had to make his own choices. I would accept them and go on.

When he pulled away, I felt all of common thought shiver. He had been so open, it was almost like a death when he went away. I imagine losing love, too, is almost like death. How is it that we learn to die so often during life, see it coming, feel it, and yet refuse death so violently when it arrives?

Lewis stood up, his energy revived. I looked inside him. There was no communication between us. He had felt us all and held onto the feeling, yet not the contact. We were spirits, untouchables, to him, and I was the Indian pointing. I was also the tree. He felt protected, watched, helped, even though we never offered help. As through meditation, he felt completely rejuvenated. He had control of his life like never before because he thought he was being protected. My protests had done no good. I watched him leave, went with him. He did not go home. In the hot darkness of summer, Lewis walked to the stone fence and over it, into the field. Above him, the sky opened into sparkling stars, a glimpse of the Milky Way. The woods appeared deeper and more haunting. The field had dark patches of leafy grass, and hid field mice exploring the weeds for food. Lewis danced in his happiness, around and around. He had love, he had art, he had protection. The world was a better place, a happier place for him. When he felt ready, he ran and jumped the stone fence, rushing breathless into the woods. He had to curb his excitement quickly and slow down. The darkness didn't permit carelessness. His eyes had to adjust. He skipped when he could see well enough, tried to break into a jog, but eventually accepted an excited walk. When he reached me, he caressed my trunk, hugged it. He knew it was me, felt my presence as that of his Indian guide. Inside him, some sort of metaphysical metamorphosis had taken place where I could be both tree and man to him. Just to be a part of him was enough. At least he knew of my presence.

In the woods, Lewis relied on the darkness which sprang from him, as well as around him. Where people tended to be afraid while in the woods in the dark alone, Lewis felt comfortable. He knew the dark, understood it, and now felt protected in it as well.

In all the time he spent exploring common thought, he still did not get a straight answer as to whether he should or should not marry Brittany. He knew only that he must paint. That night he came away with more canvases in his head, larger ones, and felt the pressures of them. Marriage, he decided, did not matter. It would be fine as long as his art came first, as long as she didn't interfere. He still thought he needed her, so would take her the way which meant the most to her, regardless how he felt. Jeffrey was right in telling him to swallow his doubt.

In a matter of weeks the wedding took place. Everything went along as planned by the three women. The men didn't have to do anything but show up, say their piece, get drunk, go home and sleep. That is all except Lewis, for as the groom his responsibility was to the beautiful bride. As a joint gift from their parents, the newlywed couple had received a honeymoon in the Florida Keys.

By the time they returned from the honeymoon, Brittany's pregnancy was more apparent. It seemed almost overnight to me, and certainly surprised, yet also delighted, Lewis. The vacation had been good for them. They had spent all their time walking the beaches, eating, and copulating, just as tradition demands. It was a beautiful memory every time I viewed it. Lewis retained details well, and the time had been so extraordinarily wonderful that the memories were deeply etched into his mind. Finally, at home, Lewis walked over the threshold of the cottage, Brittany held high in his arms.

A new life, the first morning of which Lewis dutifully began in his loft, painting from memory, from common thought experience, his first series of abstracts as a married man. His hand felt good holding a pencil, then a brush, lightly sketching over a new canvas, the shapes indicative of deer and mouse, the mystery of death, how it differs for man, plant and animal. Occasionally he added the short lives of insects, the scales from the snake or gills of fish. Lewis knew nature like no man has ever known it, in inner sight and sound, inner color and odor, and he made it became real in every painting. Lewis was the best at what he did, and after his recent encounter inside common thought, he had secured that position.

I am still exhilarated every time I remember the strength and knowledge Lewis put into his work. There never was and will never be such a keen depiction of such a finely spun world as that of thought, natural thought.

Everything remained almost perfect for Lewis, until the first signs of irritation began. Whether the actual buildup came from within Lewis unnecessarily, unprovoked, or was something that Brittany emitted, I dare not try to comprehend, for I don't want to find it inside Lewis. However, even before the baby was born, something began to wedge between them.

Chapter 12

It happened just before Christmas. Brittany was just too elated with everything: the oncoming holiday, the possibility of snow, their first Christmas together, the miracle of life inside her.

Lewis had been working late hours, from before sun-up to well after dark. What he couldn't remember, he created new; what he didn't know, he extrapolated from what he did know. Every piece sold, or had a place to hang. The J. J. Max Gallery gave him an extended contract for originals, serigraphs, and prints, through an agreement made by Jeffrey. Lewis ignored all business transactions.

In the early afternoon, on the 22nd of December, Brittany labored up the stairs to the loft. "It's snowing!" she exclaimed happily.

"Good." Lewis lifted his arm to brush paint across the canvas.

"Well, look at it."

He had his back to the window to let the gray light from outside effect his painting. "I'm working."

"But, honey..."

He laid the brush onto the canvas, but it wasn't right.

Brittany, oblivious to Lewis' deep concentration, came over and took his elbow. "Turn around. Look."

"What the fuck for? It's snow isn't it?"

Brittany's glee faded quickly. Her eyes dropped, figuratively, to the floor. "It's our first snow together," she said. "I thought you'd want to see it with me."

"I'm trying to work," he repeated.

She stood beside him, both of them facing the window, one with eyes downward, one with eyes scanning the ceiling over the window, neither looking out. There was a long silence while Brittany waited for Lewis to apologize, something he had cultivated the last months, every time something went a little wrong. But this time he was working, it wasn't a missing plate he had left in the living room, or a kiss he forgot to give her before he stepped out of the house. She had never been in his territory, the loft. He acted differently, thought differently. He wanted to work and be left alone.

The silence continued for a long while.

Finally, without uttering a sound, Lewis turned and began to paint again. Brittany's hand slipped from his elbow. She remained facing the window. Eventually, tears trickled down her face and she sniffled. "I'm going downstairs if you're going to work."

"Please do."

"You don't care?"

"Actually, I wish you would. I've been telling you, I'm trying to work. What do you want me to do, quit when you want me to look at something?" His strokes got more strained, but he continued, just so he didn't have to focus on her. That's what she wanted, he thought, for him to break down and give in. Even the tears were just manipulative. He wasn't buying it, and wouldn't allow his sensitive side to focus on her wrinkled nose, her sniffling and her tears.

Brittany turned around and walked past him. A paintbrush he was hardly attached to anymore slipped over the canvas in front of him. "You're mean." Her pace picked up and she went downstairs.

Lewis stopped painting and stood back to look at what he'd done while his concentration was shifted. He turned around and looked out the window at the soft flakes, like marshmallows, falling, just outside. He sat down on the sofa and turned so he could watch the snow. It touched him and he began to cry. He didn't want to be mean to Brittany, yet he didn't want her to interrupt his work any time she wished. He'd get nothing done. He had already lost this painting. In a fury of energy, Lewis stood up and kicked the easel over. The canvas fell, hitting its corner against the floor. Lewis heard the sound of snapped wood. The clank and boom of the easel and painting was loud. He sat back down and resumed crying.

On the stairs, Brittany's footsteps could be heard. She came up to the door and waited.

Lewis waited.

There was no sound on either side of the door. Then, eventually, Brittany walked in. She ran over to Lewis. He felt good and bad about what had happened: his sharp tongue and rejection, her interruption and tears. Maybe the painting could have been salvaged, but not now as it lay face down on the wood floor.

Brittany saw that he had been crying and sat on the edge of the couch with him. "I'm so sorry," she said through tears of her own.

"So am I." He stared past her, at the lost painting.

"Did you ruin it?"

He nodded.

"Oh, Lewis." She held him.

"I needed to be alone."

"I know. I've always known, and I should have let you alone. I was being selfish."

"No, it's okay." He knew he shouldn't say those words even as they came out.

The loft had gotten very dark. The evening sky's haze, and the snowfall, blocked the sun. His working light had diminished as only reflected light echoed from snowflake to snowflake into the loft. Shadows that stretched from tables and chairs began to merge. In the half-light, Brittany's face seemed to glow. Tears had fallen onto her cheeks and her eyes were wet. They flashed at Lewis. He lifted his hand and ran it over her face, brushed the hair from her forehead. The air was cold in the loft, so he used an electric space heater. It kicked on and a red glow from its filaments added to the minimal light. The right side of Brittany's face now reflected red. He kissed her moist lips and let his hand rest on her milk-full breast feeling the nipple rise below her blouse.

"I just wanted you to see the snow."

He looked past her. "It's beautiful."

"Our first."

"I know." He rubbed her belly. "For all three of us."

Brittany's lips curled into a shy smile. She turned to face the window with Lewis.

Lewis made a place for her between his legs so that they could sit together. He put both his arms around her and placed his hands over her stomach.

"He's active tonight," she said.

"Where?"

Brittany moved Lewis' hands to a place where the baby was kicking.

Lewis felt a small push and laughed.

Brittany laughed too.

"It's so wonderful, isn't it?" he said.

"Having you as the father is."

"How did this ever happen?"

"Let's just be glad it did."

Lewis felt excited about the baby and their life, the three of them together, yet, deep down felt the loss of a painting. He remembered what Jeffrey had told him about swallowing his doubt and was glad he had listened. His mind wandered. Brittany began to talk about her day, mostly spent alone downstairs, but Lewis' fatigue from long hours of painting and the expense of energy on getting angry, caused his eyes to close. His hands slid down Brit's belly to her thighs.

She turned to find him dozing and quietly kissed him. She slid his arms away. His head leaned far to one side, so she forced a cushion between his head and the sofa. Then she went over and lifted the painting from the floor. She leaned it against a small table where he kept paint and brushes in petite drawers, and stepped back to look at it in the glow of the heater and the fading dusk. She twisted her face and cocked her head. I wondered what she thought of it, an abstract depicting the rise of life from the ground. She didn't look happy. "Lewis," she said. "Lew!"

Lewis opened his eyes, "I'm sorry, honey."

"What is this?" She pointed at the painting.

"Worthless now."

"What was it, then?"

"I can't say."

"And why not?"

"Not until it's out of me."

"You said this was ruined."

He sat up. "That painting, not the idea. I like to keep it inside until I'm through. Especially with abstracts. They're so difficult."

"It looks like an abortion."

"Well, it is now, I'm sure. Still."

"You painted an abortion? Don't you want this child?"

"No, you don't get it. The painting isn't of an abortion, it is one. I may be able to fix it, but I'd rather start over. Something in me says that one's over."

"You're not happy, are you?"

"I'm fine."

"Then why this awful thing?"

"It's not awful." He came around to look at it. "It shouldn't be. Maybe that's what screwed up. Maybe that's why I can't use it."

"It looks like you're unhappy. You must be, how else could you carry such a thing around inside you."

"I carry everything inside me. It's probably the light."

"You carry this inside you?" She pointed at what she saw as a disgusting painting of an abortion.

"Even that. It's not right, though. I'll start again tomorrow."

"You were going to spend tomorrow with me, remember?"

"Okay, then I'll start the day after tomorrow, but I've got to paint it. It's got to work or it'll stay inside me."

"How could you do something like this?"

"What?" He spread open his hands as if to question her.

"It's awful."

"Fine. You said that. You think it's awful. I don't." There was a pause in his voice. "You never objected to anything else I did."

"But this."

"You act as if I've created a graphic representation of your mother's murder." He laughed and shook his head. "An abortion. That's ridiculous. There's no blood in this."

"There's red here." She pointed.

"That's brown. Very little red. Umber. It's the light, too."

"It's red."

"It's earth, dammit, earth, not blood, not abortion, not anything. It's ruined. It was no good to begin with." He began to walk around the room screaming. "It's a fucking painting. There's earth and sky and nature. There isn't a human element in there. Not one." His arms were raised high. "So there. Now what the fuck do you want?"

"Then don't paint it," she said.

Lewis bent and whispered hoarsely, "What?"

"Don't paint this one. Do something nice. I don't want people thinking you're unhappy with me."

"I have to paint this over. It has to be finished."

"Then don't use red."

Lewis just stared at her.

"Make yourself happy. Do happier paintings. For the baby."

"The baby?" he whispered.

"That painting's awful. I hate it."

Lewis breathed shallowly. The electric heater shut off and the loft went dark. "No," he said, "It has to get done."

"I'll hate it."

Lewis swallowed. He should never have let her in, or said that it was all right for her to interrupt him. He shouldn't have opened that door for her. Not now. But he had known that she'd eventually interfere. He said nothing more. Fine, he thought. He'd do it anyway. He had to.

Brittany got in the last word. "I hope you love your child, if not me, enough not to do this one thing." She walked out as though nothing had gone on between them that was problematic. She kissed him gently and rubbed her hand down his arm on the way out. "Come down soon," she said.

"I will."

When the door shut behind Brittany, Lewis turned the heater off. Outside the window the snowfall had gotten heavier. Small flakes had joined together to create a mass of tiny snowballs. Lewis could not see the field. He could barely make out the stone fence, which seemed to emerge, as dark rocks and crevices, from the slate gray of the air and white puffs of snow. He sighed. He didn't want to remember Brittany's comments about how much red he used in his painting, but he knew it would stick. If he could only keep it from entering the next work, keep it stuffed, like an old rag, in the back of his mind's closet, not to be seen. He brushed a hand through his hair and walked around the room. His eyes adjusted to the darkness. The cold loft air made him shiver. He took his brushes over to the sink in the corner and began to clean them. Tomorrow was another day, oh, but there was Brittany, he thought. He was spending the day with her. Was it Saturday? He shook his head and shrugged his shoulders. The sink water was cold, so he adjusted the faucets to a warmer temperature. In his mind he saw his own personal shapes and colors for warm water, for the movement of water over his sensitive fingertips, the movement over his wrists, around the brush tips. The brushes clacked together. He dipped them in and out of a solvent, and washed them with a degreaser. When he was satisfied they were clean, he brought saliva to his mouth and dipped each brush, one at a time, into his mouth and then slipped it out slowly to form a point. He then placed each brush onto the drain-board. When he was through, he went downstairs. It had been an early night for him, but he felt tired from the long hours he had been putting in. Brittany sat in the living room on the couch. Her big belly and full breasts appeared to overwhelm what used to be a skinny frame. Her face looked very small, placed in the middle of her hair which was curled out and fell fully around her cheeks.

"Are you coming down now, honey?" she asked as if what had happened earlier had been forgotten, or had never happened at all.

"I might go to bed," he said on his way to the kitchen.

"Get me some water while you're there."

"Okay." Lewis grabbed a glass and filled it, letting the water run unnecessarily long as he watched the snow outside the window. He took the glass to Brittany.

"Thanks." She looked up from a toilet paper commercial. "You missed dinner, as usual. Why don't you get a bite to eat? You're probably hungry."

Lewis was amazed at the change in her, how she snapped back to normal like a rubber band. He nodded and went back to the kitchen where he made himself a sandwich. In the living room, Brittany smiled as she watched the people in a sitcom go about their abnormally funny life.

Lewis sat down next to her.

"You look tired."

"I am."

She touched his face. "You know my mom came over today?"

"I didn't know."

"You were up there," she pointed.

"Oh."

"Anyway, she said we should entertain more often. I know this isn't a big town or anything, but you are pretty well known, and it'd make things a little jumpier around here."

"I'm only well known in certain circles. Anyway it's not me, it's my paintings people know."

"But they might want to know you, and it'd be fun for me, give me more to do." She turned her attention back to the television.

Lewis wondered if he was even heard when he talked. "If they want to meet me, introduce them to Jeffrey. He knows my work as well as anyone. They'll never know the difference."

"Uh, ha." She laughed at the TV. "Mom said, I'd love it. And you know she's right."

"Can I stay upstairs and paint?"

"Sometimes."

She heard that question, he thought. "Then you can do what you like."

"Oh," she bounced her big, oversize body, and clapped her hands like a child about to receive ice cream. "I'm so glad."

"Me, too." Lewis finished his sandwich and stood up. "I'm off to bed. I'm sorry, but if we're spending tomorrow together..."

"We'll go to the mall and shop."

"Yes, well, I'll need some sleep."

"I'll be back in an hour or so. Love ya."

Lewis bent down and kissed Brittany. "Good night."

"Good night, honey. I hope you had a good day."

Lewis looked at her. She had forgotten. How could anyone do that? And he still remembered it all too well.

Chapter 13

Abstracts were difficult for Lewis to paint. More so than realism, abstracts had to be perfect to be effective. Realistic paintings only had to hint at the realism, colors could be skewed, shapes out of perspective; as long as the idea came across clearly enough for the viewer to piece it together logically, it was fine. But abstracts had to pull from a different force, a different center. They had to fit more precisely than a double-sided jigsaw puzzle. Abstracts had to pull, from inside the viewer, the meaning, or near meaning, that the painter intended, even if the viewer wasn't conscious of the meaning at all, which was often the case.

Lewis fell into his internal, mysterious palette for just the right shape and color, arrived at through continual submersion into common thought mixed with his talent for connecting to the visual. When he tried to re-paint the abstract he and Brittany had argued over, this time altering his use of the color red, the painting failed miserably. He tried painting it again and again, the final attempt using gobs of red and pushing the painting over the edge of comprehension.

He quit. The series was incomplete, never to be finished. He wondered where to go next, remembered the Indian pointing, and decided to consult with nature. He laughed at his own idea, a disheartening fact for me, then discharged himself to the cold out-of-doors.

The snow of a few days previous had not stuck, but a healthy frost and cold wintry air kept the leaves and weeds in a crispy salad state. Lewis crunched and crackled through the small yard to the stone fence and into the field, its dried, dead weed stems lying at every angle, knocked over by wind, rain or animals. The few weeds that stood were only waist high. He heard a loud knock behind him and turned to see Jeffrey at his front door. Come to announce another sale, he hoped. Lewis lifted an arm, but just before yelling, he changed his mind, plunged both hands deeply into his pockets for warmth, and walked off. Behind him, Brittany opened the door and greeted Jeffrey.

The air smelled of winter. The tart odor of rotting leaves from the woods and the odor of dried field grass mixed to create its own fragrance. Lewis sucked it in through his nose, adding its uniqueness to his repertoire of painting materials. The sun pushed through clouds and cast a light shadow across the field. Trees glowed, the gray haze of an aura around them. Most of the leaves were gone from the maples, but many still held onto the branches of the oak and beech trees.

The image of the Indian flashed in and out of Lewis' mind. The answer to all his problems, he thought, but I knew better. It was a crutch, on several levels. First of all it was a way for Lewis to accept me, common thought, the raccoon, everything inside him which seemed illogical to his human-trained mind. Also, the Indian was a guide, a helper, a person with answers to difficult problems. Finally, it represented part of himself, part of the mystery of Lewis, a part which he didn't have to be responsible for. It was that part that he thought could help him finish the painting he had not been able to complete. It was that part, which connected closely to him, that he searched for, inside and outside himself, as he walked over the hollow, crunching forest floor towards me. It was that part which he would not find.

Nature does not have the answer. It understands life and death only as it is happening. Signatures of what is about to happen here are merely the early parts of what is already happening elsewhere. It's a fact. It can't be changed. Nothing said can change the facts. Humans have mobility and analytical thought, and no matter how close I become to Lewis, they are difficult concepts to understand. The way his mind worked was, even after all those years, foreign to me. Lewis still saw the Indian pointing as a spiritual guide. Yes, he still connected me with the guide, but only in that changeling, mysterious, god-like way. I often wished he'd see the truth more clearly.

He sat down and leaned against my trunk after brushing damp leaves away from the ground. It was very cold, but Lewis bore the discomfort. He closed his eyes and brought back the Indian. "You," it said. It always said the same thing. Lewis interpreted this as, you are important, you are the artist, you must go on. It was, in a way, the only thing he really believed in that told him to go on, the only thing he listened to. It gave him an identity he felt he didn't have in life. Jeffrey had identity in life. Externally, Lewis' was only a mirror to Jeffrey. His real identity was inside himself, where he did look different than Jeffrey. Inside, he was like everything else he made contact with, each emotion was translated into its separate parts and used in pieces to create a unique finished work.

While sitting, eyes closed, on the ground at my feet, Lewis considered his differences. Then the answer, like a bird flying by, flapped into his mind and landed within reach. He would add himself to the painting, an element of himself which depicted life from the Earth. It would be in keeping with the intent of the painting, plus it would use no red. Not that there wasn't red in his makeup, there were all colors, but he could choose only his life force, or the life force within him which did not need red. He could, in this painting of the series, drop the paganism and rise to a more spiritual life force. Lewis shook his head, rolled the back of his head against my rough bark. The Indian pointed at him, "You," it said, and Lewis added, "become a part of your own painting."

The answer was his own. I didn't attempt to push a thought into him. There was no Indian except the one he invented inside himself. There was the raccoon, me, common thought and all that went with it, but there was no Indian. Somehow, he resolved his own problem with a combination of mental image, or vision, and deep-seated analytical thought which allowed him to rationalize himself out of his dilemma.

He placed a piece of himself inside the painting. While sitting there in the cold, he conjured it up from the ooze of his mind, like a witch doctor or a sorcerer would do. The entire painting, not exact, for his mind was always much more vivid than life, but near exact, fell out before him. In his mind, Lewis could alter shapes and colors at will to adjust the outcome. He always had an outcome in his mind, and once he did, it had to be put down. His ideas haunted him if he didn't put them down. Eventually, he completed them to his satisfaction, or near satisfaction, for if truth be told, Lewis was never totally satisfied with his paintings and could hardly understand why anyone would pay for one. It was good that Jeffrey took care of that for him.

Lewis sat for close to two hours, opening his eyes several times just to glimpse the branches and minimum number of leaves against the gray sky. If someone were to walk up on him, they'd be sure that he was asleep, but there was much more than dreams going on inside his head, there was the creation of another world outside his, or mine, or the animals, either outside or a combination of them all, separate and together.

When Lewis was through deciding, accepting false guidance from the pointing Indian, he got up and slowly made his way back through the winter-cleared path to the stone fence, over its cold, pitted and grooved surface, where his hands lingered long enough to register texture, then through the browned field to his home. When he went to open the door, it was locked. He turned the knob and pushed harder, then kicked the bottom as though it may have been stuck. He peered in the door-glass, but saw no movement, so he pushed the doorbell. Nothing. "Dammit," he said, feeling his empty pockets. He went around back and felt above the door for the spare key, brought it back to the front and let himself in.

"Brittany?" he yelled.

No answer.

"Jeff?"

He walked through the house, into every room. Nothing. Walking back towards the front door, he saw the long sheet of yellow paper hanging below the window, taped to the wood. It read: Took Brit to hospital. She had pains. Couldn't find you. Jeff."

"Good God," Lewis said. He threw open the door and ran around the side of the house. Jeff's car was gone. He patted his pockets. "Shit." He rushed back into the house, got his keys, and left for the hospital wondering what time they had gone, and what was wrong.

It was hours before he got back. When he returned that evening, Jeff pulled in right behind him. I hadn't noticed Lewis coming until he was in the drive. I was concentrating on the woods, reacquainting myself with my own territory. I had, of late, been spending too much time following Lewis around.

Anyhow, Brittany was all right. The doctors were holding her for observation. She had had pains she mistook for early labor. Mostly, it had frightened her.

"Where were you?" Jeff asked as soon as the door closed.

"Out thinking."

"I called and called."

"I was at the tree. Sitting."

"You should have heard me."

Lewis shrugged, his hands out, palms up. "I didn't."

"Consulting with the Indian spirit guide again?"

Lewis looked at him. "What's bugging you?"

"You should have been here. What if I hadn't come by?"

"It was a false alarm."

"What if it wasn't and you were gone?"

"Jeff, for Christ's sake, most men work all week long. I'm almost always home. It was an accident that I wasn't here."

"Yeah, yeah, I guess you're right." Jeff looked up and smiled.

Lewis turned his eyes away. He didn't want to see himself smiling, to see himself with Jeffrey's eyes, and Jeffrey's obviously better grooming, trimmed hair, shaven face. Lewis reached to scratch his own two-day beard, and to brush his hair back.

"It scared me," Jeff said.

"I'm sorry I wasn't here."

"I know. And I'm sorry, too."

"For what?"

"Being snide about that Indian thing."

"You don't like it."

Jeff followed Lewis into the kitchen. "I admit, I have a problem with a few things: talking raccoons, seeing trees as individuals, Indian tree spirits, but if that's what you need to be able to paint, I accept it."

"It's not what I need." Lewis pulled two beers from the refrigerator and threw one to Jeffrey. "It's what I have, so I use it. I use everything. Everybody. " Lewis twisted the cap off the beer bottle. Jeffrey's popped loudly.

"Yourself?" Jeff asked.

"I'm about to."

"You never have?"

"Not really."

"What do you think you'll find?"

"I don't know, but he said..." Lewis looked up.

"Go ahead. I'll get used to it."

"He said it was okay to put myself inside this painting I'm working on."

"The one you and Brit argued about the other night?"

"How'd you know?"

"She told me on the way to the hospital. Talking kept the pain away, I guess. She said you've been acting funny ever since the fight."

"You know me."

"Yeah, you have to get it out of you. She interfered." He shook his head. "The way I used to when we were younger."

"But it's okay now. I'm the answer."

"I'm glad it worked out." He sat down. "Then things are fine."

"I think so. I'm working a lot of the time."

"Brittany talks a lot when I'm here. You don't think you leave her alone too much?"

"She doesn't complain." Lewis sat down at the kitchen table and Jeffrey did the same. Lew brushed his hand through his hair and tilted his beer bottle at a slight angle, and rolled it around on its bottom. "She's always talked a lot. Besides, now she says she's going to start having people over. Parties."

"She told me. What do you think of that?"

"Don't care, I guess. She said I can still work sometimes."

"You'll have to clean up more often."

"You mean shave?"

"Shave, get a haircut. A little sleep might brighten up your face. You can really afford new clothes. It's not like you're broke."

"They just get paint on them." Lew looked up. "But I could."

"I think sleep's the big thing. I don't want you to collapse again."

"You still worry about that?"

"I thought that today when you didn't answer."

132

"I'm sorry."

"You said that, but that doesn't matter. What matters is that you stay healthy. You're starting to get thinner already."

"I was too fat anyway."

"You were fine. For God's sake, you really need to take more care. For Brit's sake, the baby's. Look at yourself."

"I am." He looked up.

"Don't start with that shit." Jeff stood and put his empty bottle on the counter next to the sink. "That's self pity, or some such shit. You have a life. You have a family! That's more than I have. What are you going to put into your paintings, now that you've started? Self pity?"

"There's other things in there."

"It was a rhetorical question. So was, look at yourself. I just mean take care before you collapse again."

"When I need to paint, I paint. What if suddenly it wasn't there anymore? Before I even reach thirty, it's gone? I couldn't take it. The rest of my life would be empty. I've got to keep going."

"Keep the fire burning, huh?"

"Yeah, keep it burning so it doesn't go out."

"Lew, it'll never go out. Not yours."

"You don't know."

"I'm damned near positive. What I think is that you've got to worry about living long enough so you can get it all out. If you die, all that stuff is left inside you. Unfinished. Forgotten. Never seen by anyone. You've got to live long enough to paint it all."

Lewis clapped. "Nice little speech."

"Really, Lew, take a break. Promise me."

"What?"

"Promise me you'll slow down."

"I'm not going to promise."

"Please."

"We're not kids."

"So, promise me."

"Good God, Jeff."

"Well."

"Fine. All right. I promise."

"Start today. Tonight."

"I've got to work tonight. Start that painting."

"Don't you know what you're going to do with it?"

"Sure I do."

"Then start tomorrow. You have a promise to keep."

"I didn't say I'd start right away."

"You promised though, and you can wait for this painting. You said so yourself. Besides, Brittany needs you to be strong when she gets home."

Lewis shook his head back and forth. "All right, stop badgering me. I'll begin painting tomorrow." Lewis raised a finger, "At daybreak. Right away in the morning."

"Deal, just get a good eight hours tonight."

"Bargain. Then you'll stop bugging me?"

"Promise," Jeff said raising one hand and placing the other over his heart. "Now, you want another beer?"

"Sure." The refrigerator light blinked on, then off as Jeff got two more beers. Lewis glimpsed the light, caught it before and after it went on, could see all the food inside on the shelves, square boxes, packages, bottles, yellows, browns, dark, light.

"Here," Jeff handed him a bottle. "When's this series going to be done?"

"Why, you sold it already?"

"Hey, this is a part time thing for me until I finish up with school. I transferred closer to home, what more do you want? When I'm finished, I'll become your personal agent, okay?"

"Sure. Who better than you? That way you can pretend to be me. I won't have to deal with all those snivelers."

"God, Lew, they're not all snivelers, you know. Some of them are pretty decent, others are just doing their job. You can't blame them, anyway. It's more of a compliment. They want to see you, talk to you, learn about how you work."

"See what makes me tick like some lab animal is more like it."

"That's not true. Besides, have you thought about the girls wanting to fawn all over the great artist."

"I have Brit."

"I didn't say fuck everybody, I said take it as a compliment. It's flattering. You could probably use some attention too, get your head out of the woods."

"For my work, I need to keep my head in the woods."

"Where all your inspiration is."

Lew looked at his watch.

"Getting late," Jeff said.

"Not yet, but soon. If I'm going to put in eight hours and still get up by the time the sun does."

"Don't forget Brit. They'll probably release her tomorrow afternoon, too. You'll need to pick her up."

"I don't think I'll forget my own wife."

Jeff looked a little embarrassed. "No, I guess you wouldn't."

"You think I'm totally out of it, don't you?"

"No, just absent minded sometimes."

"I'm not bad. I function pretty well."

"Alone."

"What's wrong with that?"

"Nothing if you're single. And don't have kids."

"I don't yet."

"But you will."

"I'll change."

"And if you don't?"

"Uncle Jeff will be here." Lew laughed.

"That's not funny."

"You worry too much. Brit and I have talked about it. In a normal family, ours for instance, the kids don't get to see their dads that often. We didn't see Mom much either, remember? They both worked most of our lives. We made it."

"But you're in the loft a lot more time than Dad or Mom was at work."

"But Brit won't be. She'll be right here."

"She's not going back to work?"

"She doesn't want to, and I don't care. I'd just as soon she were

135

around. There's plenty to do. She goes shopping, to her mother's, her friends', cooks, cleans."

"Sounds like you guys have talked it over."

"I'm not absent all the time, just a lot of the time. I work slowly. Van Gogh could whip out a painting. I can't."

"Yours are better," Jeff said.

I felt a twinge of something inside Lewis. He took great pride in his brother's praise, and that had been a boost to whatever he thought of himself as well as what he felt his brother thought of him. "They're not that good," Lew said, still feeling proud, and genuinely satisfied with Jeff's appraisal.

"You must know they are, Lew, deep inside somewhere, you must."

"Not really, but I'm glad you think so. I'm glad something I do for the outside world works. I know I don't work too well out there."

"So that's the part of you we get?"

"I'm just lucky you like it, people like it, it could be my only existence in the outside world and be hated."

"Never, Lew," Jeff said. "I just think it'd be great if you could bring out more of yourself."

"I will be soon."

"I don't mean in the paintings."

"I know, I know."

Jeff slapped his hand to the table. "After the baby's born, me and Marsha will baby-sit and let you and Brit go out. You can use a night or two together, just the two of you."

"Brittany say that?"

"Hinted at it."

"You don't think Marsha would mind?"

"Naw, you know Marsha."

"Not really." Lew looked at his watch again. "I know you've been dating her a long time, but you don't talk about her much."

"Yeah, we're always sort of preoccupied aren't we?"

"If by that you mean the conversation is always aimed at my paintings, yes. There is quite a focus on my work when we talk. It makes me uncomfortable a lot of the time."

"Does it?"

"Yeah, but that's okay."

"Well, Marsha's a great girl. Like you said, we've been dating, off and on, mostly on, for quite a while now. She's real easy going. Nice personality, smart, I think you know that."

"Yeah, she probably thinks I'm dumb."

"No, she takes you as you are. Artistic. You're not dumb by any means, you just choose not to learn certain things."

"Right," Lew sat back and laughed.

"Anyway, she's perfect for me and I love her a lot."

"Oh, do I hear wedding bells?"

"Maybe, we're both careful."

"Practical."

"That, too. We'll wait 'til we're out of college, then tie the proverbial, nuptial knot."

"You guys will be great together."

Jeff stood up and put his empty beer bottle on the counter. "I'm gonna go so you can sleep. You promised, remember?"

"I remember."

"It's a relief Brit's all right."

"I know. It scared me when I saw the note. I got pretty upset and worried. All kinds of things went through my head."

They walked out to the door together where Lew put his hand on Jeff's shoulder, something he rarely did. They seldom touched at all. "Don't worry, I'll be a good father. I won't let you down."

"Just don't let Brit down. She loves you a lot."

"I hardly know why."

"That's not important."

Lew slapped Jeff's shoulder once and smiled, "I guess you're right."

After the door closed and Jeff was in his car letting it warm up, Lewis went back to the bedroom and got ready for bed. The hum of the car pushed past the closed windows, and eventually the crunch of tires over hard earth distanced and faded. It was a relatively short walk, but Jeffrey always chose to drive. This time the choice had paid off.

Lewis lay back in bed on top of the blankets. The room was chilly and he let the cold touch his body. All was quiet. He remembered back to when he sat against my trunk and called on the Indian. For a time he had gone into common thought, where he imagined the forest and the animals to be slightly askew from the real world. That place where the pointing Indian resided.

How wrong he was. Common thought was the real world, only the Indian was false, possibly in a realm of its own, an imaginative one. In common thought, Lewis could actually see more, hear and smell and taste more. The Indian was a figment, and I was associated with that figment. It was attached to me. He was beginning to mix all his worlds together into one.

Chapter 14

A child was born, Christopher Stewart Marshal, on January the third. Months later, the season folded over from winter to spring. The white and gray turned to yellow and green. Birds returned, chipmunks and squirrels played in the morning sunlight. April produced showers which brought the flowers in May, just as it should be.

Lewis stuck close to Brittany and Christopher those first months. He took a morning walk and an evening walk to think and meditate. He worked a scheduled six-hour day and produced the earthbound paintings he had become more and more well known for. He worked at being the ideal husband and father, changing diapers, washing, cleaning. He still stayed up late and got up early. For days at a time he appeared as though he hadn't slept at all, though I know he had slept a few, light hours.

As far as his paintings were concerned, they became softer, more nurturing, during that period. Quieter, was the word he used to describe them to Jeffrey, and in turn was the word Jeffrey related to whomever was interested, most importantly gallery owners and magazine editors.

Lewis was an attentive, caring father those first months. Neither dirty diapers, nor vomit bothered him. In fact, Lewis was more able to take care of Christopher than Brittany, in those messier categories. But she knew how to dress Christopher, and shopped often just to fulfill that all important function of making sure he was presentable whenever someone visited, and whenever she had people over.

The parties, "Finally," she had told Lewis, had begun late that first spring after Christopher's birth. For Lewis, it suddenly became a time of retreat. Brittany wanted to show off their child, and Lewis "...could stay and talk or go to the loft, or take a long walk," whatever he chose. Brittany could handle Christopher during parties until he went to bed, at which time Lewis could sneak back to the boy's room and rock him or just sit with him until he chose to go to bed, or work, himself. Many nights Lewis fell off to sleep in the bedroom chair, Christopher holding onto his finger, the loud party noise winding down in the small living room.

Occasionally, Lewis visited the party, more by the insistence of Jeffrey than Brittany. Jeffrey realized the marketing importance of a visit now and again. He knew that if the mysterious Lewis wandered through the room a little worn for the event, all the better. And on one occasion, Lewis' appearance was even more of a blessing to Jeffrey. Having been asked question after question about his recent abstracts, and after dodging those questions like flying tennis balls aimed at his head, Lewis announced, formally, that it was Jeffrey they should talk with. Lewis actually hailed the room first, "Hey, hey, everybody," his arms high in the air, his hands waving inwardly, motioning them closer. "I have something to say."

Brittany's face had a surprised look on it. Jeffrey's looked more like he was in shock to see his shy brother so boisterous, and in front of so many people. Neither knew what Lewis was doing, there was no warning what-so-ever. "Get closer, dammit!" The small crowd tucked in, a few elbows got bumped, but no real drink spillage happened. "I've been asked a lot of questions tonight, as I often am at these little events. I have very little to say to them. Why this, and how that, doesn't even register with me when I'm asked. It isn't until later, at some odd time: in the woods, at night in bed, at the dinner table, when answers to these questions finally hit me." He waited. Jeffrey shook his head back and forth slowly in bewilderment. "That's when I call my twin brother, Jeffrey. I tell him everything, and with this information, he translates the unusual and twisted thoughts I have into something useful and coherent to the rest of the world. He interprets not only with his common sense, but with the other half of my mind, that twin-connection you've all heard about. He knows the answers. He knows how I think and what I think." Lewis pointed at Jeffrey and everyone turned to stare. "Only he can answer your questions." And that was all. It was over. While everyone at the party was just beginning to relax again, and talk to one another, Lewis left the room and walked up the stairs to the loft. He had set things straight, he had hoped, and Jeffrey was now in charge, fully, of Lewis' destiny. Jeffrey thanked him for it later, but Lewis ignored him. The job was done. Lewis had done it for himself, for his own sanity, not for Jeffrey.

That night, walking up the stairs, something clicked in Lewis' head, maybe from the pressure build-up before his little speech, maybe from the pressure of the speech. Something clicked and Lewis saw the wall move, and the stairs shift right. He almost fell, but grabbed hold of the stair rail. He stumbled again near the top of the stairs and grabbed the doorknob to the loft. He swung open the door and fell onto the floor, rolling over onto his back and staring at the ceiling. He closed his eyes for a minute, but the room felt as though it was spinning like a top. When he released his eyelids, the ceiling burst into view through the faded light coming in the picture window at the front of the loft, the window which overlooked the field. A sliver of moon formed minimal light. The visible beams of the ceiling sagged like they were under a great weight. They twisted and creaked. Dust puffs escaped in odd spots along their lengths and Lewis threw his arms over his head to protect himself as they fell toward him. He turned over and scooted closer to the couch which sprouted a hand and tried to touch him. Suddenly, the lights went on and Lewis screamed.

Jeffrey ran over to him, "Lew, Lew, what's wrong? I heard you fall or something."

"The roof, the roof."

Jeffrey looked up. "What about it?"

"It's caving in. Look." Lew pointed.

"Where?"

"Where pieces are falling."

"My God," Jeffrey said. He put his arm over Lewis' shoulder and helped him to the couch.

Lewis' feet stepped, one, two, three little steps over to the right, then back left. "Tell it to stop moving."

"It's not."

"It is, it is!" he yelled.

"Wait here." Jeff put his hand on Lew's knee. "You'll be okay."

"Quick, get something to hold the roof up."

Jeffrey went downstairs and came back up only moments later.

Lewis was deep inside common thought on the one hand and deep inside himself on the other. All I could see inside him was what he conjured up himself from the chemicals mixing and turning inside his brain. Through his eyes, I could see reality, and I could see it through Jeffrey's eyes, too, but it was more difficult to do so.

In a matter of moments, an ambulance came and took Lewis away.

It seems I'm always covering arrivals or departures, but those moments are the most vivid. His departure was quick. He was shivering from non-existent cold. His eyes jutted back and forth, fearful of things that were not there.

He was back in less than a week. His mind calm, sedated. Jeffrey and Brittany brought him home in Jeff's car. Brit sat in the back seat with Lewis, holding his hand. Marsha watched little Christopher and waited for them, holding the door as the three walked into the cottage.

"I'm fine, I'm fine." Lew waved away all the hands trying to help him into a recliner. The chair gave and creaked as he plopped down.

Lewis was clean-shaven and wore a cotton dress shirt and slacks Brittany had just bought him. On the outside he looked fine, better than fine; he looked like Jeffrey, except for the distance in his eyes. On the inside, he hung in limbo. A man hung by the shoulders from a high tree limb comes to mind, swaying in a light breeze. That's how Lewis was, just swinging slowly, not on the ground or in the air, connected to reality by a rope and to free fall by the loosening of a knot. When he swung into common thought he wandered into the enchanted forest where he was first able to relax on the pine needle carpet, and when he swung back, he talked, not necessarily coherently. "It seems warm out today. Do we have any peanuts? I'm hungry. Thanks, Jeff." The medication kept him slightly too relaxed and unable to concentrate.

Jeffrey, Marsha, and Brittany made small talk and rustled around the house. Brittany made lunch while Jeff and Marsha played with Christopher and kept an eye on Lewis.

At one point, Lewis got out of the chair and went to pick up Christopher, then suddenly, on the roller coaster of drugs, felt too loose even to stand up and tumbled to the floor. Jeff caught him before he landed on the baby. Lewis was already gone again, and Jeffrey placed him back in the chair as though he were cleaning up the house and the chair was where Lewis belonged.

"Tell Brit we're staying the night," he said to Marsha.

"Are you sure?"

"We can't leave her alone to worry about both Lew and the baby, she'll never sleep."

"You're right." Marsha got up and went into the kitchen. In a moment, the two of them walked into the living room, Brittany carrying a tray of sandwiches, Marsha holding three glasses of lemonade. "You really don't have to hang around here all day and night, Jeff," Brittany said. "I do appreciate it, but I'll be all right with Lew."

"Did she tell you what he almost did?"

"Yes, but if you weren't here, I'd have had Chris in the kitchen with me."

"Still, I'd feel better."

Brit sat the tray down on the coffee table. "Well, look, stay as long as you like. If you feel comfortable in leaving later, then do that, but really, I'm not worried."

"That's fair," Jeff said.

"If we stay, I need to get us some clothes," Marsha said.

"That can wait. I think you'll see everything's okay," Brit said.

Jeffrey watched Lewis as he ate. The recliner was leaned back perfect for sleeping, and soon Lewis' eyes closed and he became still. "What happened in the womb that made him a genius and not me?"

"You're just different people, that's all," Marsha said. "I know I wouldn't want you like that anyway."

Brittany looked over.

"I don't mean anything by it, Brit. But, you've got to admit, living with Lew's got to be a challenge."

"Not usually. Probably no more than anyone else. He has his moments because he's around a lot more than most men. Still, he's fairly preoccupied. He pays attention to us, takes care of us just fine."

"You insinuated to me that things, well, weren't going very well," Jeff said.

"When was that?"

"Right before the baby."

"Things got better."

Jeff looked over at Lew, passed out in the recliner. "Have they?"

"Don't be like that! It's not his fault he's like this."

"It's no one's fault," Jeff said. "It just is. But how can you live like this? How do you survive? I'm not suggesting you divorce my brother, I love him and know that you do, too, and he loves you, but maybe you should think about help. God knows you can afford it. It might ease your mind. You wouldn't have to worry so much."

"I don't worry now, you do!"

"Don't get mad, Brit, we're only trying to help."

Brittany turned her head, avoiding eye contact. Looking over at Lewis, she said, "It's only the drugs right now, that's what has him like this. We're reacting to his present state, not his real self."

"He had a breakdown for Christ's sake," Jeff said. "People like that have relapses. Don't you know that sort of thing doesn't just go away easily? Do you know how long he's been this way? Do you, in your carefree, ah, ah, mode of life? You know how you are."

"Superficial?" Brit said.

Marsha's hand moved over to Jeff's knee to stop him, or calm him down, but he continued. "Not just superficial, but you don't seem to notice what is going on inside him. He's your husband."

"He needs to be left alone."

"Does he?"

"Maybe I know better than you."

"Do you know about the Indian pointing?"

"Yes."

Marsha looked puzzled, her face positioned, as to say what or who the hell?

144

"Do you know," Jeff continued a little louder, "that he takes walks in the woods to meet this, this spirit? That he talks to him about his paintings, about what he should paint, how, what to include?"

"No," Brit said quietly. "I thought that was over with."

"A temporary illusion?"

"Yes."

"Well it wasn't. It isn't. It's part of his everyday life. Every day!" Jeffrey emphasized by pounding a finger into the carpet.

Brittany put her hand on her husband's knee. "Why didn't he tell me? Why do you know?"

"I'm sorry," Jeff said. "I went too far. I didn't mean to bring it up. Shouldn't have. Please don't tell him or he'll never trust me again."

"Doesn't he trust me?"

"It's not that, I'm sure."

"No?"

"This started long ago, when we were kids. The trees started to have lives of their own. A raccoon spoke to him."

"A raccoon," Brittany began to cry. She got up and went into the kitchen.

Marsha stood and followed, but not before she turned to Jeff and said, "This is getting weird."

Christopher slept on the carpet next to Jeff. Jeff turned him over and picked him up. Christopher began to cry.

Brittany came out and took Christopher from him. "You can stay for as long as you like," she said, holding Christopher up to her shoulder. "I need to put him down for a nap." She left the room.

Marsha stood inside the kitchen doorway staring at Jeff. Thousands of questions must have been running through her mind. Her brows were creased tightly, her eyes inquisitive.

"We'll talk later," Jeff said. "I'm sorry this happened."

"Me, too."

"I didn't mean to get you involved, Hun."

"Too late."

"God, don't get pissed at me now, I'm in enough hot water."

"I tried to stop you."

"I know, I know." He paused and sighed, looked at Lewis peacefully asleep in the recliner. "I hope I can sort things out with him."

"You always seem to."

"It may look that way, but that's not the case. Besides, if he finds out I said anything, told everything, he may stop confiding in me. Then who will he talk to? How will he let it out? I think the last thing he needs is to hold everything in. That might just make it worse."

"You don't know that."

"No, but it makes sense, doesn't it?"

"I don't know," Marsha said, "I'm not his psychologist."

"Maybe you're right."

Lewis moaned and twisted in the chair. Jeff looked over and began to stand, then sat back down on the floor where he was. He hadn't eaten any of his lunch.

"I don't want to be right, I want Lew to be okay," Marsha said.

"So do I," Jeff said rudely, shocked that Marsha would insinuate otherwise.

"Then maybe you should tell his psychologist about all this."

"She's probably right," Brittany said from the hallway. When she appeared, her tears were dry and her face fresh. She had cleaned up: combed her hair and fixed her makeup while she was gone. "Dr. Slater should know all this."

"Do you think Lew told him?"

"In his condition?" Brit said.

Jeff looked at the floor in response. "Who should tell him?"

"You seem to know everything," Brit said.

Marsha shook her head when Jeff looked at her for support. "Sorry, Honey, but she's right. You have all the information."

"But, if the doctor wanted to know, wouldn't he ask us?"

"He asked me," Brit said, "but all I told him was about the Indian spirit, and that it happened a long time ago. I didn't know about all this other stuff, or about his continual contact with his, his illusion." She appeared as though she were going to begin to cry again, so Marsha went over to her and held her hand. They walked into the living room together and sat on the couch.

Jeff was quiet. He didn't seem as sure about what they were proposing he do as they apparently were. "I'm still not sure if it'll help," he said.

"It really isn't up to you to make that decision," Brit said.

A breeze came through the house and blew across Jeff's face. It was a cool breeze, filled with the scents of the forest and field. He visibly relaxed. "I'll do it," he said.

"Thank you."

"I'm sure that Dr. Slater won't bring it up to Lewis point-blank. He'll probably try to get Lew to let it out a little at a time."

"I'm sure he'll do what's best," Marsha assured him.

Brittany smiled and patted Marsha's hands with her free hand. Marsha still held onto Brittany.

The wife and brother, like veins in a leaf, felt equally responsible for Lewis, but each saw things moving in different directions. Brittany thought that complete exposure of Lewis' thoughts, feelings, and illusions, would save him from those very things, where Jeff felt that exposure would be even more threatening to Lewis' well being. That Lewis had to decide who would be let in on his little world. But once Jeffrey had promised, it was as good as done, and Lewis was thrust into a number of years of psychoanalysis. Nonetheless, he continued to paint. Nothing seemed to stop him.

Chapter 15

Lewis had not been blessed with a strong enough will to force his own personality ahead of all else inside him. He lacked personal assertion. That was what allowed him to let nature in so easily. He found common thought within himself, and put its personality, multiple as it was, ahead of his own. When he did allow his own personality out, it was for short periods of time only. He functioned in the human world, and then, through a long dark hollow tube. Jeffrey said that Lewis was an introvert. Brittany explained that he was just quiet, always thinking of his paintings. Both explanations were based in truth.

For the next eight years, Lewis went in and out of the psychiatric ward at the hospital twice. His relapses were relatively minor, nothing so horrifying as the first time. He felt them coming on, saw them visually as they approached.

Brittany continued having parties, but they were getting to be too much work for her to handle. She wrinkled quickly around the eyes. Her upturned mouth reversed so that she often appeared to be angry when she wasn't. The parties got boring. The same people, the same discussions. Lewis almost never appeared and Christopher was no longer a focal point, instead he was off playing with friends or in his room playing alone. Sometimes he sat with Lewis, watching him paint.

It was the enormity of life that caused Lewis to break down, just as it was the enormity that caused Brittany and Lewis' marriage to break down. Nothing so fragile, built so large, could run perfectly. The love, or need, that Brittany and Lewis once shared deteriorated almost completely before either one had noticed. One day, it was just gone and they both realized it at once.

Jeffrey wasn't happy with the situation. "So, you're going through with this?"

Lewis shrugged. He felt happy and sad about the divorce, just as he had felt about the marriage at its beginning. He had once wanted Brittany in his life without totally understanding why. Then, still uncomfortable with them as a couple, he married her. Now, with an equal amount of discomfort, he was allowing a divorce to take place. They had agreed. It had been an easy decision, really. Neither Brittany nor Lewis wanted it to be difficult for the other.

"What about Christopher?" Jeff asked.

"He doesn't quite follow what's going on."

"Sure he does. He's nine years old."

"Almost."

"That's plenty old enough to understand divorce. Has anyone talked with him about it? Have you?"

"I have. He wants to live with his mother, but he says he wants to visit often. Wants to see his cousin."

Jeff smiled. "I want him to visit, too. He's turned out to be a good kid."

"At least he's not an artist."

"Don't be so hard on yourself."

"I'm too much trouble anymore."

"That's not true."

"It is. Brittany's had enough."

"Your heart was never in it. No one can blame you for that. You have your art. Brittany knew that when she married you."

"She said that?"

"Not in so many words, not to me. She was talking with Marsha one day when she brought Chris over to visit Rob." Jeff stepped around the kitchen table and pulled a chair out. He moved slowly and rubbed his forehead with his hand after he sat down. "I would like them to grow up together."

"Me, too," Lew said. "I'm glad Brit's not taking the house."

"You're paying her enough for a mansion. Besides, I think she wants to move closer to town, closer to her parents."

"If that's what's good for her."

"Yeah." Jeff rubbed his forehead again. "So, you're for this whole thing?"

"Back to your original question."

"I just don't know whether I should believe you. You seem a little unsure."

"It'll be hard getting along without them," he admitted.

"Have you told Brittany?"

"She's basically lived a life alone the last few years. I've been traveling quite a bit."

"Off and on."

"Yes, and it seems to me that when I'm not traveling, I'm painting, and when I'm not doing either, I'm in the nut house."

Jeffrey noticeably cringed when Lewis said that. He had protested before about Lewis' nonchalant expressions concerning his condition. It always seemed inappropriate to Jeffrey, at least that's what he had told Lewis.

But Lew didn't care. To him it was a fact of life. He wished it wasn't, but it was, and it only confirmed his own belief that he wasn't fully of this life, human life, that is.

"None of that's true of course," Jeff said. "I'm sure you spent a lot of time together the past ten years."

"But not the best of times."

"Does it always have to be?"

"It should be sometimes."

"So, what happened?"

"I think I never really accepted that she loved me."

"What? Of course she did."

"No, I've been thinking about it a lot. She may have loved me, but I never saw it, never accepted it fully. You know what I mean?"

"You never thought you deserved it?"

"Yeah, maybe that. Since I was never really her type."

"Her type? For Christ's sake, she loved the shit out of you, you just couldn't see it. God damn, Lew, you let everything slip because of a lack of self confidence? It that what you're saying? You're famous, for Christ's sake. Doesn't that increase your confidence in yourself? Doesn't that build you up?"

"My art is not me."

"No, it's everything else."

"Right."

"Lew, I hate to break it to you, but there's more to you than you think, more than just your paintings. I hate to see this happening to you. I know it must be hard."

"It is, but I think Brit's right, it's for the best."

"Who's going to take care of you?"

"I can cook and clean."

"But you need someone around."

"What, in case I have another breakdown? I'll tell you when it's coming, okay?"

"Right. That's fine. I'll just wait for that to happen."

Lewis felt that Jeff had more to say about the subject and was holding back. It wasn't just the divorce or Lew's mental health that was on his mind, there was something more. There were other questions he wasn't asking. "What else is there?" Lew said.

"I don't know."

"Something's bothering you."

Jeff looked into Lewis' face, and in complete, naked honesty asked, "Will you be able to paint?"

Lew felt a shock of instant recognition. "You depend that much on my work?"

Jeff's head nodded, "Pretty much." He tried to smile, "I get commissions you know."

"I didn't really think it was all that much."

"You're the star. You have been for a number of years now. Why do you think we did that video for the galleries last year? And the trips, the interviews?"

"Still."

Jeff shook his head again. "You pay no attention."

"I try not to think about it. I don't need the pressure."

"And now this pressure."

"No, you're not a problem. It's the public, the dealers."

"Don't try to convince me."

"It's true. I can't talk to other people very well. I can't control a conversation the way you do. I need you around as much as you need me. Remember when you were still in college and I had you reading my mail? I couldn't stand dealing with those people even at a distance."

"I remember."

"Believe me, whatever you make from what you do, you deserve. I'd fail miserably without you."

"Not true. You could get a business manager."

"One who didn't know me well enough to speak for me. You're just as important in all this as I am. You're the personality. I'm the recluse."

"I never said that."

"I did. It's pretty fucking well true too, isn't it?"

"You're funny." Jeff laughed and shook his head, "You're probably right. They think you're a recluse."

"They're right." Lew bent over the table and got close to Jeff's face, "They're probably glad, too. I could be an obnoxious fuck-head like some of the other artists out there."

"True."

"With you, it's business, just the way those dealers like it."

Jeff stared as Lew talked on about their unique situation, how much Jeff's personality meant to his own sales. How being twins had offered them the added benefit of the public and dealers being able to see the eccentric artist without having to deal with any of his quirkiness. Lewis was in a very articulate state and went on to praise Jeffrey for the salesman and businessman he was, and for their inevitable closeness. "I am the artist in you," he said. "If we had been born one instead of two, it may never have come out, or it would have been stifled. You are my 'in-this-world' common sense, my business mind, my outward personality. You are technology, I am nature."

"Christ, that was beautiful." Jeff began to clap. He got up from his seat and hugged his brother. "When we were younger," he said, "I used to resent your talent, used to hate it sometimes."

"I used to hate how you were. Always captain of the team."

"We are like one person sometimes."

"This separation has allowed us to reach our peaks in both directions, something most people never get to do. I need you around."

"Thank you," Jeff said.

"You could never add pressure to my life. I paint better because of you. When you carry that part of me, I don't have to."

"So, you'll continue to paint?"

"More than ever."

"Don't get run down. We don't need another illness."

"Check on me from time to time."

"I will."

The divorce went through quickly and easily. Lewis felt the loss more than he put on, crying privately for hours at a time over the loss of Brittany and Christopher. In many ways they had stabilized his life, and now were gone. In a confused rush of unspent love, he painted several works of Brittany from memory: her eyes were most important in them. It would be difficult for people to keep from looking into those eyes.

Just as he had told Jeffrey that he was nature, so it was, and without humans around to hold him to that world, he delved deeper into nature. In a few years, all traces of Brittany were gone from him. Christopher remained as the child in himself. Common thought welcomed him daily and his paintings became frantically wild and unforgiving, yet traces of childhood could be found in an odd shape here or the twinkling, playfulness of color there. The paintings became compelling and innocent, but with death just around the corner, unforgiving. It had quickly become his best work, and sold as such.

Jeffrey wanted Lewis to move or enlarge the cottage, but Lewis was perfectly happy where he was. "There is something missing, though," he told Jeffrey.

"What? Anything." They were walking around the field in autumn. The leaves had begun to change and the tall weeds were brown and dried. Lewis touched the stone fence every twenty or so feet, because he liked the different ways the rock felt. He was in and out of common thought, so lacked the acute attention to follow too closely to what Jeff said. Up until that point, it had only been business anyway, and Lewis frankly wasn't interested.

"So, what is it, Lew?"

"I sometimes miss having..." Lew was lost in the bushes following a snake which was sliding slowly towards the brook.

"You okay?" Jeff asked.

"I'm sorry. I'm preoccupied. Thinking, I guess."

"Are you sure you're okay. You've been in and out all afternoon. I think you could use some sleep."

"Yeah."

"So, what was it you were saying?"

"Oh, that. Companionship."

Jeff laughed. "Companionship? Don't you get laid enough when you go on trips?"

"I don't mean that."

"You don't mean a real relationship, do you?"

"I think I do."

"You think? Well, do you have anyone in mind?"

"No."

"You ought to start with that."

Lew snapped himself out of common thought, away from the snake, the rocks. "I need to meet people, someone."

"I can arrange that, but God knows, I'm no cupid."

"I know." Lew lowered his eyes.

"You okay?"

"I think so," Lew smiled. He was kidding Jeff, but it took Jeff a minute or two to realize it.

"You're spooky sometimes."

"I'm just tired."

"Then sleep. Why have you been overworking? God knows you don't need the money. By the way, talking about money, I pulled some out of stocks to..."

"Do what you think you have to. It's your problem."

"Just thought I'd tell you."

"I know." Lewis looked around at the treetops for color, registering patches here and there. Nothing happened by any organized plan, and each year the first signs of color came from different trees, different areas in the small horizon that surrounded the cottage.

"I'll have a small party, invite some single girls I know."

"You know? What about Marsha, she have any friends I haven't met?"

"I guess," Jeff said. "I'll ask her."

"Or we'll go out once in a while."

"This isn't a very big town, Lew. And if you want to go to the city or anything, your chances for meeting someone might go up, but the chances they'd be willing to move out here with you, well that's another story."

"You said I'm getting better known in the private sector."

"Yes, but you want someone who loves you, not someone who loves your money, or loves the art alone."

Lewis turned and looked into Jeff's eyes, "Do I?"

Slowly Jeff said, "That's what you should want."

"My art is me."

"I know, I know," his arm went up to brush the words away, like swatting at gnats. "A woman's love is different."

"You've said that sometimes you think Marsha loves you for the money."

"Lew, for Christ's sake, that's said only as a joke. I don't really think that."

"Oh. So how do I tell whether they love me or my art? With me it's as though both are the same."

"It's not easy. They lie."

"Nature doesn't lie."

"What's that got to do with anything?"

"Nothing, I guess, just the truth."

"Fine, Lewis, but you can't fuck nature."

"No, but it can fuck you."

"Ha, ha, ha," Jeff belly laughed. "You're a riot. I'd say you're right though. In a lot of ways, it's fucked you."

They were on their final stretch around the field, on their way back to the cottage near the part of the fence that opened up to the old tractor road.

"Let's go this way," Lew said.

"Past the tree?"

"Yes."

"Do you still..."

"I do."

"But..."

"It's been a long time since I had a breakdown. Is that what you're thinking?"

"Yeah, that's what I was going to say."

"I was thinking about that the other day."

"Do you think talking to the tree will bring it on?"

"No, not at all. I come out here and actually become part of the forest now. Not totally, I know that. Only through the tree. I see the Indian all the time, even in the house, the car. I see snakes, opossums, porcupines, all the time. I know the trees, not by where they are, but by what they look like, feel like, what they are, you might say. People don't really look at trees, or try to recognize them, because they don't move. People remember where they are, not what they are." Lewis stopped in the path. "It only happens the right way sometimes." He pointed down the over-grown road. "Wouldn't you recognize that tree anywhere? If it was up-rooted and put in New York City?"

"You're right." Jeff stood next to Lew. "I remember the first time. That same branch. Doesn't that tree ever change?"

"It hasn't for a while. Even if its appearance did change, if it lost a limb..."

"A branch."

"Whatever. It would be the same tree."

"I suppose so, but that doesn't convince me of its personality, that it's a spirit or anything."

"But you admit to its uniqueness."

"In appearance only. Just visual."

"Well, there's more," Lewis said with such authority and confidence that Jeff left the subject alone, just dropped it.

Chapter 16

Finding lovers was easy for Lew. He and Jeff were both very good looking. Plus, he had money, plenty of it. And there were always art students, fledgling artists, and women just looking for part of the mystery. But Lewis had a difficult time getting to know these women, and he didn't open up often enough for any of them to get close to him. Nonetheless, he found companionship, serial companionship. Every six months or so, he found himself dating, or living with, a woman he no longer wished to have around. Each relationship began similarly, with whomever was aggressive enough to approach him. Seldom did he drive himself to make first contact. Marie was one of those few.

It happened, in fact, in the grocery store. Jeff, Marsha, and Robert were on vacation in Europe. There was no one to buy groceries for Lew, Marsha usually did that, so he decided, rather than use the maid for that purpose, to go into town himself. He seldom shopped, but was feeling fresh and adventuresome.

Marie had moved into town eight months earlier. She had transferred in from Denver and was having a hard time adjusting to the new location. The grocery store wasn't crowded, and she seemed to be wandering: removing shelved items, putting them back, then going on again with very little in her cart.

"Are you looking for anything in particular?" Lew said, after seeing her pick up and read the label of almost every pasta sauce container the store carried.

Her hair, he noticed from the back, was long and black and curly, maybe permed. When she turned, the hair glistened as it twisted in the air, then fell slowly back down to rest. It even looked soft, like goose down, not sprayed with hair spray until it was almost a solid clump. When she turned to answer him, her eyes were sad, blue highlights around brown eyes, blue mascara on black lashes, pale lipstick which matched her blouse, a well-worn copper-pink color softened through multiple washings.

"Do you work here?" she asked in return.

Lew made a small laugh, "No, you just look like you're searching." He pointed, then retracted his arm and touched his stubbled chin and quickly became embarrassed about his surly appearance.

"I'm nutrition-conscious." Her full lips moved more slowly than it took the words to get out of her mouth, leaving them still in motion after the words had stopped coming.

Lewis fumbled, but, as I said earlier, was in one of his more aggressive, talkative moods, perhaps because he had been let alone for a while. "I probably look like some derelict," his eyes focused downward, guiding her eyes also, first to his pulled loose shirt, then to his unbelted and slightly sagging jeans. He also rubbed the stubble of his cheek and brushed his uncombed hair back with his hand. He quickly began to tuck in his shirt.

She laughed. "Don't bother, it ruins your look."

Lewis laughed too, "Which is?"

"I'm not quite sure, half clown, half politician. I'd say, a politician trying to look casual." She looked up into his face then, and said, (he has always remembered this) "You don't look like you'd fit, quite right, into anything."

"I don't even fit into this world most of the time," he said.

"I believe it."

"Do you?"

The conversation got too serious suddenly, so Marie asked if Lew had a job in town.

"Not really."

"Not really?" she asked. "I thought maybe we worked near one another."

"I work at home, kind of."

"Insurance!" she said, pointing a long, perfectly manicured finger at him.

"Artist."

"Really?" She cocked her head and looked sidewise at him, in curious disbelief.

"Lewis Marshal," he held out his hand.

"I know that name."

"Thank you."

"You live here?" she said, as though it was unbelievable that anyone would choose to live where she had felt so uncomfortable for the past eight months.

"Outside of town. In the woods."

"In a tent with no water?" She laughed quickly as though she were now embarrassed to be in his presence.

Lewis found her change towards him adorable. "You live here?"

"For the past eight months. I transferred in from Denver."

"Beautiful city. Nice countryside. The mountains and all."

"Yes."

"Look, I could, well, show you around."

"Not much to see."

"The park, the mall and the grocery store," he said laughing.

"There's always the movies."

"And dinner. Nutritious dinner," he alluded to her label reading with a nod of his head.

She stared at him for a few moments, as though sizing up the situation. "All right," she said, and they exchanged phone numbers and addresses.

Later, remembering a sort of awkwardness between them, Lewis questioned his own instincts, so he called Jeff in his hotel in England, just to talk with someone, to get approval. Oddly enough, even on first meeting, Marie didn't seem like just another object to have around for a year. There was something to her, unlike the other women, something strangely hidden and sad. He had seen it in her eyes. It was more than just loneliness, more than just a mild shyness. Lewis wanted to reach into her, as he had learned to reach into common thought, and understand her more fully. That, to Jeffrey, was reason enough to pursue Marie. "You're interested?" he said. "That's a first. I'd say go for it."

"You think?"

"Show some of that Marshal charm, she'll love it."

"Not from me."

"What do you need, for her to grab your crotch? Haven't you had enough of those women? Just do it. It doesn't hurt. Do you good."

"Okay!" Lew said, slapping his hand onto the table.

While he was still enthusiastic and excited, just after slamming the phone down after his short talk with Jeff, Lewis picked the phone back up and dialed Marie's number.

She picked up almost immediately. "Hello."

"This is Lew."

"Lew? Oh, from the store. Goodness, I didn't expect a call this soon."

"I just thought, like we were talking, tonight maybe."

"Tonight?"

"Well, you don't have to."

"No, that's fine. I just didn't expect... Actually, I didn't think you'd call. I'm glad you did."

"Are you?" he said lamely.

"Don't sound so down about it. I'd love to do something with you tonight."

"Dinner?"

"Great, I'll be waiting."

"Thanks," Lew hung up then and started to walk away. Just then he remembered he didn't tell her what time he'd be there. As he reached for the phone, it rang. He picked it up and said, "Seven."

Marie laughed. "Fine," she said.

Lewis liked the way things, even the phone call, fell into place, the way they seemed to roll smoothly.

During the hours before seven, Lew unpacked his groceries, had a beer, and took a walk. The cottage felt especially comfortable that day. The sun washed over the field like a benevolent lover caressing it with warmth. The stone fence showed through the field grass, its heaviness, its mass, a permanent wall inside Lewis. In his imagination, he could be next to it and see into its dark crevices, see spider webs and ants, see the dust of dried pollen and dirt carried from the forest to the fence. He knew the fence like a friend, which stones were loose, which were not. He knew its many colors: white, red, black, blue, and its many geometric shapes.

The trees in the enchanted forest called to him, asked him to visit with more than just his mind. So he went there and sat: the familiar pine needle bed, the rock and run. Only a trickle of water flowed. A breeze pushed down from the sky and brushed across Lewis. Memories, like old photographs, flipped one after another through his mind. A tree lifted its roots out of the ground and danced, its branches swiping dangerously close to his face. The rock he leaned against rolled, trying to crush his fingers, the stream spit water at him, and he knew, while he struggled to pull from common thought, that it was happening again.

He crawled to the fence and lowered his head onto it much too hard. His hands grasped at the solidness of the stones. The hallucinations had stopped, but he still felt them, all around him, a sensation at the edges of his skin. He lifted himself up and glanced out over the field and it calmed him. He waited, thought about Marie, thought about himself. He needed to paint what he had seen, get it out of himself. Pushing himself to his feet, Lew rushed back to the house. Upstairs, he took a canvas and penciled out what he had seen, rushing the pencil lead over the textured surface. He faced the large window overlooking the field and used the field to hold him calm and keep him centered while he worked. At one point, he wiped his arm across what he thought was his sweaty forehead, and found blood there.

He hesitated. Was it real blood or just another vision? He touched his forehead with his fingers and found it sore. There was a lump and a small crevice, sticky with blood. At the sink, in the mirror, he saw a lump and gash going down over his right eye. He put down his pencil and washed his face and head, holding a towel to his forehead to compress the wound until the bleeding stopped completely. It wasn't a big cut, but the bump was already black and blue.

Lewis went back to the rough. As he worked, the feeling of craziness waned as though his working it out reduced its effect on him. He looked

161

at the clock and realized he'd have to get ready to meet with Marie soon, so he rushed the rest of the work. He had drawn in enough to work with, plenty actually. He had gotten so serious about putting it down that he overworked it, spent much more time on details he would normally, if working on any other painting, have left out. He stepped back and sighed in relief. He felt so much better inside. Calmer. The impending danger had been spit out onto the canvas. He would be done with it, get it outside himself, so that it was part of the real world and not part of him.

I tried to help him, tried to push deeper inside and make myself known, but all that happened was that Lewis saw the Indian pointing. It smiled favorably and then vanished. I tried again to appear as I was, not as a spirit, and just as my own image began to coalesce inside his head, he turned his thoughts and mind away, went downstairs and began to get ready for his date. I let loose, but rejoiced in knowing I had gotten as far as I had.

While he was gone on his first date with Marie, I explored the enchanted forest for a trigger, something which might have snapped him into his hallucinations, a key of some sort. I actually expected to find what it was in nature that had pushed dear Lewis over his crumbling edge. There was nothing there I had not already known intimately. In fact, the pines and shrubs were also concerned about him, as were nearby squirrels, snakes, raccoons and opossums. During the time he was inside common thought, he had affected the whole area. They had seen his illusion and were frightened by it, not only for themselves, but for him as well. It confused them and alarmed them. Lewis had opened so widely into common thought during this particular incident that it was easy for every plant and animal in the area to become part of him. Easily confused, a few young squirrels and opossums shivered in the underbrush in misunderstanding and fear. The raccoons, on the other hand, took it all very well, as though they themselves were some sort of oracles and were used to such things. Something I didn't know about raccoons was their quick belief and sure understanding of human thought. When I inquired, it all became clear. The one raccoon, from Lewis' past, and ones before him had had such contact. It seemed that raccoons passed on their experiences, not in stories and tall tales, but biologically and psychically.

Certain experiences were passed from parent to child, not specifics, but enough to allow a sort of deja vu, which, in turn, leads to easy adaptation.

We all agreed to try to help Lewis this time, even though there was much fear spread into pine needle and underbrush from being exposed to seeing nature in a distorted manner. We had all grown used to him. He was the first human who entered into common thought in this area, and his presence had created a mountain of learning, a mountain of new experiences for us all.

When Lewis returned from his date, I was careful to probe him slowly. Sometimes, after long contact with other humans, he stayed in their thought and refused common thought. He had to loosen up or fall asleep for me to enter.

Late that night, he began working on his painting. There was no trace of the feeling which went with the hallucinations, none of the boxed-in, hard-to-breathe sensations which had followed him around for the next hour or so after the incident. There was only the visuals, and that is what he wanted to get down. But he didn't actually have the pines pull out their roots and walk, nor have the rock already in motion, stopped by a stop-action photograph. What Lewis painted was the ability for the rock to move. He put in the brush strokes of a tree about to lift its roots from the ground. He put in fear and horror, centering the work on dirt and ground, the possibility of catastrophe. He put in the most primitive and frightful aspects of nature, the most dangerous, all in a series of colors and shapes, and he left out all understanding, all innocence. He worked through the night, making pot after pot of coffee in the small drip coffee maker near the sink. He worked the paint into the canvas like stain works into the grain of a wood plank. Some natural items, a bush here, a series of leaves there, were painted in the way they actually were present in nature, balancing the skewed area, placing innocence amid disaster, tension along with release. Let me relate the sensation in human terms: it was as though you were walking down a dark alleyway alone and had to pass by several rough looking men standing in a group. Fear would rise up inside you, even though, to that point, they posed no danger. Furthermore, you would try not to show any fear by walking as casually as possible. That is what the painting portrayed.

Late the next morning, Lewis collapsed onto the couch in the loft, but not before he watched the sun rise and the light climb down from the trees and along the grass in the field. A fog rose from the floor of the woods and from the dense grass of the field. Lewis wished for the momentum to go outside and experience the morning, but it was not in him. His exhaustion overtook him and he fell asleep almost immediately after he lay onto the couch.

The cottage creaked as wind broad-sided it. The morning had awakened the insects to another day, flowers bloomed in the field, and all the trees drank from the sun. Time had passed sufficiently enough that the enchanted forest became calm, the animals played freely as though Lewis' hallucinations had never touched them.

Lewis dreamed short rushes of images and people throughout his sleep, and I experienced his date of the night before almost as though I had been there with him.

It had started out well. Marie invited him into her apartment for a drink before dinner. "Scotch? Wine?"

"Wine," he said.

"White?" Her eyebrows rose in question. Her black hair held to her face, curled around her cheeks, and her brown eyes opened wide to accept him.

"White's fine." Lewis rubbed his hands together as though it was cold outside. He looked around nervously, sucking up image after image from the apartment. It was a color-coordinated, one bedroom flat. The sofa and chair matched in pattern and style, prints were framed and hung to augment the furniture and to add depth and color to the room, not for their individual artistic value. A doorway, without a door, led into a kitchen barely large enough for a small table. Marie offered the drinks from a portable bar located along one wall of the living room.

"Thank you." Lewis took the wine and turned away immediately. "Nice place."

"Thank you. Coming from an artist, that's a compliment."

"I'm not a decorator. If it's not on canvas, I'm lost. Really, I don't much care whether a house is done-up perfect." The tone came out harsh, and he recognized it immediately after he said it. He turned and Marie looked a little distraught. "I'm sorry. That came out all wrong. It's just that..."

"You don't care about home decorating," she finished the sentence for him, while staring into his eyes. Her tone was just as sharp, and Lewis didn't know how to respond. Finally, she said, "Don't be alarmed. I care more for home decorating. So we don't agree. You know, I've only been acquainted with your name, I wouldn't recognize one of your paintings if you pointed to it. Don't be embarrassed." She drank from the wine glass, her eyes still on him, peering over the glass.

"Oh," Lewis searched for something more to say, but found nothing.

"Don't think about it, we have other things in common." Her whole expression changed to warm and inviting. It was done with a turn of her head, a slight closing of her eyes, a nod.

Lewis wondered how he could duplicate the change on canvas.

"We do frequent the same grocer." She smiled, then walked over and took Lewis' arm. "Come along, we'll sit on the sofa together and get acquainted. I just hate going to dinner and trying to introduce ourselves during the constant interruptions. It's better if we're well acquainted. That way we can talk around the interruptions without worrying all that much about impressing our date."

"Impressing?" All Lewis seemed able to do was repeat a word.

"Yes, don't you want to impress me in some way? I know I want to impress you. Otherwise, why date at all? If I'm not interested, I don't go out. I can buy my own dinner."

"You probably can." They sat at opposite ends of the sofa, both turned facing the other."

"Bet on it."

"What else should I bet on?"

"That I'll let you know if I'm not interested."

Her frankness didn't help to calm Lewis. His nervousness also increased when he realized she could care less about his paintings. To that point in his life, except for Brittany, whom he never felt he deserved, women were there because of his work, in one form or another. Marie posed a new situation, a new problem. Yet, with her outspokenness and honesty forcing them down the road of conversation, to this point mostly hers, Lewis eventually relaxed and began to talk. From childhood to marriage to breakdown to divorce, if one wanted to know facts, they were available in magazines. There was nothing factual about his life that he could hide even if he had wanted to. But he didn't want to. Marie was much too open for him to care about holding anything back, so when he talked of Christopher or Brittany it was because it was fact and Marie accepted it all in stride.

"You miss them," she said.

"Christopher."

"Not Brittany?"

"At first," his voice was calm, his knee up on the cushion between them, his hand loosely holding the wine glass. "Eventually I got over her, I guess. It's an odd thing. I'm not sure if I really loved her."

"All men say that when it's over." She mocked him with a wave of her hand. "I never loved her anyway."

"It wasn't like that at all. I was a fanatic about having her. For a while I believed I couldn't paint without her. By the time I found I could, she was pregnant and we married."

"You didn't have to."

"I know, but there was still that," he shrugged, "need of some sort. I don't know how to explain it."

"You don't have to." She touched his knee, then took his wine glass from him. "A refill?"

"Yes, please." Lewis followed her with his eyes, turning to sit straight on the sofa. Marie was slightly hippy and had a broad back, but you'd never get that from looking at her face, which was thin and well-high-lighted with reasonably high cheekbones and full lips. She had small ears and a rounded chin, dark eyebrows, which lifted and fell at choreographed moments throughout a conversation, and which were used to bring out the warmth of a smile or the seriousness of a statement. Her brown eyes could be quite large or quickly turn to slits like a rodent's. Lewis tried to get a sense of her from behind as she poured the wine. He envisioned a short stump and a hay bale, an odd combination, but he was converting her, slowly, into more or less natural elements. When she turned to greet his intense stare, she turned her eyes away quickly, then as though re-adjusting her skirt, her face came back with an equally intense expression. This was the second time she had looked at him in such a manner and although it should have put him off, and, in fact, would have had he been in a different situation, such as inside a large room with many other guests, he actually felt excited by her. There was a feeling of intrigue and danger that she emitted that threw Lewis into sexual fantasy land. Without thinking, he said, "You're amazing."

Her expression changed as she asked what he had meant.

"Oh, I was just, ah, thinking out loud."

"I hope it was a good amazing."

"The best. Really." He sat forward to take the wine glass from her. "I mean it," he said, his hands shaking.

"I believe you," she giggled, an odd sound coming from her, but fitting under the circumstances.

Her hair bounced nicely just as it had at the supermarket, and Lewis translated its movement onto canvas. It had been some time since he'd actually thought of painting a woman as he once had with Brittany, but a work was building inside him. Lewis serendipitously rose his glass, "To a good dinner together."

Marie was caught off guard, but retrieved the expression and lifted her glass to his. "A good night, then."

A little more small talk and they went to dinner. Lewis drove, opening doors for her before and after the drive and at the restaurant. "I hope you like Italian food," he said.

"I eat anything," Marie said smiling. When they were seated, she said, "This is really wonderful."

"It is?"

"Yes, I only met you this afternoon and here we are having dinner," she said.

"Was it too rushed?"

"Not at all, that's what I mean. There was none of that long wait for a phone call, that scheming to see you at the grocery store again, none of it. I love this. This!" she pointed towards the middle of the table, "is how relationships should begin. At a run. Just meet someone, ask them out

167

and get to it." She laughed loudly.

Lewis laughed along with her even though he knew that it had all happened by accident. Still, he enjoyed his time with her immensely. The rest of the evening they talked and laughed like old friends. Lewis felt euphoric and, by the time coffee was served, they knew more about one another than mere facts. They had a meeting of minds. They found that they both loved to walk in the woods, only I'm sure Marie didn't include common thought in her life, and spend long evenings gazing out at the sky and stars. Because of that, they decided to walk through the park after dinner. It was a clear night and the stars would be plentiful.

When they arrived at the park, Marie got out of the car almost before it stopped, a by-product of too many drinks. She twirled around in the lot, looking up to the sky. "This is beautiful."

Lewis' energy level was wearing thin. His outward self began to retreat once in the presence of the trees and squirrels.

Marie didn't seem to notice how quiet he had become because she was still rambling about the coolness of the night and the brightness of the stars. She ran ahead, then returned.

Lewis walked slowly and watched how fluidly she ran from him and how excitedly she ran back. He tried to stay alert, "You don't get out much, do you?" he joked.

"Not like this." She held his hand with both of hers and walked backwards down the path. "Are we going to go by the lake?"

"To see the stars shine off the water."

"Do they?"

"You haven't seen?"

"Not here."

"Then you're in for a treat."

Marie rotated herself smoothly around to his side and placed one arm around his waist. "Hold me," she said, turning into him.

Lewis stopped and held her. The sensation was unusual. Most of his female accomplishments were interested in his hands, wanting to be touched by them, or interested in going to bed, right away. She seemed to want to be cuddled, an unusual situation, vaguely reminiscent of his relationship with Brittany. He held Marie tightly and could feel her breathe. Her hair smelled sweet, almost like candy. Lewis rubbed his hands up her back and, upon impulse, took her face between his palms, to look at, to study, but her reaction was from what she understood him to be doing, and she forced her face close to his and they kissed. Lewis felt her nose touch his, felt her teeth when she moved her mouth from side to side. His eyes closed and they held one another for a long time.

"Oh," Marie said, almost like a sigh.

"We should see the lake."

"Should we?" she whispered, then kissed him again.

It flashed through Lewis' mind that Marie was making all the moves. He felt as though he should do something, so he reached around for her breasts. They were larger in his hands than he had remembered them being from sight.

She pressed into him, then pulled away. "You're right. We should see the lake."

Her sudden change surprised him, but at the same time was a relief. He felt odd letting her be so aggressive, yet even more odd taking her breasts in his hands. He liked being with her, but felt at odds with those feelings.

As they made their way to the lake, they stopped to kiss and hold one another three more times. Lewis managed to unbutton one button on her blouse and push his hand in over her bra, feeling her flesh bulge over the top of it. He was glad when they arrived at the lake and she buttoned herself up. They stood together, almost like statues. Lewis, at least, felt like a monument placed into the world, to reflect the inner meanings of nature. He actually thought that, that he was on the earth for that reason, to teach, in a way, even though he felt he had so much to learn himself.

Chapter 17

Jeffrey was mildly shocked when he heard of how tight Lewis and Marie had become in such a short while. "This is hard to believe," he said.

"What, that I found someone without your help?"

"No," Jeff wrinkled up his face. "I'm positive that's happened before. It's just that..."

"She's normal?"

"Well..."

Marsha appeared in the kitchen doorway. She looked tired. "I like her already."

Lewis had visited Jeff and Marsha almost as soon as they returned home. Robert was outside with friends.

"So do I," Lewis said.

"Hey, I feel like you two are ganging up on me." Jeff looked at one, then the other. He had a peculiar expression on his face, half joking, half serious.

Marsha laughed. "We're not ganging up," She said. "We just don't see what's wrong."

"I didn't say anything was wrong. I haven't even met her. She's just not his usual. That's what I said."

"You should be happy. You're always saying he should find someone more average."

"Average? You say that?"

"Lew, I only mean..." Jeff glared at Marsha.

"Forget it," Lew said. "She's not an art bimbo. I know that. She doesn't, or didn't, even know my work."

"She probably doesn't know, or hasn't even heard of half the people I handle, then," Jeff said.

"That's only five artists," Marsha put in.

"According to Lew she's never heard of three of them. And I shouldn't count him. That leaves two."

"Nobody knows Barnaby. Does he even sell?" she asked.

"Thanks. My wife, my friend," Jeff said to Lewis, introducing Marsha sarcastically.

"He's right to handle Barnaby Schott's work, it's good," Lewis said in Jeff's defense.

"Yes, but he's still not well known."

"You're right, Marsha," Jeff announced. "Anyway," he said, "we were talking about Marie. I like what I hear about her, too."

"It didn't sound it a few minutes ago."

"Sorry, dear," he smiled.

"She's pretty important, huh?" Jeff addressed Lewis, "or we wouldn't be discussing her like this."

"I've only known her two weeks."

Jeff pumped his arm insinuating the human sex act, and glanced at Lew out the corner of his eyes.

"Jeffrey!" Marsha yelled.

"Well?" Jeff said.

Lewis smiled and got up from his chair. "I think I'll keep you guessing."

"Oh, boy, my fantasies are pretty graphic." Jeff got up and followed Lew past Marsha and down the hall. "They include nude bodies, paint, lots of earth colors pasted on unearthly parts."

"Are you going to follow me into the bathroom?"

Jeff laughed out loud and stopped just outside the bathroom door. "Don't think about Marie in there. I don't want pee on the walls."

"Jeffrey, for goodness sake," Marsha said.

"I'm only joking."

"Does Lewis know that?"

The bathroom door opened and Lewis stepped into the hall with them.

"I'm sure of it. He hardly has a serious bone in his body."

Jeff put his arm around Lew's shoulder. "I'm glad you two found each other. And we know love when we see it. Don't we, hun?"

"You've said that about two other women just this year," Marsha said.

"But Marie's different, remember?" Jeff said.

"She is," Lew agreed.

"So, what's the pointing Indian say?" Jeffrey joked.

"He loves her." Lewis didn't always like the way Jeffrey just blurted out about his inner life, particularly in front of Marsha, but he got used to it. He knew how married couples kept no secrets, but still, it was his private life, his way of coping. "Try not to say anything about that around Marie."

"Oh," Jeff looked at the floor. "I am a little loud sometimes. Don't get it wrong, I'm only joking. I know how seriously you take it. I just can't."

"Just not in front of her."

"I know, I know. Don't worry."

"I don't blame him for worrying," Marsha said, "the way you blurt things out."

"I said I wouldn't," Jeff protested.

"I believe you."

"I'll just make sure he remembers," Marsha said.

Lew winked at her in response.

"Hey, that's my wife you're winking at."

"Sorry, didn't mean for you to see that."

"Yeah, didn't you know we had a secret life together?" Marsha said, putting her arm through Lewis' elbow.

"I should have guessed."

"Okay, enough fun," Lewis said, separating himself from Marsha. "I've got to go."

"Work?" Jeff asked.

"What do you think?"

"I'll come by tomorrow. Don't stay up too late."

"All right, Dr. Jeff."

"You look good, Lew. Really, I think she's okay for you," he said.
"Not back to that."

"I'm done." Jeff raised his hands into the air, stopping himself from going on any longer about Marie. He followed Lew to the front door, Marsha right behind him. Shaking Lew's hand, he said, "Good-bye," then out of concern, added, "everything else going okay?"

Lewis knew what he meant. It was Jeff's way of asking about his mental health. Lew almost told him about his most recent incident, the one that happened before his first date with Marie, but seeing Marsha behind Jeff, her head on his shoulder and her arms around his waist, Lew held back. He'd wait until Jeff came to visit, or he'd just forget it. Nothing had happened since. He had promised to tell Jeff if anything suspicious happened, but it may have been only a flash in the pan. Nothing to worry about. "Everything's fine," he said. "Have a good night, you two. Tell, Robert I said good-bye."

"Will do, see you tomorrow."

"I'll be there." Lew stepped into the moist evening. It was about to rain. The signatures were everywhere, turned up leaves on the trees, cool breeze, humid night air. He looked up. Clouds were thickening overhead. An hour or two, he figured, or perhaps he knew, he had become so attuned to nature.

During the short drive home, he thought about Marie, her beautiful black hair and wondrously wide brown eyes that seemed to widen even more, engulfing everything, even swallowing him, when she had an orgasm. The look on her face was enough to make him come with her. It was great, yet he was still trying to figure out how to paint it, explain it to the world in color: burgundy and beige, a thread of pink, sky pink, almost orange, working its way down through the painting from the left top corner, stretching thinner and thinner to the top center of the canvas, but not thinning to a smooth end, but blunt, a very thin, blunt end, indicating a peak, then an explosion of blood reds, thunder cloud blues, ocean greens. As his mind worked away, he almost ran off the road. He stopped the car and got into the trunk for a large sketch pad he kept there, and began to work by dash light. He was quick, using his own form of shorthand to express the shapes and colors he imagined. Inside his head, the work was almost complete, he would work on the painting itself to find the missing elements. As he sketched, he felt what he portrayed. The excitement of the piece, the erotic conclusion. He ran his pencil over the pad with perfect coordination between mind and muscle. When he was through, he drove the rest of the way home with the radio blasting.

Lewis went straight to the loft. The room had been closed up most of the day and smelled musty, paint-musty, with a touch of paint thinner and linseed oil. He opened some windows to allow a cross breeze to air the place out, then rummaged through his paints and brushes for what he needed. He was rushing and clumsy and kept dropping things, bending down to pick them up. At one point he thought his back went out. His hand flew back to put pressure where the pain rushed, like lightning, through his side and back. Bent at the waist, Lewis made it over to the couch to sit down. He breathed heavily and massaged with his fingers. The pain felt deep inside, unreachable even when he pressed very hard. He tried to twist, crack his back into position, but the pain intensified with movement. Then, as should have been expected, he focused on the pain and tried to translate it. He twisted slightly to the right, then to the left, to see if the piercing changed to pinching, or vice versa. He wondered if the right side of his body translated the same pain differently than the left side. He pushed back then, after he felt he understood the left and right pain.

The whole procedure, like scientific experimentation, made me uncomfortable. I wanted him to crawl downstairs to a phone and get help. I didn't understand the aches and pains of humans, how it felt during movement. Even with all the years inside Lewis, it was still difficult to understand. We acted as buffers for each other. He never touched all of common thought at once and I never felt all of movement at once. Our contact was limited to concentrated areas or movements.

Inside his head, I saw him constructing an image half made of flesh and blood and bone, and half mechanical ball and slide joints, as he tried to see inside himself for the problem. Then, miraculously, he transferred all his pain, his biology and science, into shape and color. His own body had become, in its misery, another tool, another faucet to turn on.

I tried, at that time, to push inside him. He didn't recognize that the pain was increasing, yet I could feel his face grimace reactively, even as he focused inward, towards that canvas in his mind. His meditation away from the pain, did not reduce its intensity or its effect on his body. I wanted him to snap out of his little experiment and get help, fast. I tried to create the image of the Indian. If that's what he recognized as a sort of guardian, I no longer cared. I just wanted him to get help.

Lewis rolled onto the couch. The pain had pushed through. He tried to relax. Without movement, the pain subsided. He let his back slip into the cushions and tried to get the rest of his body to relax. He closed his eyes and tried to forget about his back. The painting he was about to do flashed through his mind, the urgency of its movement made Lewis try to get up. The pain slapped him back down. His face became the image of a tortured man.

Lewis gave in to the pain and lay there as still as he could. It was getting late and Jeffrey would be by the next day, but he didn't know when. Late morning, he thought. Lewis tried to lie still and sleep, but as soon as he became unconscious enough to recognize he was uncomfortable, he tried to move. His eyes would jerk open and he would cringe. Then, near dawn, terrible things began to happen. He felt the couch move across the floor, saw his easel dance, the loft ceiling ripple and churn. He knew, consciously this time, what was happening to him and tried to ignore it, tried to tell himself it wasn't happening. At one point, he focused on his pain just to extinguish the other thoughts, but it didn't work. Dust from the ceiling came down to suffocate him whenever he moved. The couch cushions massaged his back, then suddenly threw him onto the floor. He tumbled to the hardwood and screamed in agony.

I only saw and felt what he imagined. When I pulled out and confronted common thought, I saw him roll over onto the floor by what appeared as his own volition. Inside his head things became confused. He lost control of his own movement, attaching it to objects outside himself.

I asked common thought for help, to push, with me, the image of the Indian, into his contorted mind. Both animal and plant, from his childhood home to the enchanted forest, together, we concocted the Indian. Lewis' own salvation image, and we ground it, along with all the insanity his own mind was creating, into his head. As a sole light in a black cavern, the Indian appeared. Only now it was our image, not his alone. "The phone," it said, pointing to the stairs. "Jeffrey."

His mind fought to distort our image also, but we held tight, adjusting to his inner shifts in consciousness. "The phone!" the Indian said.

Then, from deep inside common thought, another image crept up the long dark stairs of the cottage. Along with common thought focusing on helping me keep the Indian whole, a warning of Jeffrey's arrival flashed through. I did, along with the help of the trees, what I thought I had to do. The Indian motioned for Lewis to roll over, as though warning him of immediate danger. When he rolled, he screamed in pain. Suddenly, Jeffrey ran to the top of the stairs and burst into the room. In a moment, he was at Lewis' side.

"Don't let it happen," Lew said as we pulled back the image.

"Nothing will happen." Jeff held Lew's head between his hands. He tried to lift him up.

"My back!"

"I'll call an ambulance."

Lewis closed his eyes. His mind told him that there was movement all around him when there wasn't. He closed his eyes tighter. Somehow, the knowledge of Jeffrey being near helped him to reject the horrible sights he had imagined. Then the Indian appeared, this time through Lewis, not common thought. "Thank you," he said aloud.

"They're coming," Jeff said. "So who are you thanking, me?"

"The Indian." He opened his eyes and saw himself looking down at him, as though he were dead and hovering above his own body, except that the central consciousness was in the dead body, not the hovering one. It was only Jeffrey.

"Good God, Lew. I don't care, just be all right."

The ambulance came in fifteen long minutes. Jeffrey listened as Lewis told him how he was thrown from the couch, how he hurt his back in the first place. Lewis was positive that brushes had been pulled from his hands or leapt from them, so he'd have to bend to pick them up. "And the couch cushions threw me to the floor," he repeated for the third or fourth time.

"I know, you told me," Jeff said. He kept his face turned. There were tears in his eyes. One hand pet Lewis' forehead. He listened for the ambulance's arrival.

Lewis rambled about nature and his paintings, about the rippling ceiling and how much better he felt now that Jeffrey was there. "You are me," he said to Jeffrey, "the outward half, just like we always thought. You're the balance, the other end of the see-saw. Did the Indian call you?"

"No. I told you I'd be by today."

Jeffrey was right in not lying, but I felt doubt in Lewis' mind when Jeffrey insinuated I had nothing to do with his arrival. I didn't, but I didn't want to lose Lewis' faith in me either, even as the Indian spirit.

"Oh," Lewis said. "He was here, though."

"I bet he was."

"You don't believe it?"

But before Jeff responded he heard the ambulance pull next to the house. "I'll be right back. They're here."

"Can't move," Lewis smiled.

The ambulance crew was careful with Lewis, not to shift his body too much. Back injuries were sensitive things.

Again, I waited for his return. There was nothing for me to do except watch dust accumulate onto his canvases and easels, crud accumulate in the sink's dripping drain. Jeffrey had not returned to close the windows for a long while, and papers scattered throughout the room. Cans of soaking brushes were pushed over by wind. Even the easel he used most often fell over. It was eerie to watch the empty room as it was molested by wind and rain. It seemed to degenerate, become something new, not a room, but an empty box left open to the elements.

Chapter 18

Lewis was gone nearly a year and a half, during which time a maid was hired to clean the cottage. Eventually, the windows were closed upstairs and Lewis' equipment cleaned up and arranged in a mechanical, squared, even manner. Everything was kept 'in place' and dusted daily until no sense of Lewis remained. Jeffrey cleaned out all the paintings and sold them, put them on display, whatever, it didn't matter. Nothing mattered. Brittany visited the cottage on several occasions, once with Jeffrey, never with Christopher. During one visit, they talked briefly about Lewis, how he held things in, how he loved nature. They looked through the remainder of his paintings.

"This painting," Brittany held one up. "I remember Lewis being afraid that it didn't work the way he wanted it to. I loved it."

"His use of color is extraordinary," Jeff said.

"You talk like a salesman."

"But I mean it. Besides, everyone says it. It's like there's some sort of life blood in his work. He puts colors together that should wash out, cancel each other, but they don't. Instead they curve around, caress each other until you feel good about it, about how they don't belong, but fit anyway."

"Jeff."

"Yeah, Brit."

"Do you think this is what has to happen?"

"What?"

"If you have genius, it's only as a trade-off with sanity? Like somewhere there's this universal law?"

Jeff continued to rummage through the paintings.

"Do you? Or do you think he drove himself crazy?" she asked.

"I don't know. I can't answer any of those questions."

"Does he still insist on being one with nature? Do you suppose that's why the cottage attacked him?"

"No, not now. He's a lot better. You should know," Jeff said.

"But he doesn't talk to me when I visit, not like the two of you talk."

"He doesn't say much to me either. It's been rough on him. The back operation, pneumonia, all while he's hallucinating wildly, calling out for the Indian. For God's sake, I'll never understand that." Jeffrey lowered his head and brushed back his hair with his right hand. "Another couple of months, they say."

"So you said earlier. What about him, though? What's he think? Will he want to come back here?"

"He doesn't think there's anywhere else to go. He just wants to come back to where he belongs, he says. The doctors say it's okay. This is where he feels secure, regardless of what's happened in the past."

"And his painting?"

"You saw the stuff he's doing in the hospital. I can't sell that."

"I like it. It's nice."

"Nice," Jeffrey let the canvases he was going through fall back against the wall. "Nice isn't art. There's no tension in that stuff, no mystery." He waved his hand at the canvases they were just going through, as though to dismiss them all. "There's nothing left here that I'd want anyone to see, nothing he'd be proud of. I refuse to embarrass him by selling inferior work."

"I like some of it," Brittany said.

"There you go again, you like it, but that's not good enough. Not for me, and definitely not for Lewis. It has to fill you up, that's what his paintings do when they work." He took her hand, "Sorry, you can have what you want, Lewis said so, just, for everyone's sake, don't sell any of these."

"I understand."

"I knew you would." He kissed her on the cheek.

Several months later, Lewis returned home. Jeffrey drove while

179

Marsha and Robert and Christopher sat in the back. Brittany waited at the cottage where she had prepared a big welcome home cake and large lunch. Marie had faded quickly and quietly from the picture once Lewis ended up in the psychiatric ward of the hospital. She had visited him there only once, which was very uncomfortable for them both. At the meeting, according to his memory, Lewis had felt embarrassed about his condition. But, on his way home, that first day back, he had no regrets. He couldn't blame Marie for leaving, and he felt only admiration towards Brittany for the way she weathered through everything. There was more to her than he had ever imagined, and he wondered if perhaps he just hadn't looked deeply enough.

He got out of the car and breathed in the sweet, cold November air. Jeffrey was quickly at his side, Christopher had his hand inside his father's. "I had to return after the leaves had fallen," Lewis said, sorry he had missed all the colors of autumn.

"It's a nice day, anyway," Marsha put in.

"It's gorgeous. It's perfect just to be back. I'll look forward to the first snow, then spring." Lewis looked around, feeling a little too much like he was still being watched, like his whole family had taken on the doctors' roles. His smile, to him, seemed too broad, too childlike, and he imagined that they thought him childish after his stay at the ward. But he was just happy, very happy. Extraordinarily happy! Euphoric! He could hardly believe his good fortune. Furthermore, he was in total control. He remained in human thought purposely, so that he could deal with his family. Yet, during lapses in conversation, he slipped in and out of common thought, just, it seemed to me, to test himself and his home.

Brittany stood at the front door with her arms out. Lewis hugged her. "It's so good to have you home again, Lewis," she said.

"Thank you. You really didn't have to go to the trouble."

"I wanted to."

"Well, I appreciate your being here, Brit, and for bringing Christopher." Chris had let go of Lew's hand and was helping Jeff collect his dad's things from the car. "He's grown into a fine young man," Lew said.

"He's a teenager," Brit said, "but he still acts like a child sometimes."

Lewis followed her into the cottage. "We all act like children sometimes."

Brit turned to face him. She looked surprised and hurt. "I didn't mean anything..."

"No, no, I know that. Neither did I. I was only making conversation."

Chris, Robert, and Jeff came in carrying bags, paintings, easels. "Where do you want all this shit?" Jeff yelled.

"In the bedroom for now. I'll move things upstairs as I need them."

"Into the bedroom, it is," Christopher said, leading the others down the hall.

"Talking about that, I'm going to run upstairs real quick. Make my peace with my old studio."

"Okay," Brit looked into his face, then touched his shoulders with her hands. "It's good to see you."

"Thanks." Lewis walked up the stairs and opened the door to the loft. His first feeling was shock. Nothing felt familiar. He walked slowly over to the window and let his mind drop into common thought. He was suddenly overcome by the rush of concern, interest. All of common thought missed him. The overwhelming love and elation concerning his return washed over him, bombarded him, and forced him into sudden tears as he looked out over the field.

"Dad?"

"Oh," He wiped his eyes and turned. "Christopher. I'm sorry."

"You okay?"

"Yes. I'm just so happy to be back. Everything's so strange, though. I'll get used to it." He had snapped out of common thought so effortlessly, that it let us all down, making us feel upset, like having the telephone hung up on you even though you knew there was an emergency on the other end.

Christopher took his father's hand. There was a comfort in his son's touch. "You want to go downstairs with the others or stay up here?"

"We'll go down."

"Mom made a nice big lunch."

"More like dinner."

"Yeah, well it's after lunch."

"That's good," Lew put his hand on Christopher's shoulder and hugged him close to his side, "I'm starved."

Chris wiped at something in the corner of his eye, while Lew dried his eyes on his sweatshirt sleeve. "I love you, Chris."

"I know, Dad. I love you, too."

They walked down the stairs together, then into the kitchen.

"Surprise!" The rest of them stood around the table, a big sheet cake lighted with sparklers read: Welcome Home.

Lewis smiled. He held back more tears and felt a terribly large lump in his throat that he couldn't swallow. "Thank you all so much," he squeaked out, and everyone laughed and smiled. This time their faces wore the broad childlike smiles. Christopher stood back and held onto his father's hand, and Lewis felt as though he had really been missed.

They sat down and ate, then made their way, coffee cups in hand, into the living room. At first, they talked about how happy they all were to have Lewis back, then about themselves, filling him in on family matters. But finally, the conversation worked its way around to art. Lewis started it by asking, "How's business?"

Jeffrey and Marsha looked at each other. "Your older pieces have gone through the roof. You saw the prints of your "Land and Sky" series. They still sell well, especially in the Midwest."

"That so?"

"Business is fine, Lew."

"They want more?"

Jeff cocked his head and shrugged his shoulders in a half-hearted affirmative. "Don't think about it."

"The stuff I did in the hospital is crap."

"Now, Lew..." Jeff began, but was cut off.

"I like it," Chris said, "and so does Mom." Brittany nodded.

Lew smiled, but what he felt was sadness. "I couldn't work there. I had to make them understand I was all right."

"You could have walked out any time you wanted. You know that," Jeff said.

"I know. I just wanted them to realize I was ready."

"Fuck them!"

"Jeff!" Marsha screamed at him.

"Sorry kids," Jeff said. Robert snickered. "It's not them that matters, though."

"I know, but I feel better knowing they believe it."

"Fine, but it's got to be for you."

"I understand Barnaby Schott's work is gaining ground."

"It's not a race."

"I didn't mean that. I just meant you were right to pick him up."

"Oh, yeah, he's doing well."

"I was surprised," Marsha said, "because I'm not crazy about his stuff. But you two were right."

Lewis smiled, he felt happy for them. He didn't want to be the reason for things to go wrong. He wanted everything to be all right. "I'm going to get started again," Lewis announced softly, dramatically. "You'll see I still have what it takes."

"I know you do," Jeff said. "Just take it easy."

"I will. I've thought a lot about it. I've got to get back into it, familiarize myself with my hands, this place, put it all together again. I know it may take some time."

"As long as you know that and don't rush it."

"I'll take long walks, go to bed early. I won't stay in front of an easel for more than four or five hours a day." Lew leaned forward in his chair. "That suit you okay?"

He and Jeff smiled at one another.

"Can I walk with you, sometimes?" Chris asked.

"Any time," Lew said.

Everything went fine that afternoon and evening. Mr. and Mrs. Marshal appeared late in the day, and Mrs. Marshal held Lewis for a long time while Mr. Marshal looked on. He must have said, it's good to have you home, son, a dozen times. When they arrived, like a light switch being flipped, the conversation jumped into small talk. There was a new mall being built. Land was sold nearby and townhouses were going to be put up. The townspeople lobbied against the location of the new garbage dump being so close to the Lake. And on and on until the evening disappeared into darkness and stars.

The air was cold when everyone left. Afterwards, Jeffrey offered to stay the night with Lew. It was a kind, generous offer, Lew felt, but he refused. "I've got to do this alone," he said.

"Just thought you might want to ease into it."

"I'll be fine."

"I could stay," Chris offered.

"Not tonight, son, it'd worry your mother." He winked at Brittany. "Besides, like I said, it's something I have to do alone. Next week, okay?"

"Okay, Dad." They hugged.

"Everybody have a good night, now," Lew yelled behind them.

"You, too." Marsha kissed his cheek. "If you need anything..." she left it open-ended.

"I appreciate all you've done. Everyone. If I need something, though, I'll call."

Brittany held him for a long while, before letting go.

Lewis shut the door and the noise of their conversation was gone. "I'll be fine," he said aloud just to hear how a lone voice sounded inside the cottage. He noticed how spotless the cottage had been kept, yet how it still looked lived-in, as though he hadn't been gone so long. It was beginning to feel more familiar. It looked perfect. He imagined that he had been shifted off the canvas of his own life, or had chosen to stand far back and to the left, hidden by a year and a half, obscured by all the things that had gone on during his absence.

He thought back to earlier that evening when he had wanted to watch the sun set over the field, but couldn't because of all the excitement everyone was exerting in his direction. He had to be attentive. He was on stage for the evening. He had to be untypically conversational, animated about things he found unimportant. Yet, it was good for him to deal with them. They were a large part of his life and he had to learn to live in their world if they couldn't live in his. That, briefly, was the decision he had made while in the hospital.

Lewis went around cleaning up the odd pieces of china and silverware sitting in the living room. Brittany had cleared the earlier dishes and they were all nestled nicely in the dishwasher. Lew filled it by squeezing in a few more coffee cups and two plates the kids had used for extra cake, then turned the knob to normal wash and pulled. The dishwasher's timer clicked once or twice then the loud hum of gushing water swallowed that corner of the kitchen.

Lewis turned out the kitchen lights, grabbed a jacket from the front closet and stepped outside. Down the path towards the stone fence, which still surrounded the field, Lewis heard the momentary rustle of a small animal, probably a chipmunk or field mouse, as he walked. At the field, the sky opened into a great mass of stars.

Slowly, as if testing the ground before him, Lewis lowered (or raised) himself into common thought. This time he was not so overwhelmed. Common thought recognized his caution and, in return, allowed him to explore first, to widen his grasp, before rushing in. So, while sitting on the stone fence, his face skyward, Lewis began to accept, first tree, then bush and field, then animal. He searched in common thought for colors. That's the only way to explain what he did. Each thing which touched him, each that he felt, had its own color. As though looking through old photographs, Lewis opened to all portions of common thought he had been away from for so long. One by one, from the trees to the animals, he reached out and accepted them. When he got to me, amazingly, for I have never seen the acceptance of common thought while he was at the hospital, even though he must have practiced somewhere, he accepted me not as the Indian spirit, but as I truly am. Before long, Lewis was engulfed in common thought, but without the anxiety he had once experienced. It was as though he was born to it, that common thought was his natural world and he was glad to be home.

An hour or two passed. It was as though he took each individual into his grasp and re-acquainted himself, yet he couldn't have done so because of the shear numbers. Nonetheless, like shaking hands at a party and gazing into familiar eyes, Lewis moved among common thought with his hand extended to meet a receiving line of life beyond human life.

Much of the time, if this can be understood, even though he sat physically on the stone fence, he mentally stood beside me. When finally he turned to me, I wanted to consume him, but could not. He had learned much, yet without a trace of it in his memory, or without allowing me to see that portion of it. I opened up and placed the image of the Indian in his head, holding it out to him as a way of acceptance. He took that image in the grip of his own mind, then added himself and allowed them to hug. It was the most amazing sensation I had ever received from Lewis, but it didn't stop there. What he did next took calm, patience and mental dexterity. The Indian, while still being held by Lewis' strong arms, turned into me. First the arms bulked and textured into wood branches, then the head faded into life and growth like only plants can understand. Finally, the body changed into a trunk and grew, pushing the branches up and out. Lewis stood back, then, and embraced me in common thought.

His journey ended, Lewis pulled away and remained sitting on the fence, looking out over the field for a while. When he returned to the cottage, he was exhausted. He cleared his bed of the things Chris, Rob, and Jeff had haphazardly thrown there, then undressed and collapsed on top of the bedspread and fell quickly off to sleep.

Chapter 19

For weeks, Lewis tried every evening to recreate the feel and sensation of the field he had experienced in childhood. On one occasion, he set up two easels and worked paint into two versions of the same painting. Both were technically good paintings, but both lacked the tension apparent in his older works. Lewis practiced with line and color what he had remembered, but reached for something much greater than a remembered technique. What he reached for, and did not receive, was a mind-to-hand connection, a knowledge of the field's existence, its being, not its appearance. He hoped that through a return to his childhood, he could gain back what a year and a half in the hospital had stolen from him. But the return to childhood was proving to be impossible. He stood back from the two paintings in front of him, both the same, yet both slightly different, neither of them working the way he wanted. Both lacked the feel he so desperately tried for. He looked around the room. Sketches were scattered over the couch and floor. More paintings of the field leaned against the wall, facing the wall, away from his view. He pushed one of the easels over and it clattered to the floor, but first hit the corner of the stand where he stored his paints, pushing a hole through the painting. He heard the canvas tear. A small pain pushed through him at the sound, but he quickly rejected it. The painting was no good anyway.

He lifted the torn canvas from the floor, removed it from the easel and placed it with the others against the wall. He removed the second painting and did the same. That night he slept on the couch in the loft. At sun-up, Lewis sat up and looked around the room, at how the morning sunlight stretched over the couch and scurried into dark corners. The sun beamed from well above treetop level. Orange clouds had already turned back to white. At a distance, a far mountain showed light and dark green where the sun lay across it, and where shadows spread over it, cast from the clouds above. The field was crisp with morning frost, and sparkled as though pieces of broken glass had been spread over it. Lewis stood close to the window and could feel the cold permeate it. The anxiety in him expanded and swelled. Had he lost it, completely?

Lewis walked downstairs and made coffee rather than refill the pot upstairs. Out the kitchen window, the dark trunks of trees shot up from the ground and disappeared out of view through the window. He sat with his hands wrapped around the warm cup, the steam rolling into his face as he breathed it in during each inhaled. He looked to the refrigerator and thought of cooking eggs for breakfast, but just as quickly dropped the idea. He slammed his fist onto the top of the table in a fury which came on so quickly I wasn't ready for it. He stood and took a long drink from his cup, then set it down hard. He pulled a winter coat from the hall closet and slipped it on over his sweatshirt, then stepped into the cold, early December air and began to walk towards the field. Steadily, he made his way to the fence, walking around it to the old tractor road. When he reached me, he stopped and sat down at the base of my trunk. Once there, he closed his eyes and opened to common thought.

I could feel his muscles, his breathing, could feel the warmth of the sun hit his right thigh and the coldness of the shade on his other. He wanted help. More than any feeling I was getting was the one of grief for his predicament. He had not expected to lose what he had, only to gain control of his mind so it didn't distort his world. But during his search for control, it happened that he also lost whatever it was that gave him that sixth sense. He opened up to ask for that sixth sense back, but it wasn't mine to give. It never had been.

Lewis wished for his old self to return, the one who knew how to transfer nature to canvas, the unseen to the seen. Yet, also raging inside him was the need to be in control so that he didn't lose his mind.

If he could only transfer the tension he was feeling onto canvas, he'd have it back. That's what was missing, but there was no way for me to give that ability to him. I forced the image of the Indian into his head and he turned it into me. I forced it again, never realizing I'd ever want him to see me as the Indian, but it was the only method I had to communicate. So, I forced the image, then made it point. In the past, he had accepted that action in different ways, had transferred the pointing into a special meaning through some secret code in his head. Each time it had helped him. Would it now? I held it as long as I could, then let go, but it did not fade, which meant that he held to it also. What was it giving him. I waited to find out.

Even when Lewis accepted common thought, not everything was available to me. There were always deep thoughts, if you will, that couldn't be picked up. Memories were easiest to obtain, or open-thoughts, feelings, immediate things. So, until he began to accept an idea, I couldn't just reach in and grab it, not easily, and definitely not if he kept me out, which he often did. He let common thought in so he could explore, not to be fed images as I had done, yet he had held the image of the Indian.

Lewis explored every nook and cranny in common thought he had access to, looking for the hook he needed to bring his paintings back to life. In his head, he converted tree to line, squirrel to color, just as he used to. Everything had its own personal, shorthand, stroke or hue, its own signature, but even in his mind the pieces were not fitting together perfectly. For hours, he connected item to item, forming and reforming shape and color into completed works, but nothing climbed off the canvas to grab you, nothing was even 'about to happen'.

Lewis let go of common thought and stood up simultaneously. He reached out and held to my trunk to steady himself. A quick dizziness came over him. After his natural balance took over and his eyes re-adjusted to the light, he walked back to the cottage. He turned up the heat, then went to the kitchen and made himself a sandwich, had a beer, and paced the floor. He was beginning to make a connection between craziness and art. Once he had conformed to the normal, he became the normal. And, consequently, lost his special talent. Did it have to be that way?

Pieces of bread fell to the floor while he tore into the sandwich. His breathing picked up. Tears welled into his eyes. He did not want to be horrified by the world. He did not want himself to disappear into the world. He had to have both! His arms raised and lowered and jutted out as though he were talking out loud, but all the talk was going on inside his head. He spilled his beer and retrieved the final third, drank it down in one big swallow, then pulled another from the refrigerator. He bit into the sandwich and filled his mouth with its texture and taste, tried unsuccessfully to transfer it into compelling shape and color, got only an idea of its reality. He shifted the translation, first one way, then another. Tears burst from his eyes. He chugged half his beer. Maybe drunkenness would let him reach that frightening side, the side where his paintings found life.

Lewis looked around to get himself oriented again. He had been blindly pacing, his eyes only seeing what was in his head. Where was he? The strong booze was in the cabinet over the sink. He reached up and pulled down a bottle of Scotch, grabbed a water glass from the dishwasher, rinsed it, and poured it half full with the thick liquid. He drank two swallows and let it burn down his throat as he opened his mouth wide and breathed in loudly. His eyes wide and his mind open, he took another two swallows almost emptying the glass. He refilled it. Common thought whined in his head, sounding like the whir of a tornado dropping to the ground and slipping along a field. He let the sound howl, eerily through his head, waiting for something to hit, for something to happen. He swilled down more Scotch and felt its texture in the pit of his stomach. He felt like spitting it out. His throat burned. His eyes watered. He grabbed the beer bottle and drank half what was left just to cool down his throat and remove the nauseating smell that crept into his nose from his stomach. He tumbled into a chair and put his head down. Consciously, he pulled color and line into his mind and began to create a painting.

He slipped from one thought to another, one painting to another, then, as though he had forgotten why he had been drinking in the first place, his mind cleared of art and he dropped into common thought and staggered through the trees and underbrush, frightening small animals with his confusion. Common thought began to reject his presence. It didn't want to be a part of him, didn't want to give him access to what it felt.

I agreed. The illness coming upon him was revolting. I pulled away,

190

too, and connected enough to where only strong images came through. All other feelings of mobility and consciousness were pushed away. I watched him from the trees which stood outside the kitchen. I saw his head rolling from left to right, back and forth over his arm, which lay across the table, the beer bottle near his fingertips, the glass slightly to its right and almost empty for the second time. He looked up shortly and let his head fall back down. His shoulders slumped as though he had lost consciousness, but he hadn't, he'd only fallen into some sort of tiredness, a fatigue brought on by the overabundance of alcohol.

Lewis tried to get up, but fell back down. He heard someone knock at the door, then passed out for a moment. When he came to, Jeffrey was there shaking his shoulders.

"My God, Lew, now what are you doing?" he said.

"I had a drink."

"I can see that. Have you eaten?"

"Lunch."

"What are you trying to do, get yourself put back into the hospital?"

Lewis wrinkled his nose and knitted his brow in confusion.

"Because they'll see this as a harmful act," Jeff answered Lewis' questioning gaze.

Lewis put his finger to his mouth and made a shhh sound.

"I won't tell, don't worry." Jeff put his hands under Lew's armpits. "Now, let's get you up and into a comfortable chair."

Lewis tried to help but fell limp. His tolerance to the alcohol was much less than he had thought it would be when he took that first drink of Scotch.

"You're a mess." Jeff said, as he dragged Lewis into the living room. Once he felt confident that Lew was all right, he got a blanket from the bedroom and threw it over Lewis' limp body. Then he got a bucket from under the bathroom sink in case Lew vomited. Jeff sat down in the living room and watched as his brother slept for several hours. He got up once to get himself a drink of water, but the rest of the time just sat and stared. The sun moved through the sky shifting the light and shadow in the cottage's living room in slow motion. Shadows crept in and out of corners, from under furniture, dependent on the sun's position. Jeffrey let the shadows overtake his brother and himself until, finally, he turned on a light. He moved the bucket away and bent down and put his hand on Lewis' chest. He shook Lewis to wake him.

Eyes opened. "Jeff," a quiet whisper came.

"How do you feel?"

"Drunk."

"Still?"

"Weak."

"I'm surprised you didn't get sick all over your carpet here."

"My head hurts."

"It should. Can you get up? I'll help you to a chair."

Lewis lifted the blanket with his hand, then rubbed his forehead. "Thanks for the blanket. What'd you do, drag me in here?"

"Yes. By the hair." Jeff couldn't help but laugh at Lewis.

Lew followed suit and laughed with him, albeit much quieter and in some pain. "I was trying to get the muse back," he admitted.

"Did you?"

"Not that I can remember. Wow, it just hit me like that." They both fell quiet. Finally, out of discomfort, they both spoke the same word: "Well..."

"You go," Jeff said.

Lewis took a deep breath. "It's been a while since we've sat across from one another. You look just like me."

"Does it still bother you?"

"Not like it used to. It used to feel like you were me and whenever you were around, I wasn't. Now, I'm here, too, maybe weaker, but here."

"I'm sorry."

"It has nothing to do with you."

"I didn't think it did. I was just sorry you felt that way when in reality it should be just the opposite. But we've covered this ground. You're the genius, you're the gifted one. I'm second, if one of us has to be."

"Do you really feel second?"

Jeff looked away. "No, I really don't."

"Well, I do."

"Always?"

192

"No." Lew sighed and rubbed his head. "But, like you said, we've been through all that before, no need to go through it again. What's important is my work and what I'm going to do about it." He paused, looked over at Jeff, his hand still cupped over his forehead, massaging his own temples. "I still feel a little drunk."

"You want to lie down?"

"No."

"What do you want?"

"It's a big decision, Jeff. I don't know what to do."

"Still having problems?"

"If you could see the shit I'm producing, and it's getting worse."

"No."

"Yes!" Lew struck the arm of the chair with a weak fist. "Dammit, I can't paint for fucking shit. I've gone through my preliminary work, reacquainting myself with this," he swept his hand across the air in front of him to indicate the cottage, the forest, the field, and in general, the lifestyle, "but nothing's happened." Seriously, he looked at Jeffrey and asked, "Do I have to be crazy to paint?"

"No. You weren't crazy, as you put it, when you started, and your work was great then. In fact, this time, when you had a problem, your work went down hill. Look at it. Even before you went into the hospital, it started."

"Maybe when I'm on the edge, teetering?"

"Don't do this to yourself. For Christ's sake. Maybe it's anxiety, fear. Maybe you're afraid that if you paint well you'll go back into the hospital. Subconsciously. Well, it's not true. That part of your life is over. Done with. That's why you stayed this time. To make sure. You keep up with your appointments, right?"

"With the psychologist?" Lew nodded.

"Then that's it, you're safe. Don't let fear stop you from doing what you love."

"I have to get back to nature."

"Do you?" Jeff looked like an old man to Lewis, sitting there across from him, safe, secure, staid.

"Yes, that's how I feel. I feel like I'm," he struck his chest with his index finger, "too much in control. I've got to let loose."

"But you're afraid."

"Maybe."

"What do you really want? I hate to repeat myself, but if you want to continue being in control, fearing what you may uncover, and not painting as well, then do it. Your work will get better, not like before, but compromised. It'll sell."

"I'm not worried about selling."

"Then fuck it, you have to be happy."

An expression of realization came across Lew's face.

"What?" Jeff said.

"I think you've helped."

"Good. So what'd I help with?"

"I have to be happy."

"You seem happy now, most of the time. When you're not agonizing over your work, or lack of it."

"I only look happy," Lewis said.

"You act happy. Why not lay off painting for a while. Rest. Get your head together."

"No, it's just the opposite. I need to work more, get tired, get excited, close up some and let the world stew inside my chest."

"Don't overdo it."

"But that's just what I need to do. I've been pussy-footing-it long enough. Christ, I wait until I've had a good night's rest, morning coffee, or breakfast, and I ease into it. It's like I'm still at the hospital, in the psychiatric ward. There's no fucking excitement there, there's no pain."

"I'm telling you that you don't need pain."

Lew stood up fast, "The fuck I don't. That's what makes me feel good. When it comes out." He stretched his hands out to Jeff. Lewis looked down and saw his brother, the rational, calm, old, social side of himself. He didn't need that side. He had to discard it, go back to being the balance, the recluse, the spacy one, the one on the edge, if necessary. He hated the horror of craziness, but couldn't live without the exuberance, the excitement, of his art. "I can't live like this any more."

"I don't want you killing yourself either. Got that?"

"I don't want to live dead."

Jeff looked away. He breathed heavily. "I don't know what's best."

"Then let me decide."

"Look, I can't sit by and let you destroy yourself."

"Can you watch me die unhappily? Slowly?"

Jeff had no answer.

"Don't make me live a life that looks happy to you and the rest of the world. I'm more fulfilled when I'm quiet, when I'm alone with myself. If I want companionship I have the Indian, if I want sex there's bars, parties."

"That sounds sad."

"To you! Let me live my life."

"Even if it kills you?"

"I'd rather die tomorrow after painting something I feel is great, than live a hundred years without it. I don't want a wife and family and vacations to Europe. I want to create life." He raised his hands into the air. His head throbbed, but he felt invigorated. He turned to his brother. "Leave me alone."

"For how long?"

"A couple of weeks. I need to be alone. To work. Nobody."

"What if you do something like you did today?"

"Leave me alone. I'll do what I think I have to."

"I'll just check on you. I won't bother you a bit."

"No," he said softly.

"Lew, you're being unreasonable."

"No, I'm not. I'll be fine."

Jeff stood up. "I don't know."

Lew got Jeff's coat and handed it to him.

"Now?"

"The sooner the better."

"But..."

"I need to be alone to work. I've got to shake off the world, the human world, and embrace nature."

"I don't like this."

"But you'll respect my needs, my decision?"

"I hate to," Jeff said putting on his coat.

"You must."

With little more conversation, Jeff was convinced, pushed out of the house, and into his car. He sat staring out the windshield for a minute, maybe searching in himself for the truth about Lewis. He started the car and drove home.

Chapter 20

That night Lewis did not sleep. He wandered the house, took four aspirins every few hours to cut his continuously pounding headache to a minimum, ate another sandwich, and prepared three days worth of food and water. At one point, he climbed the stairs to the loft and looked through the paintings he'd been doing. "Shit," he said aloud while flipping through them. "Shit, shit, shit, shit, shit." He slammed them back against the wall. "I can't live like this," he said. "It's worse than being crazy. Woa, now, don't over do it, here, Lew." He looked around the room at the mess. "Christ, now you're talking to yourself. Maybe you're crazier than you think." He yawned and put his hand over his mouth, then rubbed his temples. Methodically, he began to clean up the loft, placing all his sketches into the trash. There was a time where, under Jeff's insistence, he would have saved them. "This is for me," he said, responding to his memories of that time, "not Jeff and not the rest of the fucking population. For me." After the papers were thrown out, he cleaned his brushes, wiped down his easels, emptied and cleaned knives, cans, cups. He made coffee and drank an entire pot while working. He swept the floor, organized his paints and brushes and knives and palettes. By sun-up he was finished. A second pot of coffee sat near the sink with one cup already poured and half gone.

Lewis dragged the couch over to the window and watched the light increase over the trees and field. A heavy frost had accumulated and, sitting that close to the window, he could smell the clean scent of December air coming through the glass, cold and fresh. He stared and, for the first time that night, dropped into common thought. Still very much under control, he was apparently there for one reason, to experience the waking of the forest and field. Excluding the fact that many animals in the area were nocturnal, a lot of activity was aroused early in the morning. Field mice scurried under leaves around the frost, still harvesting for winter. Squirrels spent their days out and about. Opossums and deer selected places to rest. What was left of leaves on the trees perked up, the pines stretched. Lewis could hear the brook gurgle and glup. The sun broke over the treetops and slammed into Lewis' face. He squinted, letting its warmth blanket him through the glass. When the sun was well up, he went downstairs and took two more aspirins, then made himself a big breakfast of bacon and eggs, which he ate from the pan while leaning against the counter next to the sink. He felt excited about his plans, anxious, and somewhat relieved. He needed to be alone and not feel like an invalid that everybody had to check on. He was fine. He felt fine.

When the hour arose where the sporting goods store opened, he grabbed his coat and left the house walking face first into the morning air, the sun filtering through trees to run streaks across the ground in front of him. He breathed in the thin, cold air and smiled to himself, holding onto the wintry scent as long as he could.

He drove directly to the shopping center and walked into Harvey's Sporting Goods, found a tent, sleeping bag, backpack, gas burner and cooking kit, and paid for it all using cash. The check-out girl gave him an odd look and jokingly asked if he'd be doing some camping this winter.

"No, just gearing up for next spring," he told her.

Once back at the cottage, Lewis stripped and showered and made himself lunch. He went back upstairs and collected sketch pads, pencils, a small quantity of paints, thinner and brushes, an easel and two small canvases. Back downstairs with a kitchen filled with camping gear and art materials, he began to pack. Compacting everything as tightly and in as little space as possible was difficult, and took him three tries before he was happy with the results. The easel and canvases were strapped awkwardly to the outside of the filled pack. It would have been easy to make more than one trip, but he was determined to get to the enchanted forest with everything at once, just to be done with it. He wanted to walk away and not return for at least three days. Not long by most standards, but long enough for what Lewis had planned. He really didn't expect to do much work. The art materials were only in case he recovered sooner than he thought, or for his immediate impressions, if he received any.

Once he satisfactorily packed up, Lewis made another sandwich, walking around the distorted-looking backpack as he ate it. The phone rang, but he let it go. Alone. Totally alone, is what he had told Jeff.

Lewis had nurtured a methodical and controlled attitude while in the hospital. Carrying that discipline home with him, he washed the dishes after he ate and put them back in the cabinets so that the house was left just as he'd entered it weeks before: clean and well organized, as though he hadn't returned from the hospital at all.

Lewis lifted the loaded backpack by crossing his arms to grab the straps and twisting it through the air and onto his back. The weight rested on a strap he tightened around his hips, resulting in only a mild tug at his shoulders. It would be warm in the sun, but for the night and for the dark, damp of the enchanted forest, he grabbed an additional sweatshirt on his way out the door. Walking through the field, he looked like an oddly decorated hiker with utensils hanging off the backpack near canvases and an easel. He watched the sky, turning to look back at the cottage only once. When he turned his face and placed his concentration back to the journey, the image of the cottage blinked and was gone from his mind.

The soft cushion of the ground pushed back as he leaned his weight into it. The sun spread warmth over his face even though the air was cool. Trees leaned towards him, then rustled their few remaining leaves and straightened when a fresh wind blew in from the Northwest. He tucked the neck of the sweatshirt behind the backpack strap near his waist to free his hands. As he made his way along the stone fence, he touched the heads of some of the weeds standing amid the wind-bent majority. He let his left hand slide over the stone top of the fence when he could do so without bending and reaching down. For a moment, his mind slipped into common thought, but he quickly retrieved it and again concentrated on his walk. Experiencing nature without common thought was also exciting to Lewis. To him common thought was merely another way to see nature, a different path to take. Even though it offered insights he had never imagined, it remained foreign to his human sensations, the ones he was born with. Common thought, even at his level of control and understanding, was still a mystery to Lewis, just as human movements and experiences were still a mystery to me. Lewis was determined to change all that during his stay in the woods. He knew it would be dangerous, that it could thrust him back into his insanity; it could remove his humanness completely, leaving him no better than a plant himself; but it could also lead him into a realm of total experience, total understanding, a place where he could be a part of nature without losing what he needed to work with in the human world. All he truly wanted was to paint as he once had. He knew his little three-day experiment could just as easily go beyond his hopes. It could kill him. It could leave him with nothing. But it could also allow him to regain that which had once explained his life, his art.

I felt a shutter go through the forest. It was the signature of Lewis' plan. Out of all of common thought, it was only I who had spent hour after hour with Lewis. Could he accept everything at once without being driven over the edge? Could I protect him for three days if he chose to see and feel every element?

Regardless of what would finally happen, he was about to change himself and this area of common thought forever. That ripple of change would be passed from one territory to the next through an overlapping effect which could go on for distances beyond my understanding. Did he know the possible outcome of his decision? Not on the outside, but deep inside I could feel the heaviness, the knowledge. Subconsciously, Lewis carried common thought with him always. His love for the lives that clustered in common thought, his care for their ultimate well being was there, almost unreachable, but there all the same.

At the right spot on the stone fence, Lewis clumsily climbed over it by first sitting on the fence, then by swinging his legs to the other side. The easel loosely shifted from side to side. The rocks were cold and rough against his hands.

Underbrush had taken over the thin path which once wound through the woods, making the trip more difficult. The easel got caught more than once on a vine or bush, and he had to twist his body into contortions to unhook it. So, he dragged and pulled, tearing it from the loose grip of whatever vine or bush it got caught on next. Eventually, the easel was torn from the pack and Lewis plucked it off a briar bush. His walk instantly became easier without the constant tug from the easel. If he had thought to bring a machete, the walking would have been easier, but then he couldn't have chopped senselessly at that which he meant to have communion. Nonetheless, it wasn't long before the white oaks, maples, and scattered birches stopped and the white pine took over, at which crossroads, the underbrush all but disappeared and the forest floor became the solid mat of red needles. The sound of the run rose loudly in his ears, as though it came from the end of a long tunnel. The wind changed from a rustle through leaves and branches to a whisper through the pines, its soft fingers barely touching each needle, which acted like a reed, spreading the soft music of wind through the enchanted forest.

Lewis lowered his backpack when he came to the right spot. The ground was soft, the air fresh. His hair was tossed back and forth as the wind ran along the ground, back and forth, around the trunks of trees. The air seemed a little warmer in the clearing, warmer than the rest of the forest, not warmer than the direct sunlight in the field. He unpacked his gear and placed it orderly over the ground. He assembled the tent near the rock he always leaned against, which still sat in the same spot it had occupied all through his childhood, teens, and young adulthood. He breathed deeply, trying to capture his life in a breath of fresh air and the company of familiar surroundings. But his life was not to be recalled so easily. Only the present stood before him, like a barbed wire fence leading to an open pasture of golden wheat. Lewis looked around. Small amounts of sunlight dropped, in rays of yellow, onto the red needles making new colors and new shapes. As always, he plugged the images into his head, tried to pull something profound from them. Getting nowhere, he resolved himself to setting up camp.

Eating utensils clanked against the easel, the easel thunked against a stone, cans tinned against cans, and the sleeping bag plopped onto the ground and the tent flapped loosely when the wind blew. The music of activity rose from the enchanted forest, hollowed by the dense canopy of pines, and echoed through the forest like a song. The song of Lewis. His mobility doing what plants could never do, and he, totally oblivious to it.

Once set up, Lewis opened a sketch pad and began to work. During the walk there, he had decided to record a before and after sequence. He reached into himself as deeply as possible, closing his eyes, opening his mind, working to include the sun, the way it crept along the ground, changing shape as it changed position in the sky. He took notes, using the corners of the page, and his own shorthand. He recognized that there were missing elements. There remained a boring, mundane slant to his perceptions. He struggled to bring up more than was inside him at the time. On some pages, he extended his work into a skewed vision, trying, artificially, to find what it was he had lost. After finishing one piece as far as he thought he could go, he'd tear back the page and begin another. He leaned against the rock, drew in the brook, and the tree where the raccoon had come down to speak to him, then turned, shifted to another angle and drew the forest where he'd come in from, sketching in the fading path, trying to get the idea of past and present together in the way it had grown in and in the spreading of recent passage. Lewis sketched five pages from five points around the rock until he folded the sketch pad shut.

He had been sitting on his rolled-up sleeping bag to keep his butt off the cold ground, but his back was cold, and when he stood to put the sketch pad into the tent, he felt a shiver go up his back. He let his shoulders roll with the shiver as it approached his neck, then ran down his spine and across his shoulders dissipating its energy. He already wore the extra sweatshirt he had brought. It would be a cold night, but not so cold that he'd need a fire. For the remainder of daylight, Lewis made sure everything was in place, double-checked each item. He ate an early dinner consisting of cold beans, two granola bars and a cup of water. He expected to pull out of common thought long enough to eat meals, to urinate, and to assure he was still alive, but nothing more. Further, he had decided to first drop into common thought at night, while he was tired, so that he could let go easily, so that he wouldn't be tempted to rush home if anything seemed amiss.

Lewis waited as the sun fell and the dark crept into the clearing he called the enchanted forest. He got inside the tent when there was almost no light to see by, not even the shadows of tree trunks. Within the absolute dark of the tent, the brook sounded louder. His concentration shifted from the visible to the audible. Noises from deep inside the woods began to interrupt his solitude. Twigs cracked, leaves rustled. He heard scratching, something running through treetops, and birds landing and taking off. In his head, he converted sound to image, created imaginary animals to make the sounds he heard: squirrels, opossums, owls, animals that were part squirrel and part raccoon, part deer and part fox. He let his mind go. When he felt tired enough, Lewis closed the tent flap, all the while listening to the zipper's loud screech and noticing its effect on the animal sounds, its effect on the sound of wind lowering itself from branch to branch in the pitch black trees, which had as good as disappeared. Lewis was left alone in an empty, black space of nothing but sound. He contemplated turning a flashlight on to get his bearings, but rejected the notion almost as soon as it arrived. Slowly, he undressed in the cold and slipped into his down sleeping bag, pushing in until the top was all but closed around his face. The sudden cold of the material quickly warmed to an almost hot temperature. The cold air, only on his face, felt refreshing and real. He was secure. He was safe. It was time to lower himself into the unknown.

Chapter 21

Control had been Lewis' goal while at the hospital, complete relinquishment of control was his new goal. But shaking loose the control he had gained was no easy matter, not even under the circumstances he had created for himself in the haven of the enchanted forest. Like a bather climbing into cold water, he lowered himself a little at a time. First, just as the night had removed sight, he accepted only sound, but not the sound that was present prior to his descent, instead he listened to sounds far outside hearing range, external sounds relayed through internal contact with common thought, contact which allowed him to use other ears, so to speak. Just as a person falling off to sleep will suddenly hear a loud, real, sound from an impending dream and wake up, only then realizing the sound was not from inside the empty room, so it was with the sounds Lewis heard, which were outside his natural hearing range.

He followed these sounds: squeaks from field mice, chattering from squirrels and raccoons, snorts from deer. He followed the sounds to the edges of common thought territory, passing his concentration from tree to tree to bush like I'd never felt him do before. The deftness with which he moved was amazing. He wanted to explore everything, every tree and bush and vine, but it was impossible. The sheer numbers made it so. When he got to me, he lingered, felt the grooves of my bark, the crotch of a branch, touched leaves and heard them flutter in the light breezes. Amazed, from the top of my highest branches, he gazed, his first use of sight that night, at the multitude of stars overhead. His elation, his pure joy at the spectacular array, heightened the emotions of all of common thought. Already, before the first hours were up, I sensed a passing along of experience from our territory to another.

As though he were an actual form, a spirit in many senses of the word, Lewis climbed from me to the forest floor. He roamed, if that word can make sense while he remained physically inside his sleeping bag, the forest and the field. Now that he was deeper into common thought, and still very much in control of his journey, he opened his mind's eyes, and ran with raccoons and opossums, foraged with the deer, flew with the owl. He began to experience the forest in its entirety, difficult as that was to do. An owl swooped to catch a screaming field mouse, and Lewis felt the flight, the surged adrenaline of the owl, as well as the fear in the mouse, and the pain, almost to the death, of the field mouse caught in its talons, the bite to the back of the neck. Lewis left quickly, and fell, fell onto the sensations of a couple of ruckussing squirrels. He entered animal common thought as easily as plant common thought and again experienced what they experienced: the sudden racing of heartbeat, the sexual urge, the primal need for food and copulation almost like two equal forces constantly tugging against one another. With his next step, Lewis let in more sensations rather than focus on only a few. He extended himself to both ends of common thought territory. He was with owl and squirrel and deer, simultaneously. He felt the increased understanding of nature, of every tree, bush and vine, every weed and blade of grass. Like an avalanche, the whole of common thought opened up in him as he opened up to it. A bombardment of color, shape, emotion. Death, life and all aspects of both. Anger, lust, even envy, burst like a super nova inside his opened mind.

Close to his center, I could feel him struggle. His own heartbeat quickened. His eyes burst open in fear, then closed for the same reason, then they opened in excitement and closed once again. He became a part of the forest, the field, each animal and plant all at once. Deep inside, he was separating, in a furry of fear and astonishment, collecting, translating to color and shape, every emotion, sound, sight, touch and smell. It all came in too quickly, control had been lost, just as he had wanted. But was it what he needed?

I stayed inside him, as close to his center as I could. His tiredness was meant to make it easy to accept common thought and difficult to escape. That was his plan. But, his fatigue also made it easy for him to misunderstand what came at him at machine-gun speed. His ability to focus, to concentrate on any one activity, any one sensation, was tremendously limited. Finally, it became difficult for him to remain in common thought. Even without mobility, the mere acceptance of so many sensations was an act which took much energy. Lewis' own energy quickly began to wane. He had allowed too much to happen at once. His inward struggle to accept, accept, accept, drew life energy from him. The act of being a part of birth and death simultaneously, of experiencing the quirks of plant feelings as well as animal drive, took its toll. After he began to lose his grip on the onslaught, like a man dozing off during a lecture, he began also to join together unrelated feelings. The twitch of a leaf was associated with an opossum scratching a flea. A dying mouse was associated with a white birch near the corner of the stone fence. He became confused. The notion that he was having a relapse dropped into his mind like an egg drops from a tree and empties its contents against a rock. Lewis imagined himself losing control and, therefore, began to join his imaginings with his misunderstandings. The combination quickly became horrible, quickly threw much of common thought into a sort of panic. Remember, common thought had accepted Lewis, too. Together, Lewis' creation of new images, his own fear, and common thought's sudden panic, produced an uncontrollable menagerie of horrifying images, then fascinating ones.

Internally, Lewis struggled to get free, tiring his consciousness even more, causing even more confusion. He thought he had gone completely mad. That was his strongest thought, but I knew the difference between his madness and his imagination, and this was not madness. Somehow, he was willing all that was happening to him.

I tried to calm common thought, tried to pry Lewis free, and failed at both. The two were too well connected. For longer than I could have imagined, he held on. His imagination flourished, bursting from horrible to wonderful, confused in its own fatigue, until eventually, he could hold on no longer and literally collapsed into sleep. To common thought, the sensation was that of a constant tug-of-war, and suddenly one team, Lewis', let go of the rope. A quick shock of release, a falling, then complete relief fell over the forest.

Lewis, in sleep, played the experience over and over, sorting it all out like a mathematician sorts out a complex problem, or a biologist discovers a new DNA molecule, amidst his dreams.

When morning came, Lewis had only gotten a few hours sleep, but the sunlight striking the tent and placing a soft glow over his face, and the birds chirping in constant song, awakened him. His body felt hot inside the sleeping bag, while his face was moist and cold, as though dew had settled on him and turned to a light frost. He opened his eyes and, even through the canopy of the tent canvas, could tell that a low fog was present outside. The hollow sounds of morning in December crept in. When he stirred, bones cracked. He felt stiff and uncomfortable. The ground, even with the sleeping bag mat to protect him, was hard and lumpy. He dropped into common thought and said good morning, a long and low echoing sound throughout the territory. Then, he pulled away, testing his control. As he tinkered with the morning chores of changing his clothes and cooking breakfast on his Coleman burner, I pulled back to rest, entering him for superficial thoughts and feelings, just to keep in touch. The tent had been warm inside, so when Lewis unzipped the front and let in the freezing night air, he shrunk back quickly and put his coat on before going outside. Patches of fog lifted from various parts of the forest floor around him, creating an eerie, Wolfman Verses the Mummy, atmosphere. The morning was noisy with bird chatter. Although the sun brought light into the area, the canopy of pines and an accumulating cloud cover diminished its effects. The pine needle carpet was damp and tree trunks sparkled with moisture. Over the din of bird noises, the run occasionally made a loud gurgle, but then returned to its more constant tinkling sound. Lewis observed the thin barrier of ice which had set around a few protruding rocks in areas where the run water lay still, little alcoves of water where, in spring and summer, you would find minnows and pollywogs by the hundreds.

For breakfast, Lewis mixed instant pancakes by adding water to a plastic container filled with powder, and then shaking it for several minutes. The cakes cooked up satisfactorily and Lewis ate them with butter from a squeeze bottle poured over the tops. Afterwards, he ate a single granola bar from the half dozen packages he had packed for the trip. It was drier in his mouth than he thought it would be. Before turning off the burner, he warmed his hands. He rinsed the pan, plate, and fork he had used, in the run, then laid all that equipment aside.

Picking up his sketch pad, Lewis relaxed with his back against the rock as he had the day before. As he worked on one sketch after another, there seemed a certain ease within him, his attitude towards the sketches had changed, even though the work itself didn't progress beyond what he'd done the day before. This morning he didn't try to extend the sketches by skewing the images. He sketched straight from what he saw, straight from the visual part of nature open to anyone. He stayed out of common thought while he worked, finished up, and threw the sketch pad inside the tent.

Rubbing his hands together to warm them, Lewis walked around the clearing, among and around trees and bushes, he leaped over the run, walked around for a few minutes, and leaped over it on the way back to the tent. As his body warmed from the exercise, the low fog lifted, adding to the cloud cover. By noon the area was darker than it had been in morning. By the time Lewis ate lunch and cleaned up for the second time that day, a light snow had begun to fall, and a soft, constant wind had arrived to whisper sweet thoughts to him.

Why he did not go into common thought after breakfast, which had been his original plan, I do not know. For some time, I assumed he was not going back, that somehow, during sleep, his mind had decided it was not worth it. After all, during his morning sketches, there was an undefined sense of resolve about his work. That resolve could have been to remain out of common thought and to accept what talent he had as it was. He could paint the rest of his life and do well without the frantic genius he had once experienced. He still had great ability to recreate nature. But if that was his decision, why stay in the woods? For inspiration?

I must say, I had no grounds for any of these thoughts. Lewis had closed his mind to me for the time. I could only reach immediate sight and sound, traces of emotion.

Soon after the snow began to fall, Lewis ducked inside the tent and into the warmth of the sleeping bag. He propped his head and back up as high as possible, then dropped, filled with renewed energy, into common thought.

Common thought was leery of accepting him, so allowed him only partial connection: sight and sound, but no deep-seated philosophical connection, no connection to deeper emotions.

Lewis took in what he could. He roamed through the woods like an invisible being, climbed to the tops of trees, and dropped to the grasses. He took in a multitude of images from a multitude of angles. He opened as fully as he could, reaching out to plant and animal alike. Once he was there for an hour or so, individual plants and animals chose to open to him.

Lewis rose from his protected, prone position, dressed warmly, opened the tent, and went for a long walk while remaining in common thought, allowing the sensation of joints and lungs, of eyes and ears and fingers, of something very strange to most of common thought, to translate its world into theirs. He was sharing his world. Lewis walked amidst the pines while listening to the wind whoosh and whisper through dense, needle-bound branches. Much of the first snowfall didn't make it through to him. In fact, looking up, it was as though the snow disintegrated just before getting within reach. Yet, in common thought, Lewis felt the snow touch branches. As he got closer to the bare trees, Lewis listened for the moment when the sound of wind changed. At the threshold between the two sounds, he stopped, focused, and let in the juxtaposed sounds of white pines and hemlocks on the one side, and maples, birches, and oaks on the other. The two distinctly different sounds rushed through his ears for common thought to hear.

When Lewis opened again, he was everywhere in the woods, like a soft cloth brushing against you, caressing, almost erotically. He remained at ease in common thought, reminiscent of the ease with which he made his morning sketches. He physically moved through the woods to the stone fence and into the field where he opened his arms and accepted the flurry of snow falling from the sky. Common thought hummed and whined and chattered inside his head. Noise and silence. Inside common thought, there was a beautiful silence in hearing without ears, a beautiful sight in seeing without eyes. Through Lewis, there was a level of sight and sound beyond common thought. Through his eyes and ears, a fantasy world opened up. Between he and common thought, all things could be touched in all ways. Twirling around and around in the middle of the field, his face skyward, his arms out, like a child trying to make himself dizzy, Lewis accepted all that lay around him, and all that lay around him accepted Lewis. He sat, then, in the middle of the field, making sure to face away from the cottage, and began his beautiful manipulations. Cautious of common thought's reaction, Lewis gave a warning that he was about to experiment, just as the wind warns of its coming. He placed his own precursory ripples into the realm, pushing his own signatures outward. Soon, colors distorted, shapes changed, trees reached out towards him, the grass stretched and touched his hands. Unlike his horrifying hallucinations, Lewis willed these imaginings, no fear rode them like a fourth horseman, so no fear entered common thought. Without question, Lewis' adjustments were accepted. He played this way for a long while, then put things back.

Lewis stood and walked back into the woods where he stopped and repeated his experiments, this time creating paintings that showed a nature with the power of mobility, trees about to stand or bend, bushes just after reciting poetry. The images rushed out, like signatures of what was about to happen. The paintings portrayed a lively, natural world, one with thoughts and emotions. Lewis had broken through. I felt rejoiced, and that feeling spread throughout common thought like wildfire.

Lewis danced with common thought, twirled and touched and purred. Then he came to me. I was the pointing Indian, he said, not in words but in images, sounds, nuances. I felt proud and honored to be the spirit he relied on. He imagined me as the Indian, as he had before, then he imagined himself as the Indian, as though we were one. He understood that we were one, that we had been as one for a long time. As the Indian, Lewis stepped closer to me, all in his mind, then, like a real spirit of nature, he stepped inside me, became me. His final turn placing his, the Indian's, body inside my trunk. When a hand rose out of the trunk and pointed, I saw, with him, another Lewis, the outer Lewis, being asked to go out into the world. That Lewis was suddenly different. Just as he had created a newness in his paintings, Lewis had created another self, this one colored and shaped to deal with the human world. Somehow, he had managed to separate. Not that his human self was so much a part of that world that there was nothing else, as with Jeffrey, but that he could maneuver, he could journey through that world without fear of collapse.

After expecting to fall completely into common thought, crazy or not, so he could feel again the exhilaration his art brought him, he had accidentally found two worlds he could function in, neither perfectly, neither exclusively, but two, totally distinguishable worlds.

For several more hours, Lewis wandered around common thought territory experiencing and experimenting with a new understanding of himself and nature. Finally, his legs tired and his body cold, he returned to the tent, made dinner and ate. At dusk Lewis again walked out to the field, alone, without common thought. He stared at the sky which had opened to stars placed on a clean, black silk blanket. In a solitude which included common thought, Lewis accumulated his feelings towards himself, his family, and his work. Still, as difficult as emotions are, and as complex as they are, he placed temporary priorities on each. Back at the tent, chilled to the bone, Lewis undressed and tucked himself tightly into his sleeping bag. Warmth soon came back to his body. His muscles relaxed after shaking off the cold. Like a small boy on his first camping trip, he turned on the flashlight, inspected every inch of the inside of the tent, every seam.

On the third day Lewis did not sketch. He awoke content that he had finished the job he had planned to do. The morning was colder than the other two had been and he moved more slowly. After a quick breakfast, where he stayed as close to the Coleman as possible without getting burned, Lewis packed everything into his back pack. On his return home, Lewis walked with common thought as his constant companion. Small deaths seemed less harsh as he learned to recognize the signatures of their happenings. Emotions rose and lowered, anger, hate, love, lust, all at once, all within his reach. All he needed to do was reach out and grab whatever he wanted, or take it all, let it all balance inside him: hate balanced with love, pain with elation. He leaned towards one emotion, then another, as each grew to importance. From many places at once, the same emotion would come at him, from the tops of trees, from under rocks, from fish and other animals. The mixture of natural things stayed inside him.

For many years following that time, as long as he was within reach, we walked together like brothers, like friends, experiencing one another more intimately than ever before.

Lewis planted his eyes on the cottage as soon as it came within sight. He watched it grow in size while it also grew in importance. The cottage was no longer an enemy, it was his home, the place where he worked, a haven. Once inside, rubbing his cold hands together, Lewis dropped his pack onto the kitchen floor and ran up the stairs. He attached a canvas to the easel and turned so that he could look out the window at the field. Taking up brushes and paints and palette, he began to work, completely open to nature yet within human thought.

There are many degrees of consciousness for humans alone, and many more for common thought, so, having both, there was exponentially more for Lewis to manipulate and let work for him. While some inputs were blocked, others let in the world at large, whether focused or unfocused, as background or foreground. Lewis painted two canvases that afternoon and evening. Late that night, he put down his brushes and poured the last cup of coffee from the latest pot. He stood back. It had not translated as he had wanted, but he knew that it eventually would. He created from a place that had no visual counterpart. His hands were still learning to read his mind, and his mind was still experimenting. Time would allow mind and hand to grow together.

He looked over, and sitting on the couch was the Indian. He let me control the arm as I learned to lift muscle and bone as Lewis knew it. I struggled and the Indian shook, jerked its shoulder. Lewis helped by urging me on. After a while, the arm lifted, the Indian pointed. A merging of minds had taken place, an interlocking of man and nature like never before. I held the arm out for only a moment, then let it fall. I had never felt what it was like to be mobile. Such an odd and interesting machine humans are. Lewis smiled in approval before turning away, taking his cup of coffee downstairs to his bedroom, where, finally, he would sleep in the comforts of a bed.

Using his mind to help me, I stayed with the image of the Indian, tried to learn more about human mobility, how it worked instead of just how it felt to work. Lewis stayed in common thought at a location in the crook of my branch, the one he had fallen from as a child. Sitting there, he took in what I would take in, just as I would take it, trying to forget his ability to move, trying to understand immobility, while simultaneously, I learned the mysteries of mechanical movement. As you must know by now, we had joined, had learned to become one, together, yet separate in our own worlds.

Terry L. Persun was born in Williamsport, Pennsylvania in 1952. He holds a bachelors degree in science and a masters in art in creative writing. Mr. Persun is an editor for Designfax, a magazine written for design engineers. He is not only a novelist, but a poet and short story writer as well. He has published widely in small and literary publications. This is his second published novel. He presently lives in Port Townsend, Washington with his wife Catherine and daughter Nicole.